By EM LYNLEY

NOVELS

Hostile Takeover

PRECIOUS GEMS
Rarer Than Rubies
Italian Ice

with Shira Anthony
Lighting the Way Home
*A Delectable Novel*

NOVELLAS

Disguises

Brand New Flavor
*A Delectable Novella*

Published by DREAMSPINNER PRESS
http://www.dreamspinnerpress.com

By SHIRA ANTHONY

NOVELS

BLUE NOTES NOVELS
Aria
Blue Notes
The Melody Thief

with Venona Keyes
The Trust

with EM Lynley
Lighting the Way Home
*A Delectable Novel*

NOVELLAS
The Dream of a Thousand Nights

Published by DREAMSPINNER PRESS
http://www.dreamspinnerpress.com

# LIGHTING
## the way
# Home

## EM LYNLEY
## SHIRA ANTHONY

a *Delectable* novel

*Dreamspinner Press*

Published by
Dreamspinner Press
5032 Capital Circle SW
Ste 2, PMB# 279
Tallahassee, FL 32305-7886
USA
http://www.dreamspinnerpress.com/

Lighting the Way Home
Copyright © 2013 by EM Lynley and Shira Anthony

Cover Art by L.C. Chase
http://www.lcchase.com

ISBN: 978-1-62380-412-1
Digital ISBN: 978-1-62380-413-8

Printed in the United States of America
First Edition
March 2013

# Dedication

For my grandmother Rebecca, who taught me to love the traditions. I think of you every time I light candles. Shemecha wehyeh bracha. And you shall be a blessing.

And also to my chavurah, who help me continue the traditions, particularly Maya, Miriam, Marcia, and Marvin, for your help with this story. —EM

For my grandparents Jacob, Mae, Leon, and Bess. L'dor vador. From generation to generation. —Shira

# Acknowledgments

Special thanks to Judge Jackie for her help in navigating the New York State legal system.

# Recipe Index

Traditional Matzo Brei ..................................................................... 183

Josh's Gourmet Matzo Brei Variations ........................................... 183

Sweet Matzo Brei ............................................................................. 184

Jenna's Slow Cooker Chanukah Brisket ......................................... 185

Traditional Latkes............................................................................ 186

Josh's Chicken with Herbes de Provence........................................ 187

Josh's Provencal Carrots ................................................................. 188

# Chapter One

"DON'T worry. It'll be fine. I'll be fine!"

Joshua Golden couldn't begin to count how many times he'd heard his mother say those very words. This time, however, he didn't believe them.

"Mom, it's surgery. It's serious."

"You're a good boy, Joshy." She reached for his hand and placed a loud kiss on the back of his knuckles. "Don't worry about me."

He cringed at the old nickname. And the kiss.

"The doctor says it's nothing." Josh's dad gave his typical shrug. "She'll be in the hospital overnight, that's it."

"Then why did you need me to come home from France and help you run the restaurant for two weeks if it's nothing?" Josh suspected there was something they weren't telling him. He let out a loud sigh, louder than he expected. His mother tilted her head and gave him that look that said "Don't start."

Yes, he was home. He hadn't even stepped foot inside his parents' house, but he already knew everything would be the same as it had been while he was growing up, from the slightly faded drapes on the front windows, to the outdated upholstered furniture in the living room, to the worn rug in the front entryway. Everything would be the same, right down to the way his parents manipulated him, as they always did, and the way they treated him like a five-year-old, no matter his age.

It would be a long two weeks.

He already missed France. Even a week away from the restaurant now was something he couldn't afford, not when they'd just been awarded their third Michelin star—the highest rating. Only about eighty restaurants in the whole world had achieved the feat. Press and gourmets from all over Europe were flocking there, and here he was, in New York, because his mother called and asked him to come home for the holidays. She'd told him she was scheduled for surgery, and she'd explain everything once he arrived. But not to worry, which from Miriam Golden was a signal to do exactly that.

But Josh couldn't help but worry. It was the main reason he'd agreed to come home—temporarily. The *only* reason. He'd kept his distance from New York—and the memories it held—for a reason. He hadn't been back to his old neighborhood for five years, though he'd been in the States on a number of occasions he hadn't mentioned to his family. They wouldn't understand, he reminded himself at the wave of guilt that swept over him at the thought his mother's condition was more serious than she'd admitted over the phone.

She looked perfectly fine. She sounded like she had his entire life.

As they walked toward baggage claim, Josh's dad shuffled along; then his mother turned around and smiled enigmatically.

Oh yeah. Now he was really worried, but it had nothing to do with his mother's health.


"SO, TELL us all about your restaurant in Paris?"

They were in the car driving toward Manhattan, stuck on the Long Island Expressway. They had barely made it a mile from JFK. His father's shoulders were visibly tense—Josh knew how he hated dealing with the traffic. Why hadn't he just taken a cab instead of letting them pick him up? He could afford it.

"Well, Mom, it's called Le Petit Cerisier."

"Sounds very French," his mother said, in a tone that implied it might be better to sound Martian.

"It's named after the Japanese cherry blossom trees. We cook European-Asian fusion and—"

"What the hell is that when it's at home?" his father interrupted, turning his head toward Josh.

"Dad, pay attention to the road."

"We're going two miles an hour, where's it going to go?"

"That's not the point, Dad."

"Sure it is."

A taxi cut in front of them, nearly hitting the front right bumper.

"Seymour."

Just his father's name. That was all his mother had to say—in just the right tone, with heavy emphasis on the first syllable—and his dad shrugged and turned his attention back toward the road ahead of them. Amazing, really. He still couldn't figure out how she did it. It had worked on him, too, when he was a kid. *It'd probably still work now,* he thought wryly.

"Go on, Josh." His mother patted his hand. "What kind of food is it?" It was her usual smile this time, but he noticed the wrinkles around her mouth were more pronounced than he remembered. When had her hair gone completely white?

"You wouldn't like it." He wouldn't even try to explain why he was cooking *traif*—non-kosher foods Jews considered unclean, like pork and shellfish. They'd never eaten any of those things when he was growing up. He hadn't tasted shrimp until he was in college, and even then he felt guilty for liking it. And once he'd moved to Europe, it was as if an entire new universe of tastes had opened up for him.

"Fine." She let out another heavy sigh, and Josh immediately felt a touch of guilt at having foreclosed that part of the conversation. She meant well, didn't she? "Do you like it?"

"I love it. We're really hitting our stride, and we just got another star." He smiled, partly out of pride, but partly to reassure her.

"That's nice."

Josh repressed a sigh. He knew she was more proud of him than she let on; she just didn't quite understand how important his career was to him. Neither of them had understood why he'd left home, left Goldens, their family-run restaurant, and headed off on an international culinary adventure through Asia and Europe, eventually ending in France where he'd washed dishes and peeled potatoes to pay his way through Le Cordon Bleu. It wasn't all about food at the time, but he put his passion into his cooking rather than dwell on the real reason he'd left.

He'd finally got up enough courage—chutzpah, his dad would call it—to walk into Raymond Vessy's kitchen and ask for a job. He was right out of culinary school and with no experience working in any professional kitchen other than his parents' and half a dozen little places around Asia and Europe, learning local cuisines and techniques. Raymond had just stared at him as if he'd lost his mind.

"I do not hire children," Vessy said with a dismissive wave of his hand. "Come back when you have lived a little." Undaunted, and knowing no explanation of his travels and experience would suffice, Josh had offered to prepare him a meal, and surprisingly, Vessy had relented.

Josh had done everything himself, working from early in the morning to have dinner prepared for the chef. The look of happy surprise on Vessy's face had been worth every Band-Aid on his fingers.

"I've never had dumplings like this before. Duck confit pot stickers? Where did you learn this?"

"I made it up."

"Really? Why this combination? And five-spiced pineapple." He pursed his lips in the way the French had that could be interest or insult.

Josh had struggled to express himself in French.

Vessy pelted him with more questions. "What wine would you serve with the dumplings?"

"Petite sirah." Josh made sure to state it with confidence, even though he felt anything but. He could see by the raised eyebrows he'd impressed Raymond, who'd made an exception to his "no babies" rule and given him a job on the spot. He started as a kitchen assistant, tasked with the scut work in the kitchen—peeling, boning, and cleaning up after the more experienced staff—but once a week Raymond asked him to prepare staff lunch, and after six months he'd been promoted to the lowest rung of station chef.

Five years later, Josh was number two in the restaurant and all but ran the place.

The drive to his parents' house, only twenty miles, took two hours in typical traffic. They'd hit rush hour. Jet lag and the late nights at the restaurant caught up with Josh, and he fell asleep curled up on the backseat of the car.

By the time they'd parked the car in the garage and Josh's mother shook him from his slumber, it was six o'clock. Josh sat up and moved to wipe the back of his hand across his face, but his mother's glare put paid to that intention. He hoped he hadn't drooled while he slept. He ran his fingers through his hair to smooth it down as his father shuffled around to the trunk.

"Dad, I'll bring the luggage." Josh put his hand on his father's shoulder and with a forced smile, placed himself between his father and the trunk. He was here to help them, wasn't he? His dad didn't need to be schlepping his bags.

"That's okay. I'll be fine. You go and have a nap."

"You better not sleep too much, or your clock will be all messed up," Miriam added with a frown.

Josh shrugged and realized he'd reacted the same way his dad had earlier in the car. Shaking off the horrific thought he might be turning into his dad, Josh lugged the suitcase out of the trunk in silence and began to roll it toward the back door.

"I could have gotten that." His dad sounded slightly insulted.

"What happened to that nice suitcase we got you?" his mother added as she studied the hard-case spinner suitcase he'd picked up in Paris.

"Mom, that was when I graduated from college. It was years ago." He remembered the suitcase well: fake carpetbag paisley. He'd taken it when he'd left home, but it had been too impractical for his travels, so he'd replaced it with a sturdy backpack long ago.

"I still have the same suitcase I had when your father and I...."

Josh tuned her out. He loved her, but it was times like these he realized how much he'd changed since he left home and begun his own life. His parents would never understand why he did what he did, why he'd chosen a different life from theirs. He'd given up explaining himself, but then they asked so many questions. He was caught in the middle. Somewhere between the kid and the adult.

He stifled a yawn as he wheeled the suitcase in through the kitchen, letting it bounce over the raised threshold that separated inside from out. The kitchen looked the same, with its drab linoleum floors, ruffled curtains, and metal cabinets. The clock over the sink was the same one Josh remembered from when he was a kid—the electrical cord ran from the bottom up and over the pass-through to the dining room. "Why get a new clock?" his father had said when Josh had suggested a battery-operated one on a trip home from college. "This one works fine." The kitchen smelled good, though. Comforting. Familiar.

"Oh, Josh, honey. Wait a minute before you go upstairs," Miriam called to him as he made his way along the familiar hallway toward the front entryway.

Thundering feet rushed down the stairs and a blue and red blur sped past him.

Was that a kid? His gaze followed the blur toward the kitchen, and sure enough a boy of about ten was settling himself in at the kitchen table. His mother smiled at the boy and ruffled his hair, just like she had always done when Josh was that age. Whoever the boy was, Josh was too tired to have what promised to be a strange conversation with his mother about him. He turned back toward the stairs, came face to face and nearly collided with a man who had just stepped down.

Not just any man.

Micah Solomon.

# Chapter Two

IT HAD been more than ten years since he'd seen Micah, and the last place Josh had expected to see him was in his own parents' house. Micah turned around and walked back upstairs without saying a word. From the look on his face, Josh guessed Micah hadn't been prepared to see him either. It felt surreal, as though he'd stepped into some alternate universe.

Josh wiped the back of his hand across his mouth, hoping Micah hadn't noticed any drool. Then he remembered he didn't care what the fuck Micah noticed. Those days were long gone.

"Josh, I'm afraid your room—" His mother called up to him from halfway between the kitchen and the front hall, startling him.

He didn't wait to listen to the rest. He grabbed the suitcase, sprinted up the steps and flung his bedroom door open. He barely recognized his room for the clutter. The floor was littered with Legos, Hot Wheel cars, and gaming cards from one of those Japanese cartoons he couldn't name. Piles of cast-off clothes and a variety of school books and papers were scattered about, covering most of the surfaces. His bed sported Justice League sheets and a few tattered stuffed animals.

*What the hell?*

"Yeah, we didn't really get a chance to explain," Josh's dad said from the hallway.

"Explain now." Josh was not amused. It was bad enough seeing Micah here, but seeing his room turned into a playpen?

"Can you stay in the guest room? Ethan is using your room for the time being."

"Ethan?"

"Yeah, Josh. Ethan is Micah's son."

Josh was pretty sure his mouth had dropped open wide enough to fly a 767 into, but he didn't care. That was Micah's son? Sure, he knew there had been a kid. He'd even remembered the kid's name, but he'd never imagined how big the kid would get, and he sure as hell hadn't expected to meet him here, of all places. It made it all seem so much more *real.* He turned and, through the open door, noticed Micah in the guest room, tossing clothing into a suitcase.

"Sorry, Seymour. Ethan woke up late, and I didn't get my stuff moved in before you got back," Micah said. He glanced at Josh, more out of the corner of his eye than full on. "Hi, Josh. Sorry about this mess." He pushed past them and into Josh's old bedroom. His gaze flickered toward Josh for a fraction of a second before he set his suitcase on the bed. Without another word, he knelt down on the floor and began to collect the toys and discarded clothing.

Josh took the scene in with stunned surprise. *What the hell is going on here?*

"Let's put your case in here." His father's voice brought Josh back to himself. He let his dad take his suitcase into the guest room and headed in that direction, glancing back several times to watch Micah tidy up the mess in Josh's old room but carefully avoiding meeting Josh's gaze.

"Have a seat." Seymour pointed to the bed.

"Just tell me what's going on here, Dad."

"Only if you sit down."

"Dad." How many times had his dad sat him down like this? Sure, it had been on his own bed, not the bed in the guest room, but it was the same. They were treating him like a kid again.

"I'll explain." Miriam had come upstairs without Josh hearing her, and she walked into the room and shut the door behind her. Whatever the reason, it must be ten times worse if his mother was taking over the explanation from his dad. If he hadn't been so flustered, he might have laughed—he and his sister Jenna had always joked that his mother was the "explainer" of the family. She was calm and patient where sometimes their dad got flustered if you didn't immediately see his point of view.

Josh sat on the bed and folded his arms across his chest. This had better be good. Not that these sorts of lectures ever ended well, even when he was a kid.

"Micah and his son Ethan are staying with us. He's helping out at the restaurant," she began.

"What? How could you let him?" Josh nearly shouted, only restraining his anger when he saw her cringe. "Why would you? You know what he's done, don't you?"

"Sure, we know. But he needs help and we can help. It's a *mitzvah*."

A Jewish good deed? That was their excuse? "I want him out of here. And his son." Micah's son was ten? Had it been that long ago? Josh struggled to wrap his brain around that concept. But given how Micah had surprised him, surprised the whole neighborhood and half the state of New York, showing up at his parents' house with a ten-year-old son in tow paled in comparison.

"It's not up to you, Josh. It's up to us. This is our house and it's our decision." His father's voice was surprisingly firm. It had been years since he'd heard his dad sound so self-confident. His mother nodded, though her dark eyes were warm and soft and a little bit sad.

"Well if you've got him helping out, why did you tell me I had to come home for your surgery?" Josh fought the urge to use quotation marks in his tone as he spoke the final word.

"Because we do need your help. Micah's not a chef. He can't handle the cooking the way you can. He helps the other cooks. Chopping and basting and that sort of thing."

"Kitchen hand. It's called 'kitchen hand'." Josh let out a puff of frustration. His parents had run a restaurant for more than thirty years, but they knew nothing about the real restaurant business.

"Whatever it's called in hoity-toity France, around here he's our assistant." She frowned at him, and he felt a twinge of guilt. They weren't just treating him like a child; he was acting like one.

Josh bit back his anger once more, doing his best to moderate his tone and ignore the jab. "That's the best job he could get?"

"For the time being. He lost his law license, and it's taking some time for him to appeal it...." His mother's voice trailed off and she glanced at Josh's father with a pained look on her face.

"Well, I hope you don't let him anywhere near the money. You know what he'll use it for."

"Josh, you're way out of line with that." His father's voice was harsh and reproving. It had been a long time since Josh had been chastised by him and it hurt. "He's clean. No drugs. Don't worry about that. You don't know the whole story, Josh. He's doing a mitzvah too. Helping where he's needed."

"Is that so? If he's so fine and upstanding, why's he working in a kitchen peeling potatoes? And he's got a son he's looking after too?" Josh wouldn't have believed it if he hadn't seen the physical resemblance. Micah's kid. "Where's Rina? I can't see her dumping the kid with him after prison. Is she okay?" Suddenly Josh's heart skipped a few beats. He'd never blamed Rina for any of what had happened.

"Rina's got a nice, important job at that bank, and they sent her out of town for some big project...." His mom's voice went from pride in Rina's accomplishment to an almost whisper.

"So, why isn't he staying at her place with Ethan?"

Seymour glanced at his shoes for a moment before replying. "The co-op wouldn't let Micah stay while Rina's away and—"

"Damn right." Josh felt good saying it. Justified.

"They have some stupid rule about parolees."

"Damn right." Josh couldn't help repeating the phrase. "Maybe there's something to that, you think?" Why the hell didn't they care what Micah had done? Was he the only sane person in the house?

"Why must you be so uncharitable? He used to be your best friend. Why can't you show some concern for him when he needs our support the most?" His mother looked disappointed in him. He hated that. He wanted her to be proud of him. But how was Micah's life *his* fault?

"Used to be. That's the point." It was too much to deal with, especially on top of jet lag. He faked a huge yawn to the expected effect.

"You need a nice long nap. We'll talk more about this once you've slept and can think clearly." His mom rubbed his shoulder then patted the bed. "Nap."

Josh nodded obediently. Anything to get them out of the room. He needed time to himself to process everything that had just happened, and to think.

His parents shuffled out and quietly closed the door behind them. He heard soft voices in the hallway as they said something to Micah, but he couldn't make out the words. He didn't care.

## Chapter Three

IT WASN'T jet lag, but Josh desperately needed a good nap to clear his head. The old steam radiator rattled and hissed. Despite the heat being on, there was always a chill in this room. Jenna's old room. He remembered when he and Jenna used to build blanket houses and hide during thunderstorms. The room looked different without her dolls and stuffed animals. He wondered how Jenna was doing—he hadn't spoken to her in months now, maybe longer.

He kicked off his shoes, shed his jeans, and eased under the old crocheted bedspread his Aunt Rose had made a thousand years ago. It used to be white but was now pale yellow. At least it didn't smell like mothballs the way Aunt Rose always did. When she died, he'd barely believed it. He thought the mothballs would preserve her forever. He hadn't thought about Aunt Rose for years.

He hadn't thought about Micah for years either. Not much anyway. When he did think about Micah, it was always the same thoughts: "What if?" or "Why?" Josh had never had good answers to those questions, so he avoided the thoughts as much as possible. Coming home had brought up emotions he thought he'd buried years ago.

He took a deep breath, pulled the bedspread up to his chin, and settled against the soft down pillow.

Micah had been sleeping here, and his mother hadn't had time to clean the room or change the sheets. Josh inhaled, wondering if the scent was Micah's. Wondering if Micah had lain here at night wondering about *him. Yeah, right.* He didn't think Micah had thought about him that way for a very, very long time.

JOSH and Micah had been friends practically since birth. Their parents had known each other from *shul*—synagogue—and Micah's parents ate at least twice a week at the restaurant.

Josh still remembered the first day of kindergarten and how relieved he'd been to see Micah sitting at a desk in the classroom when his mom dropped him off. Josh had taken the desk next to Micah's, of course, and they'd eaten lunch together. After school, they'd played on the playground before their mothers had come to walk them home.

"I'm really glad you're in my class," Micah told Josh as they shot hoops. "My mom said I shouldn't get mad if you weren't, but I'm really glad you are."

"Me too." Josh didn't tell Micah he'd been a nervous wreck until he'd seen Micah in the classroom. He'd put his shirt on backward that morning, worrying about school and meeting new kids.

"You're my best friend." Micah flashed his usual bright smile. "I guess the teacher knew that."

"Yeah." Josh's heart felt like it would fly out of his chest. "You're mine, too."

Micah just grinned and tossed him the basketball. "Wanna come over to my house tomorrow after school?"

"Sure." As if Josh would have turned the offer down! Josh pretended he wasn't jumping up and down inside and instead tried to make a three-point shot. The ball missed the hoop by a few inches and landed near Micah.

"Cool." Micah passed Josh the ball. "Try again," he said. "You were really close that time, Joshy."

"I'm really not good at this." Josh stared down at his shoes.

"My dad says you have to imagine the ball going into the basket. It kinda works for me sometimes. Try it."

Josh chewed on his lower lip, then set himself up again for the shot, planting both feet on the three point line and focusing on the hoop. He closed his eyes for a moment, imagining the ball going in, then opened them and took the shot. The ball went through the hoop.

"You did it! You did it!" Micah raised his hand and they exchanged high fives. "That was great!"

From then on, they were inseparable, spending afternoons at each other's houses playing and doing their homework, going to Sunday school together, sitting together at shul. They liked the same things: Hot Wheels cars, Transformers, and especially *Star Wars*. They even landed in the principal's office a few times for talking too much.

It was just after winter break that they met Rina for the first time. "I'm Rina Hershkowitz," she announced after retrieving the basketball from where it had landed by the fence. Josh had missed the rebound and was chasing down the ball and laughing at something funny Micah had said.

She was a tiny little thing, but she'd surprised them both by nailing three baskets in a row, which was far better than Josh's track record. At first, Josh hadn't exactly welcomed her with open arms into their little twosome. He'd been jealous and afraid Micah would like Rina better. Micah must have understood, because although he made it a point to include Rina when they were at school, he never asked Rina to his house.

From kindergarten all the way through high school, Josh and Micah shared every single joy and pain of growing from boys to men. All but one. Josh hadn't had the guts to tell Micah when his feelings changed from friendship to love, to a desire for something physical. About how he dreamed of kissing Micah, not Rachel Kaplan, under the pier.

Micah hadn't talked about girls much, but he'd been the best-looking boy in their year, so parents and grandparents, teachers and rabbis, were always trying to pair him up with suitable Jewish girls.

"I wish they'd stop playing *yenta*," Micah complained to Josh in their last year of high school. "I hate it. It's like I'm some sort of show dog or something. What's that called? A 'stud'?" Micah's laugh was bitter.

"You are a stud," Josh teased without thinking, then blushed when he realized what he'd said.

"I'm serious, Joshy. You know, both Mrs. Rose and Mrs. Finkelstein came up to me after services last week and asked who I was taking to prom?" Micah rolled his eyes.

"So who are you going to take?" Josh asked, wishing he could be the one going to prom with Micah. *Yeah, maybe in an alternate universe.*

"I was thinking of asking Rina. At least she won't expect me to kiss her or something, and I won't be bored out of my mind."

Josh decided he could live with Micah taking Rina to the prom—at least he wouldn't have to worry about Micah making out with her. "Sounds like a good idea."

"So how about you?" Micah asked. "Are you going?"

"Nah." Who would he have gone with, anyhow? Besides, he'd just spend the whole time wishing he were Micah's date. He also wasn't sure he wanted Micah to see him with a girl. He still sort of hoped Micah might catch on and realize how he felt about him.

Two months later, the summer Josh had turned eighteen and just before they were heading off to different universities, they'd broken into the community pool at midnight, drunk on a bottle of sweet kosher wine Josh had stolen from his parents' restaurant. They hadn't planned on the break-in, and once they'd climbed over the fence, they didn't know how to celebrate their daring feat.

"Jump off the high dive!" Josh had suggested. Micah was a strong swimmer and a good diver.

"No. You jump."

"I suck at diving. No way I'll go off the top one."

"I'll do it if you do."

"Okay." That sounded good to Josh. Everything seemed easier with Micah at his side.

They headed for the iron ladder to the top level before Micah stopped dead in his tracks. "Shit. No swimsuits." Micah started laughing uncontrollably at this point. He couldn't hold his Manischewitz the way Josh could.

"Who needs 'em?" Josh slipped out of his shirt and pants before his brain caught up. He stood there in his white briefs, waiting. When Micah shimmied out of his own clothes, Josh thought he'd died and gone to heaven. He tried not to stare at his friend's near-naked body, illuminated by the strong light of the full moon. They'd changed in front of each other for years, in locker rooms, but it was the first time he'd been alone, kind of tipsy, and this close to a much more manly, grown-up Micah. Josh's pulse raced.

Micah didn't seem to notice Josh's attention, instead motioning toward the ladder leading to the high-dive platform. He started up the rungs and Josh waited for a moment, looking up at Micah's receding ass as it bobbed in the moonlight. With a deep breath, he grabbed hold of the side and stepped up.

In no time at all they stood side by side staring down at the water below, illuminated by the pool lights, shimmering and blue. Josh looked over at Micah, who was smiling.

"Ready?" Micah asked.

Josh took another breath. He was panting, but not because of the climb. It was being here with Micah that left him breathless. Even drunk, he knew one word, one wrong look would ruin everything. Josh willed his brain and body to behave. "Yeah. Ready."

Micah held out his hand. When Josh didn't move, Micah grabbed his hand and gave it a squeeze. "We'll go together. On three."

"One." They spoke in unison. "Two. Three."

Josh hesitated for a fraction of a second, but Micah's tight grasp on his hand gave him courage. They jumped off the platform hand in hand, and together descended the fifteen feet before hitting the cool surface of the pool with a splash.

Underwater, Josh felt Micah still holding tight and ventured a little squeeze of his own. Was Micah telling him something? Hands still clasped, they breeched the surface of the pool. Josh couldn't breathe, overcome by a mixture of adrenaline and fear. And something else he was afraid to name, even to himself.

Micah didn't let go, but tugged Josh's hand, pulling him toward the side of the pool where they got out, shivering in the cool evening breeze. Josh barely felt it, but he noticed Micah's nipples, peaked and dark. He shuddered.

"Time for a real dive!" Micah said in a soft voice that sent shivers through Josh. He couldn't dive.

Micah led him back to the ladder and they ascended. Once on the platform, Micah demonstrated the position. He had his feet together and he showed Josh how to hold up his arms. "Line up next to me, just like this."

Josh stepped to the edge.

"Get your toes right out over the platform, like this."

"I'm afraid."

"Don't be. I'm here."

"We can't dive together."

"No. I'll go first, show you what to do."

"No. I can't do it."

"Sure you can, Josh." Micah stepped closer and with a toe nudged Josh's feet into the right position. Then he held out his arms. "You do it."

Josh did.

"Not quite. Let me show you." Micah reached out to show Josh where to bend his knees and elbows, his long fingers leaving trails of fire along Josh's skin.

They'd never been quite this close before, at least not with so little clothing on. Josh wanted to look at Micah, stare at him, drink in his near-nakedness, but he was afraid. Even the slight touches, the hand-holding and the way Micah showed him how to stand, had more of an effect than he wanted to admit. He could feel his cock filling, and a cold dread washed over him. He tried to think of anything but Micah so close. Close enough to touch, to kiss, to love.

Josh's cock wasn't deterred, and he dared a glance downward, noticing how it started to push out the thin white cotton briefs, wet and clinging to every curve and bulge. He felt his whole body flush.

"Josh." Micah's voice was just a whisper.

Josh looked away. He knew what would happen if he saw Micah's face.

"You go first. Show me." Josh choked out the words.

"Okay. Watch me." Micah gave Josh a warm squeeze on the shoulder, then a brisk smack on the butt. He took a deep breath, edged his toes over the platform, pointed his hands, and took off from the platform.

Josh watched him execute a simple but flawless forward pike with only a small splash as he entered the water.

A moment later, Micah broke the surface with a grin and a wave. "Your turn!"

Josh moved to the edge and watched Micah do a slow crawl to the shallow end of the pool. Once there, Micah turned and sat at the bottom of the steps. It looked like a mile away from up here on the platform. Could he do this? He had to. Micah was watching. Josh's heart raced and he considered running home, avoiding Micah entirely. It was almost as embarrassing as worrying that Micah had seen the bulge in his briefs. No. He had to do this, he told himself.

"Josh?" Micah practically shouted. His voice echoed off the walls and the surface of the pool. "Just jump. I don't care if you dive. Whatever you do is fine."

Josh peered down at Micah, then at the shimmering surface of the water below him. He raised his arms over his head and pushed off slowly, trying to imitate Micah's dive. He wasn't sure if he did the right thing with his legs, but before he knew it, his fingertips broke the surface of the water and he submerged. He swam underwater toward Micah at the shallow end.

"Great job, Josh. I can't believe it. That was amazing."

"Liar." Josh pushed his wet hair off his face and wiped his eyes with his hand.

"No. Well, okay, it wasn't perfect, but damn good for your first time." Micah clapped Josh on the back, his hand slapping up droplets of water.

"Really?"

"Yeah!"

Josh sat down on the shallow steps to try to catch his breath. It had been exhilarating diving into the pool, but hearing Micah's praise had been so much better. His heart was pounding and his ears were ringing and Micah was smiling at him. And God, he loved that smile! He ran a hand through his hair and looked back to see a different expression flicker across Micah's features. He wasn't sure what it meant, but he sure knew the effect it was having on him. Micah's pale skin shone in the light from the moon. He wanted to reach out and touch Micah's face, feel the soft skin, brush the drops of water away.

Afraid to look down for fear his cock was going to embarrass him, he put his hands in his lap instead. He couldn't help but venture a glance in the direction of Micah's crotch. There was a similar bulge there. What did that mean?

Micah, still smiling, scooted over so his thigh was pressed up against Josh's. Micah's face, his mouth, were just inches from Josh's. He could feel Micah's breath on his cheek.

*Oh, God.* Did Micah maybe feel the same pull? The same connection, the same excitement? Josh was afraid to hope. He felt

Micah's hand on his shoulder, turning him so their lips were so close, he could feel Micah's breath. He looked right into Micah's green eyes, and decided even if he only got one kiss ever from Micah, it would be the most wonderful thing in the world. Josh let his lips brush Micah's, felt Micah's hand tighten on his bicep.

"What are you two doing in the pool?" It was a cop shouting from the other side of the fence, wearing a uniform and shining a very bright flashlight on them.

They jumped at the voice, springing apart. By the time the cop got down to the shallow end they were shivering and several feet apart. Josh glanced over at Micah, who was staring at his own feet.

"You boys know you're not supposed to be in here at night. Do I have to call your parents?"

"No, sir." Micah spoke up. "If we go home and promise not to do this again, will you please not call them?"

"What're your names?"

Josh looked over at Micah, who nodded. "Josh Golden and Micah Solomon."

"How old are you?"

"Seventeen."

The cop shook his head. "Pre-college pranks, huh?" He didn't wait for a reply. "Okay, I'll let you off this one time, but if I see you in here again, or hear anything about either one of you causing trouble again, you're gonna get it. Hear?"

"Yes, Officer," they replied.

"Get your clothes and get home." He watched as they collected their clothes and dressed. By the time Josh had tied his tennis shoes, Micah was already gone.

# Chapter Four

AFTER the almost kiss at the pool, Josh hadn't seen Micah again before he left for Massachusetts the following week. While Micah studied at Brandeis, Josh stayed in New York and went to NYU for accounting, thanks to a scholarship from the Hebrew Society. He and Micah barely spoke after that. A card at Josh's birthday. An uncomfortable conversation at High Holy Days, when they'd run into each other at synagogue. Josh began to wonder if he'd imagined the whole thing. But if he had, then why wouldn't Micah call him or return his calls? Why did Micah seem to be avoiding him? Or maybe he had only imagined Micah's interest? That thought was infinitely worse.

They saw each other rarely over the next few years. Josh heard about Micah from his parents or via gossip at the restaurant. Micah got into trouble with drugs. He'd been arrested a couple of times, caught with small amounts of pot and once with speed, but he was still seventeen the first time, and his father managed to keep him out of serious trouble. Micah's parents had enough money to hire the best lawyer for him, after all. Later, Josh heard Micah was using drugs pretty heavily and had even been sent to rehab one summer.

There were other rumors, too—that Micah slept around a lot, even got some girl pregnant. Then the news dried up for a while, and Josh wondered if maybe Micah had gotten his act together. But it didn't matter anymore.

Josh had all but concluded he was better off without Micah after all.

NOW, as Josh stared up at the guest room ceiling, the memories swirled in his jet-lagged brain and quickly erased any pleasure he might have gotten from the thought that Micah had been sleeping in the same bed just a few hours earlier. Micah had been disappointing him for more than a decade now. It was hardly anything new. And even when Josh thought he was completely out of his life, Micah showed up and threatened to twist his heart into knots, yet again.

Well, he wouldn't let that happen. He'd spent years running away from home, from this neighborhood, this house, his family... and Micah. He'd built his life into everything he'd ever wanted: he worked in one of the most talked-about restaurants in France. Hell, he practically *ran* the place. He was on the verge of becoming an internationally renowned chef in his own right, and a couple of weeks back home while his mom had her gallbladder removed was not going to derail his big future.

Micah had fucked up Josh's life, and the universe had paid him back big time. Now Micah was the fucked-up one, with a suspended law license, a drug conviction on his record, and an ex-wife who probably wanted less to do with him than Josh did. Except that they had a son.

He rolled over onto his side and closed his eyes, begging the oblivion of healing sleep to take over. If he was lucky, he'd wake refreshed and discover all of this had been nothing more than a sleep-deprived dream—nightmare really.

But outside the door, he heard the patter of passing footsteps up and down the hallway and low whispers of people who thought they were being quiet but were failing miserably. He thought he heard his mother's voice and the familiar low tones he recalled from the few intimate moments he and Micah had shared. Those voices were followed by a sharper, high-pitched voice that sounded startlingly familiar. Ethan's voice reminded Josh of Rina's. He hadn't seen her since college, but they'd spoken on the phone. Rina, ironically, had hoped Josh could help her figure out why her marriage was failing.

At the time, Josh thought he had a pretty good idea. Not that it would do any of them any good. Not now.

Still, there was one particular conversation with Rina Josh couldn't forget, though he'd tried to many times.

"WHY are you calling me?" It had taken him a moment when she said her name—he hadn't spoken to Rina in years. Not that he'd forgotten her either. He'd genuinely liked her, cared about her even. That, and she was the woman Micah had married. How could he forget that?

"You and Micah are friends. I thought you'd want to help."

"Friends? Where'd you get that idea?" He hadn't meant to snap, but the entire thing with Micah still hurt so damn much. It had been more than five—closer to ten—years since Micah had dumped him for Rina. Shouldn't he be over it by now?

"Oh." Surprise colored her voice and she paused, the low hum of transatlantic static heavy in the emptiness "I thought…."

"How'd you even find me?"

"Well, Micah talks about you. He told me you were in Paris and that Jenna probably had your number. He mentioned it when you got the job at the restaurant, how it was such a big step up for your career."

It was. But how did Micah know? And why did he care?

"I'm glad you're doing so well." Rina's voice jarred his thoughts. For the first time during the conversation, he realized she sounded really upset. Frightened, even. He'd never known Rina to be afraid—she had more chutzpah than any woman he knew.

"Look, Rina, I can't help him. He's never listened to me about these things."

"I'm not asking you to help him. I'm asking you to help me. And Ethan. Our son."

*Our son.* He repeated the words to himself and his gut twisted. He didn't reply. He wasn't feeling very charitable, even though he had once cared about her and worried about whatever she was going through—she had the child to take care of too. He hesitated, not wanting to get involved in Micah's family life.

Rina didn't let Josh's silence deter her. "Josh, I don't know exactly what's gone on between the two of you, and I don't need to know. But I need your help. I don't know what to do."

"Okay. Tell me." *She hadn't done anything wrong*, he reminded himself. That was all on Micah, not Rina.

"He's been acting strange. Going out at weird times, not telling me or his office where he is most of the time. He's not sleeping, even when he is home."

Josh had plenty of explanations for Micah's behavior, but Rina wouldn't like any of them. It was easy to imagine the worst about Micah after everything that had happened between them. "That sounds familiar and it's no big mystery. He's probably using again."

"I don't think so...."

"Those are classic signs, Rina. Why can't you just face facts?"

He heard a sniffle across the line and realized his tone had been even harsher than his words. He bit his lip and chose his words more carefully. "Rina, I'm sorry. I'm not trying to hurt you. I'm just trying to be realistic here. You have to think of yourself. And of Ethan. If Micah's using again, he could be dangerous to you two as well as himself."

"I know, Josh. What should I do?" She sounded desperate, not at all like the accomplished Harvard MBA he knew she was. At the moment, she was a worried mother, not a businesswoman.

"Did you check for drugs?" He realized he was clenching the telephone so tightly his hand hurt.

"No."

"Go check. Look around his office and—"

"Yes. Josh, I think I found some. Something. I'm not sure what. I was taking groceries from the car and there was a little bag in the trunk, behind the spare tire."

"In *your* car?"

"Yeah. He used it the other day, and when I got home with the groceries the next time I drove it, he started yelling at me."

"Did he threaten you?"

"No." She sniffed again. "No. But he scared me. He told me to go inside and he'd sort out the groceries. Later he apologized, and I noticed the bag was gone. But, Josh, I'm afraid. For him. For Ethan. For me."

"Can you talk to him about it?" Josh had no faith that Micah would listen to anyone. Micah could barely tell himself the truth or get himself out of what appeared to be a disastrous marriage. Josh wondered how the hell he'd managed any success in his job.

"I've tried, but he keeps saying it's something to do with a client."

"That's a convenient excuse. Keeps him from having to actually tell you anything, doesn't it?" The man was a consummate liar. He had been for years now, at least since he'd gone away to college. Josh felt vindicated, almost pleased with himself to have figured it all out for her. If she couldn't see the truth staring her straight in the face, he damned well could.

"But, Josh, he does some work defending kids with drug issues. I mean, he could be telling the truth."

*Right. And the tooth fairy lives on Staten Island!* Josh took a slow breath. At least he wasn't paying for this call. He had no idea how much calls from New York to France cost, but Rina worked for some huge bank and Micah had to make plenty as a lawyer. "If that were true, he wouldn't be acting so strange, right? It's not that he's lying, it's that he's showing signs of using. That's a different issue."

"Right. Okay, you're right. I'm glad I called you, Josh. You're helping me put this all in perspective. I'll take Ethan to my parents and then…." She didn't finish the sentence.

Josh didn't want to know how she would handle it. He didn't care. All that mattered was that Rina and the boy were safe from whatever mess Micah had gotten himself into this time.


THE next he heard from Rina was a week later.

"They arrested him, Josh. He's in jail."

Josh waited for the inevitable. He expected to feel a little jitter or even a couple of weak butterflies, but his gut was calm. Micah's power to screw with him—with all of them—was over. Thank God.

"They found cocaine in his car. A lot. They say he had dealer weight."

*Holy shit. He's dealing now?* "Are you okay?" was all he said. He reminded himself he was okay too. They'd all be okay now.

"Yeah. Except for the idea that my husband is going to jail for a really long time." She sounded shaky, as though she wasn't convinced. Micah had that effect on people, Josh reminded himself. He made them care, then pulled the rug out from under them with his selfish behavior.

"He had the stuff, Rina. You can't really argue with that. He can't pretend it didn't happen." Josh felt a sense of satisfaction in knowing that Micah had been caught red-handed. *Once an addict, always an addict.*

"It's just not the kind of thing he's ever done before. I can't figure out why he'd be dealing drugs."

"Maybe he couldn't hide how much he was spending anymore and he had to start dealing to cover his own habit." What did she want him to say? He was the last person who was going to give Micah another break. Where had it gotten him before, anyhow?

"He won't talk to me about it. He just says it's not what I think."

"And you believe him? After everything he's done? All his lies?" He sighed and closed his eyes.

"He's never lied to me before."

*Right. Sure he hasn't.* Josh wouldn't make Rina feel any worse by listing everything he knew about Micah that she didn't. He suspected she had no clue he and Micah had been lovers until their engagement. "Or you haven't found out about it yet."

"What's that supposed to mean?" Her voice took on a sharp tone that might have sliced off an ear if he'd been in the same room with her. As it was, the shrillness still echoed through his brain.

"Ask Micah. I'm done with him. I think you'd be better off without him. We all are."

"I'll talk to him and see what happens with the charges."

"Let me know if I can help you." He wanted to make it clear he had no interest in helping Micah.

"Thanks, Josh."

Luckily, she'd never asked for his help.

He'd found out from his parents that Micah had been charged with possession with intent to sell. He'd spent months in jail before he eventually pled to a lesser offense, but he'd still gotten a year in prison and six months at a halfway house for drug offenders. He'd refused to reveal how or where he got the drugs, even though they'd have thrown in the time served. He'd been suspended from the bar and probably would never practice law again. Micah had thrown everything away. His wife, his kid, his career. Josh couldn't summon up much concern even if he suspected what Micah was up to: hiding in his closet and taking drugs to ease his guilt, like he'd done in college. Or partying with the wrong crowd. Micah had made his bed. Maybe he'd find a new boyfriend in prison.

NOW, Josh was back in New York and Micah was out of prison, virtually unemployable and supporting his kid by sponging off Josh's too-generous parents.

And he'd taken up residence in Josh's old bedroom.

The perfect start to Josh's first trip home in years.

*Chag sameach. Yeah, happy fucking holidays.*

THE following day Miriam was admitted to the hospital for what was very routine surgery. It was the recovery that would be tough. She'd be off her feet for a few days, and she'd need to take it easy for another couple of weeks. Working at the restaurant was out of the question. Hence, the need for Josh to call in a shitload of favors from Raymond Vessy to get time off.

The three of them took a taxi to the hospital, and even without his father behind the wheel, the short trip from Alphabet City in lower Manhattan to the hospital in midtown pushed Josh just about to his limit.

"I left some hamburger in the fridge for Ethan's dinner." Miriam patted his father's shoulder from the backseat. "Oh, and there's one load of laundry still in the dryer—I didn't have a chance to fold it before we left this morning."

"Mom." Josh smiled at his mother to reassure her. "You really didn't need to do all that. Dad and I can manage just fine."

"Mrs. Samuels is bringing a casserole by tomorrow morning," she continued without missing a beat.

"I could have made something, Mom."

"I didn't want you to worry about it," Miriam answered. "Besides, you'll be busy with the restaurant."

"All this stopping and starting. We should have taken the FDR," Seymour told the cabbie, who ignored the comment.

Throughout all this, the taxi wove in and out of lanes, nearly hitting a bus. Josh wasn't sure whether the headache forming between his eyes was because of the stopping and starting or his mother's worrying. *She* was the one having surgery, and she was worried about *them*.

"It'll be okay, Mom." Josh prayed it would be.


JOSH sat with his dad in the waiting room during the procedure, drinking far too much bitter vending-machine coffee. Josh's stomach protested but he needed something to do.

"You better get going, son," Seymour said as soon as the doctor had reported the surgery had gone well. His father would be allowed to visit Miriam in recovery, but Josh wouldn't be able to see her until she was in her room later on.

"I'll stay here with you, Dad."

"No. I mean you need to get going to the restaurant. You're in charge of dinner. Micah doesn't know how to run the kitchen during meals. He can slice and dice and garnish, but you have to organize the staff. They're expecting you."

Josh started to grumble and realized, once again, he sounded a lot like his dad. The thought chilled him almost as much as being reminded he'd have to work in the cramped kitchen with Micah. He barely could spare two words for him during a very uncomfortable breakfast they'd been forced to share. Only the presence of Ethan kept Josh from being as rude as he wanted. "Okay, Dad. I'm doing this for you and Mom."

"We appreciate your sacrifice."

Josh got up to leave, wondering if his dad had meant that sarcastically, or sincerely.

## Chapter Five

JOSH cabbed it to the restaurant and arrived with less than an hour before dinner service started. He paid the driver and stood on the sidewalk outside, staring up at the sign that read "Goldens." It had once read "Golden's Deli," but his parents wanted the place to sound more upmarket, so they'd dropped "Deli." Adding "Restaurant" to the sign would cost more than they could spare, and there had been a long-standing argument over where the apostrophe should go. His mother wanted "Goldens'" since it was a family business, and his father wanted "Golden's." When his parents couldn't agree, it had been removed from the sign altogether, leaving the current incarnation simply "Goldens." But the menu covers proclaimed "Goldens Restaurant" in flashy gold-foil script on fake red leather that Josh's dad hated as soon as they'd been printed. Josh smiled as he noted the same old menus were still piled up next to the hostess stand.

The interior hadn't changed much in the five or so years since he'd last stepped foot in the restaurant. An airy and bright front section with a few tables at the window offered views of bundled-up passersby, while further inside the décor shifted to leather booths and dark wooden tables with captain's chairs. It felt like it had been designed by the dad in the Brady Bunch and remained in a time warp. But it was clean, and Gina, the hostess, greeted him warmly and asked after his mother's health as he moved toward the kitchen.

He took a breath before opening the door. He'd been in this kitchen since he could walk, and he'd run Raymond Vessy's kitchen on many occasions, but for the first time in his culinary career he really was the top chef—in charge of everyone and every decision—for good or bad. The excitement coursed through his veins, made his blood pump more quickly, and his breath hitched as he put a hand on the kitchen door. He couldn't wait to take charge.

One glance around sent his mood plummeting. He'd arrived not a moment too soon with dinner little more than thirty minutes away. There was an assistant chef and a dessert chef, who, along with one or two good prep and line cooks, should have been able to handle everything. Josh should have only needed to keep everyone on task, supervise any complicated techniques, and make executive decisions in the front of the house. His father had already introduced him to most of the kitchen staff the night before, so he wasn't going in cold and expecting discipline from a bunch of total strangers. And yet, in spite of all that, half the prep work hadn't been done.

One prep cook, Martin, a guy in his forties who had worked for the Goldens for several years, had a pile of unevenly sliced onions and was sawing away at another onion in front of him, with a bucket full of whole onions on the counter beside him that should have been ready long before now.

"Martin, who taught you to slice onions? Don't you know the simplest thing about cooking?"

Martin stopped slicing and stared open-mouthed at Josh. The others in the kitchen paused in their motions then went back to work. Josh stepped up and grabbed Martin's knife from him. He looked it over. "First off, this isn't sharp enough. Someone get me another knife."

No one moved. From the other end of the counter, Micah silently handed Josh another knife. Josh took it and examined it. "At least this is sharp enough. Now watch!" He gave Martin and the others a basic lesson he'd learned on day one of culinary school. "Cut in a smooth motion like this—" He demonstrated. "—and make sure the slices are even so they cook evenly. No one wants to bite into a piece of onion that's cooked too much or too little." He picked up one of Martin's original efforts. "See how uneven that is? Every slice will be partially undercooked *and* overcooked. It's a good thing you hadn't gotten very far. Put these aside and start over. We'll use these slices for soup or something." He slammed the knife back onto the counter and moved to the next person.

"What are you working on?"

Leah, a twenty-something with a nose ring and wide brown eyes, sniffled and stammered. "Salad, Josh."

"Chef. In the kitchen, call me 'Chef'."

"But we just call your parents—"

"They're not here right now." Josh let out a loud breath and looked from face to face. Except for Micah; he ignored Micah. "Everyone back to work." He continued his way around, prompting the staff to do the jobs they should have already finished, pointing them to others they should have known to do without his supervision. No wonder his parents needed him here. They couldn't trust their own staff to get the job done without them. He'd expected far more from these people. It seemed his parents still did the lion's share of the cooking, and the staff was lost when they were expected to independently perform jobs which should be second nature to them.

He'd run kitchens in France for years, and he had to fight the urge to yell in French. He was used to a certain amount of deference and discipline in the kitchen, and he was appalled at how poorly trained this crew was. Getting dinner prepped, then cooked and served felt like a three-ring circus. Cooks got in each other's way, dropped food and pans, and if he hadn't been there to pick up the slack they wouldn't have managed. Damn good thing it was early in the week and not particularly busy. By the time they stopped taking orders at ten, Josh felt like he'd already been there a week and not six hours.

He gave the clean-up crew their instructions then sent the kitchen staff home. He spent fifteen minutes inspecting the kitchen and making notes on what needed to be done the following day. This place was a disaster! How on earth could his parents run a restaurant this way? It was a good thing he was home to get their business in shape.

He ran his hands through his hair and realized he hadn't eaten anything resembling a meal since some crappy pizza he and his dad had gotten in the hospital cafeteria during his mom's surgery. He arranged a plate of leftovers, heated it up, and headed for the dining room, stopping on the way to pour a glass of the best by-the-glass wine he could find in the bar. He had just settled himself into a table in the dining room—now closed—when he heard footsteps moving in his direction. He grabbed the knife and turned around, stopping himself just in time from stabbing Micah.

"Can I join you?"

"No." Josh was too tired to deal with Micah. It had been bad enough having to work alongside the man during dinner.

Micah sat down anyway. He really liked making everyone else follow his rules, didn't he? He hadn't changed at all. Maybe he'd learned some even worse habits in prison.

Josh took a healthy sip of wine and suppressed the urge to spit it out again. Little better than vinegar, and he'd actually tasted better vinegar. Maybe he'd need to redo the wine list while he was here. He started eating, not bothering to look at Micah.

"You didn't seem very happy with the staff tonight."

"Good guess, Sherlock." Maybe Micah would get the hint he was unwelcome at the table and just leave. "They didn't do a very good job. I had to watch everything they were doing."

"Everyone works fine when your parents are here."

Micah's words were matter-of-fact, but Josh's anger flared at the insinuation. Josh swung around to face Micah, glaring at him full-on. Damn. He shouldn't have looked at the man. Why was it when he looked into those deep green eyes all his resolve went to hell?

If anything, Micah had gotten better looking over the years. Sure, there were tiny lines around his eyes and mouth, but they only served to accentuate Micah's features. His hair was a bit longer than Josh remembered, tumbling over his ears and forehead. Here and there, Josh thought he saw a few strands of gray, but Micah's dark silky hair was still shiny and full. Josh pushed away the memory of how that hair felt between his fingers. It had been more than ten years since they'd spoken, longer since they'd been together, speaking like normal people, still lovers and long-time best friends. And now, just one glance at Micah's face had Josh's body telling his brain that nothing in between mattered. But it did matter, he reminded himself.

"Are you listening?" Micah's voice was deeper, more gravelly, like maybe he'd gotten in the habit of smoking in prison. It gave his voice an edge, a sexiness, it never had before. Another thing to ignore, Josh's brain told the rest of his body.

"Yeah. I just don't care." Josh turned back to his plate and forced himself to focus on the potatoes and not to listen to Micah's voice or wonder if Micah's lips would still feel the same as they trailed along his neck.

"Well you should. Maybe they weren't at their best tonight, made some mistakes. They're worried about your mom, too." Micah paused but Josh didn't glance at him. "No one's gonna say anything right to your face the first night, but from what they said behind your back, they're pissed—and hurt. They love your parents, but not enough to put up with two weeks of you. And it won't help your mom's recovery to find out what's going on here."

Micah's blunt words took Josh by surprise. His shoulders tensed and he shot back defensively, "So suddenly *you're* the expert on treating people right and going behind someone's back? And you're worried about the consequences? Did you learn all that in prison?"

Out of the corner of his eye, Josh saw Micah nod slowly. He still didn't trust himself to look directly at Micah. Not yet.

"I deserve that. But it doesn't change what I told you."

Josh set down his fork with a clatter. "Did you do any of those twelve-step programs?"

"What's that got to do with anything?"

Josh blinked. "Aren't you supposed to right your wrongs, or something like that?"

"Make amends. Yes."

"I guess you skipped that step?"

"No."

"I don't recall any apology from you." Resentment clawed at Josh's gut. Why the hell could Micah still make him so angry? Hadn't he moved on? He was over Micah, he reminded himself, because his emotions needed reminding.

"I tried. You wouldn't take my calls, and I guess you didn't read my letters." Micah's voice was calm and controlled, in spite of Josh's anger.

"So, it's my fault?"

"No, Josh. None of it was your fault. I already told you that, a long time ago." Micah's voice softened, still gravelly, but more intimate and more obviously sad.

"I guess you're off the hook." Josh was tired of this. It was bad enough worrying about his mother. Did he have to deal with Micah's shit as well?

"If it would make a difference, I can tell you what really happened."

"It wouldn't." What else could Micah possibly say? Why he kept living a lie and hurting everyone who ever loved him? Micah had already done a damn good job hurting him and Rina. And one day soon that kid of his too.

"Then let's not make any of this discussion personal. I just wanted to give you a heads up on the kitchen staff. I wouldn't want to make things difficult for your parents."

"My parents? How convenient of you to care about them. I guess it's understandable, since they're the only thing standing between you and a room at the Salvation Army." Josh took a long drink of his wine, ignoring the taste.

"Your parents have been very kind to me. I've been completely honest with them about everything—"

"Really?" *Right.*

"Yes. And—"

"I don't want to talk about this anymore." Josh got up and took his dishes into the kitchen, placing them in the rack for the dishwashers. Micah didn't follow him.

Josh made sure the kitchen was stowed away for the night. Breakfast was the easy meal, so he wouldn't have to be back until lunchtime the following day. He needed a good night's sleep. He worked his way around the restaurant, locking everything up and flipping off most of the lights. Micah must have already left. Before letting himself out, Josh stopped at the bar and retrieved the rest of the bottle of wine. It wasn't as bad as he originally thought. Or maybe he was in too bad a mood to really give a fuck.

Shit. He'd been here twenty-four hours and already he'd let his culinary standards slip. Who knew what a mess he'd be after two weeks? Would Vessy even take him back when he returned to Paris? He slipped the bottle into a paper bag, popped the cork out, took a swig, then recorked it and let himself out the back door. A shadow in the alley moved and he grabbed the bottle like a baseball bat. It wouldn't do much damage, but it was better than nothing.

"It's just me."

*Fuck.* Even in pitch black, Josh recognized the voice. Would the man not take a hint? "You scared the shit out of me. I thought you left ages ago."

"I did, but I was just walking around. I came back so you wouldn't walk home on your own. The neighborhood's changed a lot and—"

"And what, you were worried about me?"

"Well. Yes."

"Save it." He took a swig of wine and then moved off quickly. He didn't want a nice stroll home with Micah. He stepped into a pot-hole in the alley and nearly fell. He caught his balance at the last moment, but he twisted his ankle a little with the effort. Frustrated, tired, he sat down on someone's back steps and rubbed the ankle for a minute while he fortified himself with some more wine. He was only a few blocks from home now, but he walked over to the main street, just in case.

"Hey, dude, you got the time?"

The voice startled Josh. It was a short, thin guy wearing a hoodie, with long, greasy-looking dark hair. "Yeah. Um." He took a look at his watch. "Ten to midnight."

"That's some hella nice watch you got there, dude."

*Aw fuck.* One night back in the city and he'd fallen for this old trick? *Fuck.*

He saw the flash of what he thought might be a knife. "I'd sure like a nice watch like that one."

"Yeah, sure." Josh started to unfasten the watch. He had to put the wine down on the nearest steps to do it; then he took a deep breath and handed it over. It *was* a nice watch, he thought sadly.

The guy grabbed it and ran toward the alley. Josh heard a scuffle and a few shouts and saw a blur a couple of doors down. One figure knocked the other down and gave a sharp kick. Josh started running.

"Josh, it's okay."

*Micah.* Josh stopped. He stood there, mouth hanging open. He must have looked like a fool. Thank God it was dark.

"I got your watch back. But he might have friends hanging around. We should get going." Micah grabbed Josh's arm and tugged him in the direction of home. They ran like the devil himself was after them. Josh got to the door first and unlocked it. Micah tumbled into the entryway after him, both of them breathing hard. Josh bent down, hands resting on his thighs. He gasped, throat raw from the cold air, heart rate not yet slowing down as he fought off the wave of panic he hadn't let himself feel while he was being robbed.

"You okay?" Micah laid his hand on Josh's shoulder in a gesture of concern. Josh felt a long-forgotten jolt of heat at the contact and pulled away.

"Yeah." Josh gasped a few more times. "Thanks."

Micah shrugged. "I'm beat. Gotta get to bed. Ethan doesn't sleep well if I'm not around to tuck him in."

Josh had forgotten about Ethan. Now he recalled the neighbor was watching him until Micah got home. The woman had fallen asleep on the couch. Micah took another crocheted afghan—the house was lousy with them—and covered her up before making his own way up the stairs.

Josh locked up, turned the lights off, and went upstairs. He washed up and changed for bed, climbing between the sheets that still smelled a little like Micah.

Had he been too hard on Micah? Maybe. Sure, he'd been all nice and helpful tonight, and maybe he'd even saved Josh's life. Thankfully, the thug hadn't pulled the knife on him, but based on the way Micah had overpowered the guy so easily, maybe he could have handled the knife as well. Had Micah learned how to beat people up in prison? Wherever he'd learned it, it proved to be a valuable skill. Josh never thought he'd accept something like that before tonight. But he hadn't been thinking too clearly, either. He'd give everything a good think in the morning, after he'd slept off the wine and the fear and the surprise.

He closed his eyes, remembering the feel of Micah's hand on his shoulder and the look of concern on Micah's face. His jaw tightened as the familiar pain reasserted itself.

Tomorrow. He'd think about it all tomorrow. Only lying there in the dark, Josh couldn't help but remember how close they'd come to something more than this. For just a short time, he'd even believed they'd be happy.

THAT almost kiss the summer before college had been Josh's last good memory of the boy he thought he'd loved for many years. For whatever reason, Micah had changed. Turned into someone else. Someone Josh didn't know anymore. Still, he never stopped thinking about Micah. Or dreaming about him. Or loving him.

The summer Micah came back home after graduating from Brandeis, he called Josh at least half a dozen times, but each time Josh told his parents he couldn't talk, or he was running out to do something and he'd call Micah when he got back. It was a lie. He had no intention of calling Micah or of seeing him. Not now. Not after so long. Not after everything he'd heard Micah had done. He was a different Micah than the one Josh had known and fallen for.

One afternoon in late summer, Micah showed up on his doorstep unannounced. Josh's mom was home before dinner rush at the restaurant and welcomed him with open arms, though she had a sour look on her face. She'd passed along plenty of gossip about Micah, delivered with her usual clucks of disapproval and a sad look in her eyes that said "such a nice boy with such promise could get himself in that kind of trouble."

"Trouble" was Josh's mother's code for drugs or getting someone pregnant, or getting pregnant. She could be fairly judgmental, but Josh knew when it came to Micah, she worried a lot.

This time, there was nowhere to hide. Josh was right there in the living room when Micah walked inside. "Hey, Josh."

"Hey." Josh tried not to look at Micah but failed miserably. Why did the guy have to look so good, anyhow? Where there was just the hint of muscle when he'd last seen him, Micah's body had changed. He wasn't overly broad, but had a nice, lean look to him. *Like a swimmer.* The thought reminded Josh of the pool, and he looked back down at the book he'd been reading.

"Want to grab some pizza over at Geraci's?"

It had been Josh's favorite place, not that far from home. Just far enough to get away from the prying eyes of the neighborhood and the community. And somewhere one could get meat and cheese on a pizza without risking the hard glares of the "kosher patrol," as he and Micah used to call them. Hardly anyone in the neighborhood actually kept kosher outside of their homes, but enough of them pretended to by glaring at anyone who flouted the rules in public. Josh hadn't been to the place in years. Not since the last time he and Josh had eaten there, the day before the midnight pool incident. Why was it every thought led him back to that night?

"Nah. Mom made pot roast. Dinner's in two hours."

"Micah, stay for dinner," Josh's mother shouted from the kitchen.

Josh cringed. He didn't want her listening in on their conversation. No matter how it went, he wanted it to be private.

"Sorry, Mrs. Golden, I can't tonight." He lowered his voice. "Josh, I need to talk to you."

Josh sighed. "Sure. Your treat." He headed for the front door so he wouldn't have to pass his mom in the kitchen. She'd kill him if she thought he was going to ruin his appetite for dinner. Truth was he didn't have any appetite. Not with Micah back.

"Take your jacket, Joshy! It looks like rain!" his mother shouted, as if he were a kid who needed looking after.

He pressed his lips together then grabbed the windbreaker off the rack and slammed the front door behind him.

They walked the ten blocks to the pizza place without talking. Josh couldn't help thinking how strange it felt, being with Micah and not finding anything to say. In high school, they'd talked about everything from music, to politics, and even about their hopes for college and beyond. Josh had never felt so uncomfortable. At least, not since that night at the pool.

They settled into a booth in the back of the restaurant near the bathroom. Josh had to wonder if Micah had chosen it because it was private—they'd never sat here before. It was still early, not even close to dinnertime, and the place was only half full. Josh toyed with the red-and-white checkered placemat in front of him, folding the corners back and forth until one of them ripped off. He slid the bit of paper underneath and hoped Micah hadn't noticed how uncomfortable he felt.

The place smelled of grease and pasta sauce. The faint scent of garlic and cheese hung in the air. Josh found the smells comforting. More to avoid looking at Micah than out of curiosity, he studied the large chalkboard where the day's specials had been posted. Behind the counter, one cook was tossing a crust while another opened the large oven and slid an uncooked pizza onto the rack. It was a good distraction: Josh had always been fascinated by restaurant kitchens—except the one at his parents' restaurant, that was.

A waitress tossed menus on their table and took their drink orders—two beers, whatever was on tap—and walked away.

They opened their menus and Josh concentrated on the words rather than look at Micah. He hadn't really looked Micah in the face since the moment their lips had touched that night in the pool four years earlier. He'd been afraid to.

Micah closed his menu and leaned forward on the table, resting his elbows on the surface. "Josh."

Josh raised the menu a little so he wouldn't be tempted to look into Micah's green eyes.

Micah reached forward and pulled the menu down. "Look at me, Josh."

Reluctantly, Josh met Micah's gaze. His stomach leapt and butterflies invaded his gut. Heat raced through his body from his head to the tips of his fingers and toes, culminating with a sizzling burn in his cheeks. They probably glowed bright red—so bright they could turn the lights off in the place and everyone could still see what they were eating.

"What?" The word came out as a croaky whisper.

"I'm sorry."

"For what?"

The waitress returned with their beers and plunked them on the table. She pulled her order pad out of her apron and looked at Josh, then Micah, expectantly, but without saying a word.

"Large number sixteen," Micah said, without even glancing up at the woman. His gaze never strayed from Josh.

Josh heard her scribbling on the pad and walking away. It was all he could do to keep looking at Micah. He wanted to look down again. "Sorry for what?"

"For everything."

"Okay."

"No, it's not okay. I need to tell you something."

"No, you don't. You haven't talked to me for four years. What's so urgent now?"

"I'm heading off to law school next week."

"Law school." Josh took a sip of beer and nodded, more to himself than to Micah. "Odd choice, isn't it, given what I've heard about you the past few years."

Micah glanced around before settling his gaze back on Josh. He let out a breath and fidgeted with his hands before answering. "I know what you must be thinking."

"You don't know. But even if you did, it doesn't matter. We're not friends anymore, so nothing I think should matter." It hurt just to say it.

Micah reached one hand across the table but stopped short of touching Josh. "It matters to me. You still matter to me."

"Really?" Josh sat back against his seat, putting his hands in his lap, out of Micah's reach. His body, even after all these years, had a mind of its own as far as Micah was concerned. Like that long-ago night at the pool, Josh wanted to stay in control. The years in between hadn't erased what his heart felt, even if his brain told him how stupid it was to still care, to still hope.

"Josh, you might not believe it, but that night, that last night we spent… at the pool…. It was really… nice. Nice being alone there with you. Nice until the cops came and ruined everything. I wanted to tell you then, but I was afraid. I thought you felt the same things, so it wasn't that. It was me. I wasn't ready. And I wasted a lot of time."

Now Micah had Josh's full attention. This was the last thing he expected to hear. At least if Micah was saying what Josh thought he was trying to say. But why had it taken four years? "Go on." Josh's heart rate accelerated and his mouth got dry. He sipped at his beer, trying to quench the thirst.

"Josh, I've cared about you since I can remember. Not just as a friend. I've loved you since before I even understood what that means. And now—"

The waitress showed up with their pizza. She must have realized she'd arrived at a bad moment because she just put the pan down and left. Neither Josh nor Micah even looked at her.

"What?"

"Josh, I wish I hadn't tried to ignore those feelings for so long. I can't pretend it's anything less than that, when I think about it, really think."

Josh blinked a few times. He didn't know what to say. Micah looked pale and a little sweaty, like he used to after he'd run the half mile between their houses. He gulped at his own beer and then started serving slices of pizza. He put one down in front of Josh.

"Josh, I spent a lot of time trying to erase those feelings. Yeah, I knew how you felt, but I didn't like how much I liked it." He shook his head. "I'm probably not making sense. I didn't think I was gay. I'm supposed to like girls, supposed to get married and have kids, like our parents. I never wanted to like a guy. But, I liked you. I wanted to be with you, not those girls our parents and the rabbi and the yentas were always trying to fix me up with. At least with you they gave up after a while. No one was surprised when you came out. But that wasn't what I was supposed to do. Supposed to be."

Josh took a bite of pizza, but he didn't taste it. He chewed and watched Micah.

"I did a lot of stuff I'm not proud of. I think I was trying to get away from the feelings. But none of it worked. I want to be with you. I know we probably can't, not after everything I've done–and not done. But I had to tell you. To at least try. I wanted to come clean, at least to you, so I wouldn't regret never telling you the truth of how I feel about you."

Josh took another bite of pizza. It was cold and it made his stomach churn. Part of him felt numb. Cold, just like the pizza. And yet there was something else he felt: excitement? Had Micah just said he loved him? But Micah wasn't gay and he wasn't coming out. What did it all mean, then? He pushed the plate away and ran a hand through his hair.

"Now what, Micah? What am I supposed to do with this information?" He knew he sounded angrier than he'd intended, but he couldn't help himself. How the hell *was* he supposed to react?

"Do you still have any feelings for me?"

A trick question? Josh was afraid to admit to anything. Had he really loved Micah or had it been some adolescent fantasy? The person he'd loved before college was a different one than the man who'd gotten in trouble for drugs and got college girls pregnant. Did he care about this guy sitting across the table from him? Was this the Micah he'd loved in high school? Did he even know what love was back then, when he'd wanted nothing more than a kiss?

"Come back to my house. Let's talk in private. Coming here was a bad idea." Micah's lips parted a bit and he leaned in toward Josh.

"Your house?"

"My parents are in Israel. They're making *aliyah*, and they're doing paperwork before they move for good. They won't be back till Rosh Hashanah."

Everyone in the neighborhood knew Micah's parents were moving to Israel. Making *aliyah* was the right of any Jew to return to Israel, and the dream of many American Jews. They'd be welcomed with jobs, housing, whatever they needed to smooth their way into Israeli culture and society. For a moment, Josh imagined how he'd feel if his own parents picked everything up and just left the U.S. He brushed the thought away. It'd probably be better for Micah. He could do whatever he wanted, and there'd be nobody to call him on it. Micah's parents were far more traditional than Josh's—they'd never accept a gay son, assuming Micah ever told anyone else what he'd just revealed to Josh.

"Okay." Josh just had to know. Had to take the chance.

Micah threw some money down on the table and they left.

THEY walked in silence, and it started raining a block from Micah's house. He grabbed Josh's hand and they ran the rest of the way, both dripping wet by the time they made it under the overhang on the front porch. Josh's heart beat like timpani. Micah's hand felt exactly the same as that night years ago: warm and inviting. He wondered vaguely what he was doing, going home with Micah.

Micah fumbled for the key in his pocket and opened the door. Their clothes dripped rainwater on the rug in the entrance hall. Without turning on the light Micah slipped off his jacket and hung it on a peg near the front door. Josh did the same. He knew his way around this house as well as his own. Even though he hadn't been here in years, it felt and smelled the way it always had.

He was just turning around after hanging up his jacket when Micah's arms slipped around his waist. Half a second later, Micah's lips brushed against his. He felt Micah's breath—still coming in soft pants after their run—against his cheek, and he melted against Micah's chest. He opened his mouth and let Micah's tongue inside.

The first time they'd kissed, four years before, had set his insides on fire. This contact was a million times more powerful. Every part of his body seemed to vibrate with the touch. Micah pressed him up against the wall, erection prodding Josh's thigh.

"Josh?" Micah whispered, more a question than anything. "Can I kiss you again?"

"Yes." Before Josh finished the syllable, Micah was on him. It was glorious.

"God," Micah said as their lips parted, "You don't know how long I've wanted to do that." His voice was husky, intimate.

"Actually—" Josh laughed nervously and hoped he didn't look like a complete idiot. "—I kind of do." He wouldn't tell Micah how much he'd thought about him after high school or how he'd worried *he* had been the one who'd screwed up their relationship because he'd pushed Micah too hard.

"Come upstairs? To my room?"

Micah held out his hand to Josh, who took it without hesitation. They climbed the steps in silence, Josh's heart thudding against his chest. The entire thing seemed so surreal. How many times had he imagined this?

Micah didn't turn on the light—the room was illuminated by a streetlamp outside the window that cast shadows on the ceiling. He closed the door with his foot, then pushed Josh against it and kissed him again. Unlike the other kisses, this one was less tentative, more confident, a confidence that went a long way to reassuring Josh that Micah wasn't just playing around this time.

Micah tasted so good and smelled even better, his cologne mingling with the faint scent of musk. Josh reached out and pulled Micah's shirt over his head, stopping for a moment just to look at Micah's skin. Even in the semi-darkness, Micah looked amazing. Josh ghosted his fingers over Micah's chest, reveling in the silky smoothness of it, and then found his nipples with the palms of his hands. Micah moaned in response, and Josh saw he was hard beneath his jeans.

"Josh." Micah whispered the name against Josh's neck. "I don't have a lot of experience… with men, I mean." Josh forced himself not to think of what that statement implied: that Micah had lots of experience with women. He couldn't help but remember the rumors he'd heard. *Stop it,* he told himself. *It doesn't matter.* This *is what matters.*

"I like what you're doing." Josh hoped he'd sounded reassuring. He was half reassuring himself, he knew. Micah smiled, although he still looked nervous. With an audible breath, he pulled Josh's shirt off and kissed him again.

"Bed?" he asked.

"In a minute." Josh wanted to explore Micah's body, to take things slow. He'd hoped for this so long, and he didn't want to rush it. Even in the dim light, Josh saw Micah's cheeks redden. Josh met Micah's gaze encouragingly, then reached for Micah's jeans. He unbuttoned and pulled them down to Micah's ankles, along with his boxers. Micah's body was as amazing as Josh had imagined. Long and lean and athletic. His chest was smooth, the light dusting of hair starting near his waist and darkening as it ran over his belly to the curls below.

"I was so afraid you wouldn't want me," Micah said. "After all I've done."

"I want you." God, how he wanted Micah! "I've wanted you since that night at the pool." Before, really, although Josh wouldn't tell Micah that, at least not yet. His gaze came to rest on Micah's cock— long and cut and jutting out from his body. "You're so beautiful, Micah."

Micah's blush deepened as he reached out and unbuckled Josh's jeans. It only took a minute before Josh was naked, too, and they were holding each other. Josh shivered, but it had nothing to do with the temperature in the room. Micah's hands on Josh's skin was the most amazing thing he'd ever felt. Better than he'd imagined, down to the slight tremor in Micah's hands as they slid over his back.

"Bed now." As much as standing here touching Micah was a turn-on, he also wanted their bodies to be closer.

Micah turned and walked over to the bed, the light from outside reflecting off his pale skin and making it shimmer. His shoulders were broader than when Josh had seen him in his bathing suit, his waist a bit narrower, and his ass…. Josh's throat felt tight with anticipation. He'd never felt so nervous. What if tomorrow Micah changed his mind and didn't want to see him again?

"You okay?" Micah peered up at him and lifted the comforter in invitation.

"Yeah." Josh ignored the fear and climbed into the bed. "I'm great." He pulled the comforter over their heads and kissed Micah, who slid his hands under Josh's ass and squeezed. Josh shifted to allow Micah a better grip and their cocks touched, the pressure exquisite. Josh reached down and took them both in his hand, rubbing his thumb over Micah's slit and wetting it with precome to ease his way.

Micah's moan sent shivers down Josh's body. He pushed the covers off his shoulders and got to his knees, straddling Micah.

"What?" Micah mouthed.

"I want to see you." He trailed his fingers over Micah's chin and down his chest, found a nipple with his thumb and forefinger, and rubbed until it hardened.

"Fuck. Josh. Feels amazing."

Josh bit his lower lip as he tweaked the other nub until it matched the first. Then he bent down over Micah and licked around one nipple, then the other. Micah's back arched as he made an effort to meet Josh's lips, and Josh slipped one hand between Micah's legs to fist his erection. He brushed a thumb over the tip until he coaxed another sound from Micah's lips.

"I want to taste you," he whispered against Micah's chest.

Micah's only response was an exhaled sigh.

Josh found the tip of Micah's cock with his mouth. This time, Micah gasped. Josh looked up to see Micah's face, his eyes closed, lips just slightly apart. He couldn't imagine anything better than that perfect face, knowing he was the reason for the look of absolute bliss he found there. *I love you, Micah.* It was okay that he was the only one who knew it. For now, that was just fine with him.

Josh kissed a line up and down Micah's cock, then licked around the crown, taking time to listen for Micah's moans. He wanted to learn what Micah liked. He wanted Micah to remember this, no matter what happened. Even if he couldn't say it, he'd show Micah how he felt about him.

"Josh."

Josh took Micah in his mouth, made his way down to the base of his cock with slow deliberation, then grasped it at the base. Micah's breath hitched in response, and Josh smiled, releasing Micah, then starting from the crown again and working back to the root. The taste of Micah on his tongue made Josh's own cock ache, but he ignored it. This was for Micah.

"So good," Micah rasped as his hips lifted to meet Josh's mouth. He carded his fingers through Josh's wavy hair, pulling on it. Josh rumbled his approval around Micah's cock. "God. Josh. Gonna come if you keep doing that."

Josh just smiled and released Micah from his mouth. "Can't have you coming so soon." He kissed his way back up Micah's chest and found his lips. "I have other plans for you first."

"Oh, yeah?" Micah pushed Josh over onto his back with a playful grin.

"Yeah." Josh looked up into Micah's green eyes and whispered, "I want you to fuck me."

Micah's face registered both surprise and heat. Truth be told, Josh was surprised he wanted it so badly—he almost never bottomed. But somehow the thought of Micah's cock inside of him was about the hottest thing he could imagine right now.

"Yes." Micah appeared at a loss. "I mean, I'd like that. If you want to, of course."

Josh smiled and pulled Micah's face to his. "Fuck me, Micah," he said as the kiss broke. "Now. I've wanted you for so long. I don't want to wait anymore."

"Right. Uh…."

"Condom?" Josh prompted.

"Uh, right. I bought some today. I was kind of hoping we'd have a reason to use them." Micah pulled a condom and a packet of lube out from under a pillow. The blush on his cheeks was so damn cute, Josh could barely stand it.

Josh rolled over onto his belly, offering up his back and his ass. Micah settled onto his thighs and began to rub Josh's shoulders and upper back. His flagging erection pressed into the bed, and Josh shifted as his cock stiffened with the touch.

"Feels nice." *Understatement of the year.* Micah's fingertips on Josh's skin felt like fire, as if they had awakened his body from a deep sleep.

Micah's hands ghosted over his skin, and his lips trailed behind for good measure. Micah licked and nipped at Josh's back until he found the globes of Josh's ass. "So smooth," Micah said in an undertone as he kneaded the hard muscle there.

"Touch me," Josh nearly begged. "Put your finger inside me."

"I haven't done this before," Micah admitted, sounding a little nervous now. "I don't want to hurt you."

"You won't hurt me. Just lube it up first and stretch me." God, even telling Micah what to do was so fucking hot.

Josh groaned as he heard Micah tear open the packet of lube. He parted Josh's cheeks almost reverently and, a moment later, brushed his hole with cold and slippery fingers. Micah circled the tight opening, grazing it with a thumb and then pressing just the tip of a finger against it.

"More." Josh wanted that finger to breach him. To claim him. "Please."

"I don't want to hurt you," Micah repeated, only this time Josh thought he heard the hidden meaning in those words. He pushed the niggle of doubt at the back of his brain away, wanting just to *feel* for a change. This was Micah, he reminded himself. The Micah he'd loved for years. The Micah he'd only fantasized about being with. The Micah whose absence the past four years had left a hole in his heart the size of Central Park. Micah's strong hands on his body, his full lips on Josh's skin.

"You won't." Josh said the words more to reassure himself than anything else. "Please. I need you inside of me."

He heard Micah's inhalation as he pressed a tentative finger inside, stretching him, exploring his ass. *Micah's* finger inside of him. Josh gasped as a second finger more boldly joined the first, this time touching Josh's prostate and making him dizzy.

"Good?" Micah asked, concern evident in his voice.

"Great. But I'll be better with you inside of me. Give me another. Please. You're making me crazy." Micah pressed a third finger into Josh, who tucked his knees underneath himself and pushed back against Micah's fingers.

For the longest time Micah just worked him open, at first gingerly, but then responding to Josh's soft moans, he grew bolder, brushing with each stroke the place inside that made Josh crazy.

"Want you inside me, Micah."

Josh got onto his back as Micah tore open the condom wrapper. He needed to see Micah's face—the beautiful face he'd dreamed of for as long as he could remember. Micah rolled the condom on and met Josh's gaze. Heat pulsed in those green eyes, and Josh knew without a doubt Micah wanted him at least as much as he wanted Micah.

Micah kissed Josh once more, his cock pressed against Josh's. Josh lifted his legs as their lips parted, opening himself to Micah. Micah pressed his cock against Josh's hole, easing himself inside. The burn was hell, but as Micah pushed harder, past the second set of muscles, Josh let himself relax. The burn gave way to satisfying fullness and, as Micah began to move, turned into pleasure.

"Josh. I wanted you so much. You don't even know…." Micah reached to stroke Josh's cock. It was all Josh could do not to come at the touch. It was too much for him to take in. Micah, buried in his ass, filling him. Micah's hand on him. Micah wanting *him*. His Micah.

"Micah," he panted. "I don't think I can last very long. I'm going to come." He hadn't wanted it to be over so fast.

"It's okay. I can't hold back either." Micah's breaths felt hot against Josh's chest as he continued to stroke Josh's cock.

"Then don't. Come with me."

Josh felt Micah's body tense above him as he came with a shout into Micah's hand. Micah followed, his body shuddering against Josh's. He pulled Josh against him and kissed Josh's neck before both of them collapsed onto the bed. And in that moment, Josh knew nothing would ever be the same for them again. It would be so much better.

JOSH awoke sometime later, Micah pressed against his back, his erection pressed against one thigh. He vaguely remembered Micah cleaning them both before he fell asleep in Micah's arms.

"Hey."

"Hey." Micah planted a kiss on Josh's shoulder blade.

"That was amazing." Better than amazing, really. It was the best Josh had ever felt with anyone. It was as if everyone else he'd ever been with just faded away when he was with Micah.

"Yeah." Micah's voice held a hint of wonder and something more—something Josh was afraid to put a name to.

Josh rolled over and brushed his lips against Micah's. "I never got to finish what I started," he murmured as his hand strayed down to find Micah's cock.

"What? Oh." Micah smiled, and Josh thought he saw him shiver.

"Roll onto your back."

The edges of Micah's mouth turned upward. "Mmm. I'm thinking I'm going to like this a lot."

Josh's only answer was to lean down and take Micah's cock in his mouth, this time swallowing it down so the curls at the base tickled his lips. Then he licked at the underside, moved upward until he found the tip, and gently ran his teeth over the edge until he heard Micah groan, then pressed his tongue into the slit, tasting Micah's salty essence. The heady scent of musk and sex was stronger this time. Josh lingered at the crown, feeling the smooth skin with the tip of his tongue, wanting to make this something Micah would remember for a long time to come.

He slipped one hand beneath Micah's ass, supporting him, while tenderly cupping Micah's balls and rolling them around with his other hand. Until today, he'd always thought of blowjobs as something you did just for your partner's enjoyment. Now, he found it turned him on too. He loved the feel of Micah's cock in his mouth, the taste of him, the weight of his balls in his hand, and the way he made Micah writhe on the sheets.

He released Micah, then lubed up a finger and slid it back over Micah's perineum until he found the tight opening. Micah clenched around him as he pressed inside. He felt a hand on his head, stroking his hair, and his own cock responded to the touch, aching for its release. Micah lifted one knee so it pressed against Josh's cock, and Josh rubbed to intensify the contact, keeping himself on the edge, waiting.

Micah clenched around his fingertip. "Relax," Josh whispered. He heard Micah's breaths deepen, the soft rasps and stutters fading as his body released its tension. "That's it. Let me inside."

Micah blew out a long breath as Josh slipped his finger past the inner muscles and found Micah's prostate. Micah keened beneath his touch, and Josh smiled up at him, moving his finger in and out to brush the sensitive spot.

"Josh. Oh, God. Josh. You're amazing."

Josh's grin was lost as he swallowed Micah again, working his way back down Micah's hard shaft with the slight scrape of his teeth. Micah was close now, hissing his approval, his skin hot against Josh's body. Josh, too, teetered on the edge of orgasm.

"Please," Micah begged. "Josh, please."

Josh increased the suction, hollowing his cheeks, feeling the tension in his own ass and balls until Micah shot into his mouth. Josh greedily swallowed Micah's hot come, savoring the salty, slightly bitter taste.

"Let me help you." Micah's voice was still low and husky as he reached for Josh's cock. "I want to taste you. Make you come like I did."

Josh wouldn't have argued if he'd had the strength. When Micah's warm heat engulfed his cock, he leaned back on the pillows, a quivering lump of need. He didn't need Micah's mouth to know the only man who could truly satisfy his need was Micah. He knew it in his bones. In his heart. In his soul. He loved this man more than he would admit. And it terrified him.

"Micah!" he cried out as he came hard into Micah's mouth. A moment later they were kissing and he tasted himself on Micah's lips. *I love you so much!*

AS THEY lay in bed together later, Micah pulled Josh close. The bed was small, so it wasn't particularly difficult. It also wasn't difficult because it felt so *good* to be close. Josh put his head on Micah's shoulder. "Yes," he whispered.

The next thing Josh knew, it was morning. The sunlight was just beginning to filter through the window shade and already the room felt stuffy and warm. August in the city was hot and humid. Micah's body was warm and Josh's moist skin didn't want to peel away as he shifted on the bed.

"Yes, what?" Micah's voice was gravelly. So sexy that Josh's cock struggled to respond, but he was too exhausted, despite a few hours' sleep.

"Yes, Micah. I do still have feelings for you." Josh realized he'd fallen asleep the night before and they hadn't made it to this discussion. He was pretty sure Micah already knew how he felt, but he didn't want there to be any doubt this time.

"Me too." Josh shivered to hear this, then pressed a tender kiss to Micah's jaw in a silent gesture of reassurance.

"When do you leave for law school? You didn't even tell me where you're going."

"Harvard. I leave next week."

"Really?" Josh grinned. Maybe Micah hadn't been such a fuck-up at college after all. But would Harvard Law let him in with drug charges? "It's not so far away. We can spend weekends together, can't we?"

Micah didn't reply. He pressed his lips to Josh's and Josh's body took over from his brain. All thoughts of weekends in Boston disappeared when Micah took a nipple into his mouth. All Josh could do was moan.

Two hours later they were showered and dressed, sitting downstairs in the kitchen. Josh was making pancakes from various things he'd found in the fridge. It had been a bit of a challenge—he knew this house well, but he'd never cooked here. He managed to locate the makings of a good breakfast. He liked cooking for Micah, he decided. It wasn't something he'd done for the other men he'd been with, but then again, the other men hadn't been Micah, either.

"Damn, you're such a great cook. Your mom teach you this?" Micah asked as he shoveled another pancake into his mouth.

Josh's chest tightened with the compliment. It felt so good to hear. "No. I made it up. I like experimenting."

"You're good. You should be a chef."

Josh shrugged. He'd never been very good with compliments. "I'll work in the restaurant. My accounting degree means I can do the books for my parents. I can either cook when they need help or I can get their friends as clients too."

"You're wasted as a bookkeeper. You should be a chef. Have your own restaurant."

"Naw. I can't. Nowadays you need to go to some fancy cooking school. Like the CIA."

"CIA? I thought that was for spies."

"Culinary Institute of America. Up in Dutchess County. Kind of an American version of Le Cordon Bleu."

"You should apply."

"Too expensive. For that price I might as well go all the way to France. Besides, why would I want to go to France, now that...." He reached out for Micah's hand and picked it up, planting a kiss on the palm.

"Josh." Micah's voice wavered. "Josh...."

"What?" Josh had a sickening feeling in his stomach. Too many pancakes and not enough sleep. That's what it was. He prayed that's what it was.

"Josh. I'm going to figure out how to make this all work. I am. I really am." Micah's expression was sincere, but there was something else there that scared Josh half to death.

"What are you talking about?" They were together, right? Micah loved him. He loved Micah. What else did they need?

"Just give me a little bit of time once I get up to Cambridge, okay?"

"Yeah, sure." Josh gave a weak smile and pushed his plate away. He glanced at the cup of coffee and decided against drinking it. He was jittery enough now without it. What did Micah need time for? To tell his parents? That could never go well.

Micah stood up and came over to Josh's side of the table. He tugged his arm until Josh was standing, then planted a delicious soft kiss on Josh's cheek. Josh felt a lump in his throat and swallowed hard. Josh wanted so much for this—for *them*—to work. But Micah couldn't promise him anything, and it left him feeling unsettled, on edge. He loved Micah, and it terrified him.

Micah stooped to brush his lips against Josh's neck and wrapped his arms around his waist, pulling Josh hard against him. "Let me thank you for that delicious breakfast."

"You can clean up, do the dishes."

"Not quite what I had in mind." Micah's hard-on sprang to life against the thin cotton of Josh's boxers and his own cock responded. "Let's go back upstairs."

"Oh, yes," Josh breathed against Micah's shoulder, knowing he'd follow this man anywhere, any time for the rest of his life.

THEY spent the rest of the weekend together and most every day until Micah left for Massachusetts. If Josh's parents suspected anything, they didn't say. Josh just figured they were happy he and Micah had gotten their friendship back on track. Micah ate almost every dinner that week with the Goldens—his parents were away, his mother reasoned, why shouldn't he eat well? Josh couldn't complain. Even if they weren't alone for dinner, he was with Micah, and that's what mattered. He told his parents he was out late with Micah, and they never questioned him. He was a college graduate, after all. What were they going to say?

After Micah left, they talked on the phone every few days, but Josh never made it to visit Micah up in Cambridge.

The world imploded a few weeks after Micah left and Josh ended up in France after all. Ironic that it had been Micah's suggestion all along. Or was it?

Josh's mom had bustled into the kitchen in their family restaurant one Sunday morning. "You know, I have to take back all the bad things I said about Micah Solomon." It was one of the busiest days for them. They were closed on Saturday—the Sabbath—when most of their Jewish customers were at shul. The less-observant wouldn't want to be seen entering a restaurant—even a Kosher one. Sunday morning was big business, though, along with Friday mornings, when housewives came in for food and baked goods for the weekend.

"Why's that?" Josh's dad asked. He was busy slicing brisket for the lunch crowd and, as always, wore the slightly irritated "why are you bothering me with this" look he saved for Miriam's gossip.

Josh stayed silent as he dished out bowls of their famous red cabbage and apple salad. He hadn't said anything to anyone about what had happened between him and Micah. His parents had stopped trying to fix him up or questioning who he was dating after he'd come out two years earlier, and he was glad of it. As much as they'd loved Micah—

although they didn't love Micah quite the way Josh did—he figured they'd be fine with the truth, but Josh decided not to speak up until Micah said it was okay. As far as Josh knew, Micah still hadn't told anyone but Josh he was gay. For Micah, he'd do anything. For Micah, he'd wait as long as it took.

"I'm not supposed to say anything just yet, but there's going to be a big announcement very soon. We've been approached to cater a special event…." Her voice rose in a sing-song.

Josh recognized her tone. She always got excited about wedding or engagement parties. Generally she was a huge gossip, so Josh wondered why anyone trusted her with any secrets. But she must have gotten her wires crossed on this one. There was no way Micah's parents would be announcing anything between the two of them. No matter how much support Josh had gotten from members of the shul, customers, and neighbors, Micah's parents were much more religious than his own, and Micah's dad would blow a gasket when he heard the news. The Solomons weren't exactly planning to throw a PFLAG party at Goldens Restaurant.

Josh's mother came over and gave him a little hug. "You'll love this news, Joshy. I know you will."

What? What the fuck could she possibly be talking about? Whatever it was clearly had nothing to do with him. The memory of the look on Micah's face when he'd said he'd work things out seemed etched in his brain. The way Micah's voice had quavered when he'd talked about their future together. Josh's stomach did several back flips and he ran for the bathroom.

"Josh, honey, what's wrong? Josh?" his mom called after him.

He puked up his breakfast and stood over the toilet with the dry heaves when he'd finished. After washing his mouth out twenty times and splashing water on his face, he took a deep breath and pulled himself together. Or at least as together as he could manage. He grabbed his cell phone, but his hands shook so badly he had to sit down on the floor, his back against the wall to steady himself.

Micah's phone rang and rang until his voicemail picked up. Josh disconnected. What should he say? He slammed the phone shut and leaned back against the wall. He had to think. Maybe he'd gotten it wrong. Maybe his mother wasn't talking about some kind of engagement party for Micah. He must have misunderstood. He went back over what she'd said, but it still added up: Mom thought Micah had done something good, and she hadn't mentioned Harvard. Josh's older sister Jenna had gone to Yale, and his mother hadn't shut up about it for the entire four years she'd been there.

He called Micah again. "Micah, I heard something kinda weird from my mom and I need to talk to you soon. Like now. Please call me." He hoped he didn't sound as desperate as he felt.

Micah didn't call back till late in the afternoon. Josh didn't know how he'd managed to keep working except the restaurant was so busy he didn't have a minute to let his mind wander to Micah long enough to have a meltdown. It was a good thing.

"Josh, I wanted to talk to you first, but everything got so hectic."

"What's everything? Tell me now."

"I hate doing this over the phone."

*Please, no.* Josh's chest tightened and his mouth went dry. God, but he wanted to be up there with Micah, in his arms, in his bed. Now he knew that would never happen. For a while, he'd convinced himself the entire thing with Micah hadn't just been a temporary fling. He knew it was only his stupid hope that had made him believe it. It wasn't as if Micah had said they'd be together, he reminded himself. Micah had told him the truth, but he'd refused to believe it. Until now.

"I knew it was my responsibility, but I just.... And then my dad went around me and talked to her dad and by the time I knew, it was too late. They arranged everything."

"Arranged what?" Like Josh needed to hear any details. All he really needed to know was who and when. Then he could go home and cry into his pillow for the next year or two. Maybe longer.

"The wedding. We'd just sort of talked about it, but then our parents got involved, and you know my dad...."

"Who?"

"Well, that's kind of the funny part."

"There is no funny part, Micah." He knew he sounded harsh, but he didn't care. He'd never felt more miserable in his life.

"It's Rina."

*Rina?* He waited.

"Josh, she's pregnant."

And with those words, Micah turned Josh's world upside down yet again. Micah had slept with Rina? Come to think of it, Rina had told him back in high school she wanted to lose her virginity to Micah. That's what best friends were for, she'd said. Josh should have been insulted she hadn't chosen him, but he wasn't—it's not like he would have accepted the job if she had asked him. He hadn't really minded back then, back before he thought he ever had a chance of Micah loving him back. Only now it seemed both of them were in love with the same man.

Just what he needed, a love triangle with his two closest friends. Or two former closest friends. What do you get your life-long crush for his wedding to your best female friend?

Josh didn't stick around to ask Dear Abby. He sold everything he owned, including his Israel bonds he'd been saving since his bar mitzvah, and bought a plane ticket for France.

# Chapter Six

WHEN Josh woke up the morning after his disastrous start at the restaurant, his head warned him not to drink crappy red wine anymore. He rolled away from the window and the offending sunshine as slowly as possible so his brain wouldn't explode during the process. He cracked open one eye an infinitesimal amount to see the clock on the nightstand and instead saw an early-morning sunbeam glinting off his watch.

Watch. *Aw, fuck.* Details of the previous night sharpened into focus, intensifying the pain in his head.

The watch. The guy in the alley. Micah rescuing him.

Micah.

Mom.

Okay, those two names shouldn't be anywhere near each other in his brain, but Josh recalled his mom's surgery the day before. He'd talked to his father from the restaurant, but he needed to find out how she was this morning. He planned to stop by the hospital before he had to be at the restaurant. That would be preferable to hanging around the house where he might actually run into Micah and be expected to have figured out how the hell he was supposed to feel about everything.

He took a deep breath before trying to sit up. He stalled and took another. Then two more for good measure. Thus oxygenated, he could probably face standing at some point in the near future. His stomach roiled as he finally managed to get the top half of his body vertical.

He considered this an accomplishment.

He hadn't drunk that much, had he? Maybe half the bottle. He could easily drink two or three times that, so what was up? Then he remembered that in the past forty-eight hours he'd flown a third of the way around the world, seen his parents for the first time in years, faced his mother's surgery, and come face-to-face with an ex, well, ex-everything as far as Josh had been concerned. On the stress level scale, this had to be way up there. What a cheery thought for the morning.

Ten minutes later he'd showered and dressed. He reached for the watch on the nightstand and picked it up. Piaget Polo. It had been a gift from a former lover, a very wealthy Parisian businessman with a wife and kids who spent as much time away from home "on business" as he could get away with. It was a nice watch. An exquisite watch. And it cost at least as much as a decent car. But it wasn't worth anyone getting hurt over. He left it on the nightstand.

Josh went downstairs and headed for the kitchen. He heard the clatter of pans and figured his dad was cooking. That ache in his stomach wasn't a hangover, Josh realized, just hunger. He sped up his steps but stopped in his tracks when he realized it wasn't his dad in the kitchen. Micah and Ethan were there.

"Breakfast is almost ready." Ethan greeted Josh with a huge smile and turned back toward the stove. He had something in a pan, and Micah stood behind him, supervising.

Then Micah turned and Josh saw the bruise along the right side of his face.

"Aw f—cra—rats. Micah?"

Micah ran his fingertips along the discoloration and gave a small shrug.

Josh wished he couldn't remember how those fingertips felt on his face… and other body parts. He sat down at the table. "I'm really sorry."

"Forget about it. Just be more careful."

Josh held up his hands and showed off his empty wrist. "Look, Micah, no watch."

Micah nodded and turned back toward Ethan.

"Can I turn it yet, Dad? It's bubbling. You said wait till I can see bubbles. Look!"

"Yes. You can turn it. But be careful not to touch the pan, okay?" Micah bent over Ethan as he slid the spatula under a pancake and flipped it. The batter splashed a bit over the side of the pan, but Micah only smiled and said, "Good job." Ethan grinned.

"Smells good, Chef." Josh poured himself some coffee from a thermal carafe on the table. He took a tentative sip. Nice and strong. Not quite like they served in France, but damned close. He smiled.

"It's pancakes," Ethan told Josh, his voice filled with obvious pride. "Secret recipe."

"I can't wait." He forced himself to smile back at the boy. Whatever he might think about Micah, Ethan had done nothing wrong. In fact, he seemed like a pretty good kid, considering.

Micah helped Ethan get the pancakes onto a platter, then Ethan brought the dish to the table and presented it to Josh as if he were serving a king—or a customer in a restaurant. Josh took a look and grinned. They smelled heavenly. They were uneven in shape and color, but a good effort for a ten-year-old.

"Wow. They look great, Ethan. Thank you."

Micah stayed at the stove, working on the second batch while Josh and Ethan divvyed up the first platter.

"So this is a secret recipe? Where'd you find it?" The pancakes were good, they had pieces of nuts and blueberries and banana. He put some more syrup on and took a huge forkful.

"Dad's recipe," Ethan said through a mouthful of pancake.

"Actually, Eth, this is Josh's recipe."

Josh looked up and caught Micah's gaze, noticing the slight hint of pink on Micah's cheeks. Then it hit him. He had made these pancakes for Micah the morning after that first glorious night they'd spent together. How long ago had it been? Micah still made those pancakes after he'd gotten married and had a kid? Josh didn't know whether he should acknowledge the memory. He'd put it all out of his mind—at least until the night before—but Micah clearly hadn't.

Probably not a good idea to think too hard about that either.

"Morning, boys." Josh's dad shuffled into the kitchen, wrapped in his ancient blue terry-cloth bathrobe. His hair—what was left of it—

stuck out in all directions and his stubble was more white than gray now.

In that moment, it struck Josh how old his father looked. Funny how he hadn't realized it until today. "Hey, Dad."

"Decaf?" His father pointed to the carafe.

"No. Full strength." Micah winked.

"Good." Seymour poured himself a cup and drank half of it in one gulp. "Your mother won't let me drink the real stuff. She's on some green tea kick. Look where it got her. She's the one in the hospital!"

"I filled the decaf jar with regular." Micah held up the container with a conspiratorial grin. "Should I brew another pot?"

"Yes," Josh and his dad said in unison.

"Micah, what happened to your face?" Seymour clucked in a perfect imitation of Miriam.

"Long story, Seymour. I'm fine, but you should see the other guy." He threw a furtive glance at Josh.

"Be careful. All of you." Josh's dad pointed a finger of warning at each of them in turn.

"Okay, Mom," Josh replied.

"Ready for pancakes?" Micah brought the frying pan to the table and served some to Seymour, then gave Josh the rest. He poured another round and then started more coffee brewing.

"So, how is Mom?" Josh asked, finally getting to the point of coming downstairs in the first place.

"She didn't have a good evening. I stayed in the chair for a while and then they made me leave. I called in this morning and they say she had a rough night too. I want to get down there around ten. They won't let me see her till after the doctor does his rounds. Stupid rules."

Josh pushed a bit of pancake around on his plate. His mother would be fine, he reminded himself. If it was really bad, the hospital would have called his father. *She'll be fine.*

"Ethan, you ready?" Micah's voice brought Josh back to himself.

"Yeah, Dad." Ethan got up and put his dishes into the sink. He grabbed a backpack from the corner and hoisted it on his shoulder.

"Coat."

"Dad." Ethan rolled his eyes and shook his head.

"It's December. Put on your coat."

Ethan screwed up his face in a frown, but he came back a moment later with his coat while Micah served the next batch of pancakes. "Coffee will be a few minutes. I'll take care of the dishes when I get back."

"You didn't eat anything," Josh blurted out as Micah and Ethan started out the back door. Damn, without his mother around, everyone else seemed to be taking her place. Including himself. Micah was long gone, though, and Josh found himself hoping he hadn't heard.

After Micah and Ethan left, Josh sipped coffee and ate more pancakes with his dad while they made small talk about the front-page stories in the newspaper. The pancakes were really good. In spite of everything, he was touched Micah had cooked them. Was there a deeper meaning to serving them this morning? A tiny part of his heart wanted to ask, but his entire brain warned him not to.

"What happened last night, Josh?"

Josh's gut churned. How many times had he been asked that? By a parent, a teacher, a lover? It wasn't really a question, it was a judgment. What was his dad asking about? Had he already heard how he'd pissed off the dinner crew?

"Nothing."

"Nonsense. I hope you weren't the other guy Micah was talking about." The stern tone surprised Josh.

"You think I hit him?" The idea that his father might believe he had hit Micah made Josh slightly sick to his stomach. Sure, he disliked Micah. But he'd never hurt him.

"You acted mad enough to wring his neck when you found out he was here. Your mother and I never expected that. Such anger! It nearly made her cry."

"Really?" Josh answered more belligerently than he intended. He saw his dad recoil and he immediately felt terrible for it. The last thing he wanted was to make his mother cry. "I mean, she did? I didn't mean to upset her."

"What's wrong, son? You seem to have a big chip on your shoulder."

"I don't want to talk about it."

"Fine." Seymour's voice was tight and Josh knew he was frustrated. "But don't take it out on anyone else. This is still our house. You're both here because we want you to be here. I don't want you two fighting, especially not in front of Ethan."

"Okay." He didn't want that, either. Not that he wanted to spend time with Micah, but he didn't want to upset the kid, either.

"I'm gonna take a shower. You coming to the hospital?"

"Yeah, of course. I want to see how Mom is this morning." He needed to reassure himself she was going to be okay. He wasn't sure how he would handle getting any bad news.

"Just don't upset her."

"I won't." Now he *really* felt like a kid again.

Seymour drank another cup of coffee in silence and then went upstairs.

Josh was clearing the dishes when Micah came back. He'd hoped maybe Micah would have been gone longer. He really wasn't up to making small talk with the man, but the silence gnawed at him and he found himself trying to be polite. "Back so soon?"

"It's not very far."

"So Ethan goes to school around here?"

"Yes. PS 110." Micah's answers were short, terse. Josh figured he wasn't the only one who wasn't in the mood to talk.

That was where Josh and Micah had gone. "Gee, I didn't think it would still be there."

"It is." Micah filled a plate with pancakes and reheated them in the microwave. "Lots of things are still right here," he added cryptically. Then he sat down and drizzled syrup on the pancakes and poured himself some coffee. He ate quickly, not glancing up at Josh, and just as abruptly got up and finished clearing the table. He loaded the dishes into the dishwasher and added soap. He shut the machine and moved to the sink.

"Not gonna start it?"

"Your dad's in the shower."

Josh nodded. Micah knew his way around the house better than Josh did now.

"I'm sorry about last night." Josh thought back to his dad's asking what was wrong, and realized there was more to the question than just Micah's shiner. "All of it. You were right. About the staff. The neighborhood. Everything."

"Everything?" Micah didn't turn around. He was dumping coffee grounds into the trash and fiddling with things on the stovetop and counter. He rearranged some things that were already in the right place.

"I said I was sorry. Sorry you ended up in a fight and sorry I blew off your comments about the kitchen staff. That's the best I can do right now. Take it or leave it." It had already taken him a lot to admit that much.

Micah turned around and their gazes locked for a moment. There was just a flash, but Josh thought he saw emotion welling up in Micah's eyes, a glimpse of—was it pain? But before Josh could identify it, it vanished.

Just like their love affair.

*Lots of things are still right here.* What had Micah meant by that?

Micah glanced up at the ceiling. No shower sound. He pushed the start button on the dishwasher and started to fill the sink with hot, soapy water.

Josh shook his head to clear away the nonsense, but the constriction in his chest wouldn't go away. Or the lump in his throat, for that matter.

"Josh, I'm going to the hospital in ten minutes," his father's voice boomed from upstairs.

Josh glanced at his watch and realized he wasn't wearing it. "Yeah, Dad. Meet you in the hall!" Then he turned back to Micah and asked, "Need my help with the dishes?"

"Nope. Don't need anything from you." Micah kept his head down, hands in the sink.

But Josh noticed the way Micah's posture sagged, as if he were being crushed by a heavy weight. And unlike the chip on Josh's shoulder, Micah's worries seemed to weigh on both shoulders.

Josh drained the last of the coffee in his mug then walked up behind Micah. He reached around him to drop it into the soapy water, letting his arm brush against Micah's for a millisecond. He wouldn't pretend he didn't inhale Micah's scent when they were inches apart. He'd figure out what that jolt of electricity meant later. And why Micah's body had tensed at the brief touch.

Five minutes later, as Josh shrugged into his coat and wrapped a scarf around his neck, he thought about how the spot where his arm had touched Micah's still tingled and throbbed under the layers of clothes. As he shivered in the morning breeze, that one spot burned and a few misty memories fought back the December chill.

# Chapter Seven

THE taxi ride to the hospital was, blessedly, short and silent. Seymour dragged a hand through the gray strands of hair clinging for dear life to his mostly bare head and let out an occasional loud sigh. The taxi driver kept looking back at them in the rearview and Josh held off saying anything.

The doctor intercepted them halfway between the nurses' station and Miriam's room.

"Mr. Golden, can you spare a few minutes?"

Seymour looked at Josh, and Josh looked back at the doctor.

*You're it.* "What's wrong, Doctor?" Josh asked as he reached for his dad's elbow and gave it a steadying squeeze.

"You're the son?"

Josh blinked a few times. He'd never been into drag. Did he look like he was the daughter?

"Last time I looked."

The doctor blinked a few times at that reply, and Josh wished he hadn't said it so flippantly.

Then the doctor let out a tiny laugh. "Miriam said you came in from France for her surgery."

"Oh. Yes." Now Josh felt like a real dickhead. He examined his shoes and waited for the doc to say what he'd intended.

"I'm Nathan Silver." He offered Josh his hand.

"Josh Golden. Good to meet you." The doctor's handshake was solid, friendly.

"I'm glad you're here for your mother, Josh. Let's have some privacy." The doctor motioned them over to a small room near the tion. Once all three were settled in uncomfortable plastic chairs, he continued. "Miriam's recovery isn't progressing the way it should."

"What?" Seymour leaped out of his chair, but the doctor put out a hand to calm him.

"It's not serious, just something we're monitoring. Usually there's a little bleeding and fever after the surgery which goes away relatively quickly. Miriam's still having more of both than we like to see at this point. I'd like to keep her in an extra two days, even if she improves. Just to monitor the situation and make sure she doesn't overdo it."

"What if she doesn't improve?" Josh's gaze met the doctor's. He knew he shouldn't be noticing the little golden flecks in the brown eyes or the way they crinkled when he smiled. He was supposed to be worried about his mother, right? He fought the urge to check the doctor's hand for a ring.

"It generally means there's an infection and she'll need additional medication, which could impact her recovery. Again, the main thing here is to monitor her status and allow extra time off her feet." In spite of Josh's anxiety over his mother's condition, the doctor's manner gave him comfort.

"How much time?" Seymour asked.

"We did the laparoscopic procedure, which most people recover from in a week or so. With Miriam's age and her slower recovery, however, it might be as long as four weeks. We didn't have any reason to anticipate this, since she's in remarkable health for her age."

"Four weeks?" Josh did some mental arithmetic to determine how long he could feasibly stay home. The fact that Nathan Silver didn't have any rings and did have a very nice smile tipped his calculations a little. "I'll have to check with my boss to see if I can stay longer."

"That's premature, Mr. Golden."

"Josh," Josh insisted, warmly.

"Josh." Nathan Silver smiled even more warmly. A little beep sounded from his breast pocket, and he pulled out a smartphone and pressed the screen a few times. "Looks like your mom's ready to see you now. Why don't you visit for a while, and then come look for me before you leave and I'll answer any other questions you've got." He pulled a business card from another pocket and handed it to Seymour. He glanced at Josh and pulled out another one. "All my contact numbers are on there." Josh's eyes met Nathan's, and Josh got the definite impression at least one of those contact numbers was a personal one.

Nathan got up to leave and smiled once more before heading down the hallway.

Flowers covered nearly every surface of the hospital room. It both surprised and pleased Josh to realize how many people loved his mother and were concerned for her health. Miriam was sitting up in bed poking a spoon into a bowl of something white with a look of horror on her face. It could have been ice cream, tapioca, or a pile of newly shorn wool off a sheep. She pushed the rolling tray away and her expression brightened when she noticed them.

"I was worried. What kept you? Visiting hours started twenty minutes ago."

"We were talking to Dr. Silver," Seymour said.

Josh leaned down and hugged her. "Mom." He hugged her again, harder. "Mom." It surprised him how worried he'd been and how much better he felt to see she was okay. He'd always thought of his mother as pretty much indestructible.

"I'm fine. Stop worrying. What did he say?"

"Well—" Josh began.

"Josh, what did you think of him?" she interrupted before he could finish. "The doctor. Nathan. He's so handsome and he asked a lot of questions about you...." She singsonged in a sickeningly familiar way. "Is he your type?"

"Mom!"

"Miriam. What are you talking about?" Josh couldn't quite fathom his father's expression.

"Wouldn't you like to see your son married to a new doctor like that? A nice *Jewish* doctor?"

"Mom!" Josh's face felt hot. It was one thing to notice a good-looking man—it was entirely another for his mother to try to fix him up with one!

"Oy. Miriam, focus on getting well. Play yenta later." Now Seymour looked almost irritated with her.

"No harm in looking, just in case. It's good to have options."

"Just in case? Mom, what are you talking about?"

"Well, they say I have to stay a few extra days. I hope we don't have problems with the insurance."

Josh didn't think his mom sounded as sick as the doctor thought she was, but then again, the doc didn't know what she was like normally. At least they seemed to be looking after her.

"So, Joshy, tell me how did everything go last night?"

He winced inwardly at the nickname, but gave them both a rundown of dinner service, leaving out everything except how many covers they did and how much they made. He'd sort out his issues with the kitchen staff and not bring his parents into his problems. Micah was right about that. He didn't mention the mugging either. There would never be a good time to bring that up. He'd rather let his dad think he and Micah had a fistfight than let his mom worry about him nearly getting knifed in an alleyway. That would put her recovery back a few days at least.

He stayed for an hour, then made excuses to leave, saying he wanted to get to the restaurant before the lunch crew left.

"Oh, right, Joshy, I forgot to tell you." Seymour put out a hand as Josh stood to leave. "Sit down again." Josh did. His father continued, "There's a dinner party on Wednesday. They reserved the back room and the menus and recipes are in the party folder. I ordered the special items and they should show up today or tomorrow. If anything's missing, you'll need to go to another supplier to find it. Richie helps with the ordering, so he can give you suggestions. Okay?"

"Okay. Sure. Party tomorrow." He leaned over his mom and gave her a kiss. She reached up her arms and pulled him in for a hug, but he could feel how weak she was. Now he wished he hadn't stayed so long. Toward the end of his visit she'd hardly spoken. She must have used up a lot of her energy putting on that show when they'd first arrived.

He was glad Nathan Silver was keeping an eye on her.

"See you tomorrow, Mom. And don't worry. It's all under control."

"I know, Joshy." She waved as he left.

Seymour nodded, but his face looked as gray as his hair.

The sun was out, and Josh walked the ten blocks to the restaurant, enjoying the relatively fresh air after being cooped up in the hospital for an hour. He'd have to check that dinner party for the following night. Usually parties were good business if you handled them properly. They had a fat profit margin because there was almost no waste. You cooked a few different dishes, rather than having to have extra ingredients on hand for the full menu. You never knew what regular customers would order, and the larger the menu, the bigger the waste was. But if half the tables were being used for the party, they had probably cut their regular menu orders a little bit. Wednesday wasn't a huge night for eating out, even in Manhattan. If it was quiet, they could get started on some of the prep work tonight.

He was smiling when he walked into the restaurant. Most of the tables were full even though it was near the tail end of lunch service. The customers looked happy, and the cashier was busy ringing up bills. *That's the way it should be.*

The hostess, Marla, greeted him, and a few of the servers gave him nods when he took a swing through the dining room on the way back to the office. The kitchen staff were working smoothly so he closed the door. He noticed Micah was at one of the prep stations chopping carrots. Well, maybe he needed the extra hours. Josh didn't know how much his parents were paying Micah, and it wasn't his business.

He opened the party book and found the page for the next day's event.

It wasn't a buffet. It was a tasting menu. That was a lot more work for a kitchen, since the portions were generally small, so you needed more courses to fill people up. Nothing too difficult as far as the recipes went, though, thank goodness. He glanced at the pricing sheet, gaze skimming over his father's calculations of costs, prices, and margins. He could do this in his sleep back in France. His staff there would have this prepped in a couple of hours.

He glanced at his watch and remembered. No watch. He looked at the clock. He had two slow hours now between lunch and dinner. They'd be prepping for dinner, but it couldn't hurt to bring in an extra body to get started tonight. Maybe he could get a lunch person to stay past their shift.

He wandered into the kitchen and found Micah still chopping—he'd progressed to tomatoes. There was no one else in the kitchen. Josh glanced at the table where staff ate at the end of their shift. Empty.

"Everyone leave already?" He hadn't been paying attention to the time. When had it gotten so late?

Micah stopped chopping and turned around. "Uh, yeah. They're gone."

"I was going to ask a couple of guys to stay to help prep for tomorrow's party."

"Oh, the holiday fund benefit."

"Whatever. It needs more prep than the schedule allows."

"So, what do we do?"

"You working on tonight's dinner?"

"Yes."

Josh let out a breath. He resisted the urge to remind Micah to say "Yes, Chef." He'd told the staff yesterday he expected them to treat him with respect, and that included addressing him properly. Micah had been there, too, but apparently his memory had deteriorated from all those drugs. How had he ever actually practiced law? They were alone so he wouldn't press the issue, but once the rest of the guys came in, he'd go over the rules and expectations. Again. Still, he'd keep Micah's comments in mind and be nicer about it.

"What time does the rest of the shift arrive?"

"Three or three-thirty. On Tuesday one lunch person works through to dinner."

"You?"

"No. I'm not on the schedule. One person is scheduled to do both shifts."

"When is he coming back?"

"Uh, Peter went home for today. He's not coming back."

"Not coming back. He say why?" It wouldn't be easy with one less person, but he supposed with Micah's help, they'd be all right.

Micah shrugged. "Not really." It was clear Micah knew the reason, he just wasn't sharing it with Josh.

"What did he say?"

"He said he didn't want to work with you after what the dinner guys said."

*Shit.* "What did they say?"

"I told you last night." Micah didn't look up from his work.

"No, you wouldn't tell me." Josh's irritation threatened to get the best of him. He was tired of the runaround. He needed straight answers.

"Oh, right." Micah still didn't look at Josh but shrugged and added, "They don't want to work with you. Some of them called in sick. Well, all but one."

"Does that include you?"

"Which part?" Micah continued to chop. It was really getting on Josh's nerves now, how calm Micah was.

"All of it. Do you want to work with me and are you planning to stay for dinner shift?" Josh was starting to feel sick to his stomach. How the hell was he supposed to run the kitchen with one employee?

"I'll stay and help as long as you need it. I'm here to help out your parents, no matter what." The little of Micah's expression Josh could see was unreadable, and his voice was even.

"I'm sure they appreciate your loyalty." Josh's pulse raced and he felt a vein throb in his temple. He rubbed the spot, hoping to prevent it bursting through his skin and spraying blood all over the kitchen. He really did feel like he was going to explode. He'd never tolerate such unprofessional behavior from his own staff. He turned on his heel and headed back to the office to think about how to handle this. His head ached and he stopped rubbing his temple. Maybe if his skull exploded they'd cancel dinner and he wouldn't have anything to worry about, he thought with a wry laugh. *That would be perfect!*

Back in the office he skimmed through file folders looking for staff phone numbers. He tried to put names with faces but he couldn't remember anyone's name from the night before. Usually he was good with names, but he'd been so out of sorts with the jet lag and his mom's surgery. *No. You need to stop making excuses.* He had an hour tops to get this show back on the road. He couldn't do this alone though. He grabbed the staff list and a copy of the week's work schedule and headed for the kitchen.

He found Micah in the cooler, marking items off a list on a clipboard.

"Oh, Josh. I mean, Chef. I have tonight's prep list and everything's ready or prepped except for the two specials." He handed the clipboard to Josh and pointed to the specials. "I can do the beef, but I'm not so good with fish."

Josh took the clipboard. Beef goulash and poached salmon were tonight's specials. Micah had done a professional job of summing up what needed to be done.

"You can make the beef? Can you handle the vegetables too?"

"Yes, Chef."

Josh breathed a sigh of relief. One problem down. On to the hundred other problems. "Great. Can you help me by calling these guys and getting even one or two of them to show up? I'd really appreciate it. I'll get started on the specials in the meantime."

"You want me to call?" Micah looked at Josh with surprise.

"Yes. Please. We can't do this on our own."

"Is your dad coming in tonight?"

"No. He's staying at the hospital." The last thing Josh wanted to do was call his father. Not only did his mother need his father at the hospital, he wasn't going to admit defeat quite so quickly. He'd turn this around. He *had* to.

"How's your mom doing? I'm sorry. I meant to ask before."

Josh shook his head as he waved Micah out of the cooler. "She's not doing so well. Look, let's discuss this once we get some help. But I can't expect any help from Dad right now. He's exhausted, and he can't handle a short staff situation like this. Thank God it's Tuesday."

"Better than Friday?" Micah flashed Josh a sympathetic smile.

"We're closed Friday night. If only it were Friday!" Josh had already planned a night out for Friday. Lord knew he needed it, especially now. Keeping that thought firmly planted in his mind, he handed the staff list to Micah. "Use the office. And if you can, can you try and find out if the front of house staff is having the same issues?"

"Yeah. I'll see what people are saying. But they have their own manager, so I'm guessing they're fine."

"It's me?"

Micah gave some combination of a nod and a headshake, like the motion a bobblehead doll made. It didn't improve Josh's mood.

"Okay, I got the message. Let them know. Apologize. Promise anything within reason to get people in tonight and we'll sort tomorrow out later."

"I'll do my best." Micah pushed open the kitchen door, leaving Josh alone. Josh sincerely hoped Micah still had a little lawyer left in him. If the man argued cases in front of a jury, he'd be able to convince some of the staff to come back, right?

He grabbed the nearest empty pan—a metal container for prepped vegetables—and threw it across the room. It clattered and clanged, sounding like an entire building was collapsing.

Micah came running back into the kitchen. "You okay?"

Josh had composed himself completely. "Fine."


HE BUSIED himself with the fish dish, and once he had the first steps cooking, he started on getting the beef portions cut for Micah. Twenty minutes later Micah returned.

"I talked to three people. No one else would answer so I left voicemails. I'm pretty sure they recognized the number...."

"And?"

"I got Raphael to commit to coming in, only because he wasn't here last night and doesn't think you're as much of a dick as the crew told him." Micah's cheeks colored. "Sorry, Chef. I was paraphrasing."

"That's okay. It's not like I can fire you." *Understatement of the century!*

"Why, because you need my help?"

"Because you're not an employee. I don't think all those labor laws apply to you."

"Well, actually, even if I'm not an employee, you st—"

"Okay, fine. I forgot you used to be a lawyer." Josh was surprised to see Micah almost flinch at the comment, but he went on anyway, not understanding why speaking the truth should hurt Micah's feelings. "I guess you never stop, do you?"

"It wasn't my specialty, but over the years I helped your dad with some legal stuff."

"When you were in prison?" Josh knew his voice held scorn and a little contempt. He'd told himself he needed to back off of Micah a bit—he couldn't afford to lose what little support he had—but the staff walking out had left him in a toxic mood.

Micah looked as if he'd been slapped. "Before."

"Sorry. That was uncalled for. Look, Micah, I know you're trying. I really appreciate that." He meant it too.

"There's also Brenda, the dessert chef," Micah continued as if he hadn't heard Josh. "She doesn't have any problem as long as you leave her stuff alone and just let her do her job."

"I can work with that." He'd have to.

Raphael and the dessert chef showed up as promised.

Between Josh, Raphael and Micah, they managed to cover the entire dinner service. Both the specials turned out well enough that customers sent back positive comments. It was, thankfully, a slow night and they managed everything without a full staff.

Raphael promised to talk to the others and convince them to work their regular schedules the rest of the week. They closed the kitchen a little early, and Josh treated everyone to leftover salmon and beef since there was more than enough for tomorrow's lunch. He even cracked open a nice bottle of Cabernet.

Brenda and Raphael left. Micah wouldn't let Josh walk home on his own, so he helped the dishwashers and mopped up the kitchen while Josh did the books. But Josh couldn't concentrate after the wine, so he decided he'd finish in the morning. He made sure the deposit was ready for the morning manager and went to look for Micah.

He found him in the kitchen, working his way down the party prep list.

"Ready to go?"

"Yeah. I mean, yes, Chef."

The more Josh heard the title, the less he liked it. He couldn't exactly back down now, though. Not after the staff mutiny. He'd only made it through one night and he had a lot more coming. Especially with his mom needing more time to recover.

"I started some chopping for tomorrow's party, and put everything in the special section of the cooler. But here are the items we haven't received yet." He pointed to the clipboard. "They should come tomorrow morning, but...."

"It's been a long day. Let's deal with this tomorrow. If it doesn't show up, I'll rework the menu. No point in losing sleep over it now."

"Right. Chef."

"We're alone. You don't need to keep calling me that." Micah raised an eyebrow, but said nothing.

Josh locked up and they walked along the main street, moving briskly enough to avoid any unwanted attention.

"Micah, you really came through tonight. Again. Thanks for being there when I needed your help." Josh never thought he'd say this to Micah, but he was glad he did. Surprisingly, he felt a lot better having said it. "Sorry I fucked things up with the staff and caused all the extra work for you."

"Like I said. I'm trying to fix my own mistakes, and this is part of what I need to do too." Out of the corner of his eye, Josh saw Micah smile at him. Even with all the insanity back in the kitchen, Josh still wasn't sure he could handle looking the man in the face.

"One of those twelve steps?"

"Not exactly."

Josh wanted to ask what exactly, but he could tell Micah didn't want to say more about it. "So the neighbor is watching Ethan again tonight?"

"Yes, unless your dad is back. He said he'd send her home when he got back from the hospital. He's really great with Ethan, since my own parents aren't around. Rina's parents retired to Florida a couple of years ago, so your dad is kind of a good influence on him when he won't listen to me."

"You and Ethan seem to get on pretty well."

"You saw us for thirty minutes at breakfast."

Breakfast. Josh could barely remember that morning, although he hadn't forgotten Micah had taught his son Josh's crazy pancake recipe, and how he'd called it a secret family recipe. Oh, that was one hell of a secret Micah was keeping about when he'd first eaten those pancakes.

Seymour was in the living room when they got home, watching television in the old blue terry bathrobe.

"Good dinner?" he asked when Josh shut the door behind them.

"Fine." Josh shrugged and sat down on the couch. "How's Mom?"

"Good night." Micah headed upstairs.

"Good night," Josh said and craned his head to watch him ascend the stairs.

"She's tired. She's older and more tired than I've ever seen her looking. But she pretends she's fine. She's planning your wedding to the doctor. What's his name again?"

"Dr. Silver. He was kinda hot." Josh shook his head. His mother never gave up on her matchmaking.

"I don't want to hear that."

"Don't you want us to be happy?" For the first time that evening, Josh smiled.

"No." Seymour's gaze moved toward the ceiling and he lowered his voice. "That doctor is not the right person for you." He shook his finger at Josh the way his mom would have done if she'd been here.

"And who is? Some nice Jewish girl?"

Seymour glanced toward the second story again. "No. I know you're not going to marry a girl," he practically whispered.

"I'm pretty sure Micah knows I'm gay. I don't know why you're whispering…. Oh, right. The kid. Sure. No gay jokes around the kid."

Seymour chuckled and shook his head. "I'm exhausted, and all I did was watch your mother sleep all afternoon."

"Did you help Mom pick out china patterns for me and the doctor?" It felt surprisingly good to joke around with his father after all that had happened that day. *Just one day since he'd come home? Nonstop shock and awe, Golden family style.*

"Keep joking. I know what kind of life you must have in France. And that's fine when you're young. But you're old enough to grow up now, Joshua. Think about having a real future. Can you keep doing that for the rest of your life? Don't you want a family?"

"Not really. I've got Jenna's kids if I feel an uncontrollable urge to be Uncle Josh, which I don't expect I will." He knew his parents wanted him to move back home, but he wasn't interested. He was perfectly happy with his life in Paris. He liked going to the clubs when the restaurant was closed, hooking up with someone for the night. Having fun.

"Oh, speaking of Jenna," Seymour said, interrupting Josh's thoughts. "They're all coming for the first night of Chanukah next week. Usually your mother cooks, but she'll barely be out of the hospital at that point. We need you to take that over. I'll help as much as I can."

He couldn't imagine a dinner he'd rather avoid, except maybe his wedding reception after marrying the doctor. "Sure, Dad. I'd love to," he said instead of what he really thought. He needed to do what was good for his parents. It wasn't forever. He'd suck it up and he'd survive. They needed him.

"Good boy." He ruffled Josh's hair and hoisted himself up from the couch. "Good night."

Josh sat there with the television flashing images of some late night talk show, not really watching. He searched for the remote control and turned it off. He dragged his exhausted body up the stairs, washed up and fell asleep.

HE WOKE up in complete darkness when he heard a sound in the hallway. A strange scraping kind of noise. Was someone breaking in? What did breaking in even sound like? Not scraping. Maybe there was some serial killer out there who broke in and scraped innocent people to death.

He tiptoed to the door and listened. Nothing. He opened the door as quietly as possible and saw Micah, wearing skin-tight boxer-briefs, shuffling from Josh's room at the other end of the hall toward the light. His eyes were half-closed, and with that relaxed ease of thinking no one was watching, he gave his junk a good scratch, rearranging everything so Josh got quite an eyeful of the whole package even in the dim glow of the little night-light at the end of the hall. The hand moved up and absently skimmed across a pec, and Josh could see the hard buds of his nipples in the cool night air. He kept watching, though he moved half a pace back into the room so Micah wouldn't notice if he happened to open his eyes.

Was he even awake? Some people really did walk in their sleep. Josh harbored a secret hope that maybe Micah would accidentally come back to bed in the guest room. His cock swelled, seconding that emotion, and he couldn't help giving himself a little squeeze as Micah passed. The briefs hugged his perfectly rounded ass. Micah had grown up and filled out nicely. When he'd last seen Micah naked, they'd been twenty-two, more than ten years ago, and their bodies were still as much boy as man. Now Micah's shoulders were wide, his chest strong and well developed. He had a flat stomach and enough definition in his arms and abs for Josh to tell he exercised and did weight training. Probably in prison. Everyone lifted weights in prison, didn't they?

*Stop it.* He was being unfair by tying everything Micah was to what he'd done. But that was Micah: a list of ways he'd fucked up other people's lives. A hot body and a few good deeds didn't erase thirty years of history with Josh.

Micah shut the bathroom door and Josh shut the bedroom door and climbed back into the now-cold sheets and wished he had the superpower of time travel.

JOSH pulled at the tight collar of his tuxedo, trying to loosen the bow tie. Why did they have to wear tuxes, anyhow? They were so damn uncomfortable. He glanced to his right and saw his mother seated in the front row of the congregation. She smiled at him and patted a stack of dishes to her right—a frou-frou pattern covered with tiny roses that reminded Josh of his grandmother's china. *Probably* is *Bubbe's china.* The idea made him chuckle.

The rabbi was saying something in Hebrew, although Josh didn't quite recognize the words. He looked to his left and saw Doctor Nathan Silver standing there, also dressed in a tux, wearing his stethoscope and name tag. He looked damned good too. Nathan smiled back at him. Yeah, Josh decided, he could get used to seeing more of that smile.

The next thing Josh knew, Nathan was slipping a ring onto his finger—was that a *wedding* ring?—and reciting the traditional Hebrew wedding vows, *"Ani l'dodi v'dodi li."* I am for my beloved and my beloved is for me. *Do I end up marrying Dr. Nathan?* It wasn't a terrible thought, really. Still, somehow it felt strange. Then it was Josh's turn, but instead of repeating the words, he just stared at the ring in his hand.

"Waiting for something?" came a voice at the back of the room.

"Micah?" Josh whispered as he turned around. The ring dropped onto the carpet and rolled down the steps, forgotten.

"Missed me?" Micah wore nothing but his boxer briefs and a wicked grin.

Josh said nothing, but looked around, worried about what the rabbi and the other people in the sanctuary would say. He needn't have worried. They were all gone.

"I know you want this," Micah whispered as his hands brushed Josh's naked body. When had all his clothes disappeared?

Micah tugged at one arm until Josh lay down with him, right there in front of the Ark holding the Torah scrolls. He should have been mortified to be naked in front of the holy texts, but he didn't care. All he could think about was how Micah's body felt, how Micah's fingers felt on his own body.

"This is what's right, isn't it?" Micah asked as he laved one of Josh's nipples.

"Yes," Josh said, surprised that he didn't even hesitate. He spread his legs and let Micah in.

Micah smiled and leaned down to kiss him. "I love you, Josh. We belong together." He then proceeded to give Josh every reason to agree as he consummated their marriage. A moment later, Josh stood next to Micah in front of the rabbi, both fully dressed in tuxes.

"*Ani l'dodi v'dodi li,*" Micah said as he held Josh's hand and traced lazy circles over the ring on Josh's finger.

Josh slipped the other ring onto Micah's finger and looked into the most beautiful eyes he'd ever seen as he repeated the wedding vows.

Everyone threw rice except Rina, who sprinkled a handful of glitter over them.

JOSH woke with a start to the sound of a door closing, his belly sticky with a puddle of come the approximate shape and size of Lake Erie. Or maybe Lake Huron; he'd always sucked at geography. He could still smell Micah on the pillow. He grabbed tissues from the nightstand to clean up and realized too late it was one of the ancient doilies. He groaned and rolled, pulling the covers over his head.

# *Chapter Eight*

THE party the next night went off without a hitch. The whole staff showed up, and Josh was extra careful with them. Thursday was busier, but nothing eventful happened. On Friday the restaurant closed early, and the dinner crew prepared food for the two bar mitzvahs being catered the following day. With little time pressure, the mood in the kitchen was light and cheerful, especially when Josh shared the news that the doctors decided to release Miriam on Saturday morning.

Josh had some celebrating of his own to do Friday night after the stresses of the week. He was relieved his mom had shown enough progress the docs were going to let her come home for a couple of weeks of what was supposed to be bed rest. He suspected the hospital staff couldn't wait to get rid of her. Not that she was a bad patient, just that she hated being there and let everyone within earshot know it. Dr. Nathan Silver said that was a good sign. If she was acting normally, she was recovering. Josh still hadn't gotten up the nerve to call Nathan, and after the dream, he wasn't sure he really wanted to. Still, he hadn't thrown out the business card, either.

Josh had paperwork to go over, so he let Micah walk home on his own, after promising he'd be careful. By the time Josh got back, the house was dark, except for the Shabbat candles burning in the silver candlesticks on the dining room table. Who had lit them? Normally, his mother did, but she wasn't back yet. His dad wouldn't do it. The scent of hot wax, familiar from his earliest days, drew him into the room. He nearly collided with a stepstool placed at the end of the table. When he was little, they had put that there for his sister when she was learning the Shabbat prayers.

Had Ethan lit the candles? Why on earth…? As kids the boys never would have touched them. That was the women's job. He noticed a cup of wine and a hunk of bread on a plate. The other two main Friday night prayers: blessing the wine and breaking the bread, the bounties of the earth. Micah had mentioned wanting to get home for plans with Ethan, and maybe this had been what he was talking about.

He watched the candles burn, remembering how as a kid he used to love Friday night dinners at home, singing, getting a sip of wine, and then pulling apart the braided challah, still warm from the oven. The house didn't smell like Shabbat now with his mom in the hospital, but something about the candles gave him a warm feeling he hadn't felt for years.

The clock chimed the quarter hour, and he made his way upstairs. The second story was dark. He could hear soft whispers behind his old bedroom door, Micah and Ethan talking. He wondered vaguely what they were talking about, then pushed the thought out of his mind. It was fine for Micah to have his family, Josh was happy on his own. He didn't need Shabbat candles or warm challah—he had a career and a life away from all this domestic bliss. His parents' door was shut, and he could hear his dad's snoring. Another reminder of what he didn't want: getting old and having barely seen the world beyond the old neighborhood.

He closed the door of the guest room behind him and pulled his shirt off. It smelled of brisket and dill and kasha. He'd take a shower and check out a gay dance club his chef friends in Paris had raved about. He needed to get out and have some fun. He'd been working his ass off in the kitchen for days now. He deserved it. In France, he'd worked just as hard, but at least there he'd gone out from time to time. He was starting to feel as if he were stuck in some alternate reality. *Or maybe a monastery.* Some drinks, some sweaty shirtless dancing, making some new and temporary friends, and he'd feel a lot better.

It would be the first freedom he'd had since he came back. He laughed to think that, back in France, his crew thought he was off to New York for two weeks of fun and frolics. Little did they know how much hard work he had to do to keep his parents' restaurant running in their absence.

After showering, he pulled out a new pair of pearl-gray pants made of butter-soft leather. He'd bought them in France at a trendy boutique in the Marais, not far from his apartment, and they'd cost a small fortune. They were also worth every penny—they smelled like a new car and felt like heaven as he slid into them. No underwear. The leather was cool and smooth against his skin, cupping and caressing him in all the right places. He checked himself out in the mirror from all angles and adjusted things here and there till he liked how he looked. He slipped on a silver mesh shirt and decided a little touch of eyeliner would emphasize his dark brown eyes. He leaned in close to the mirror, wishing the light was better in here. No way he'd go down the hall to the bathroom in case he ran into his dad.

Josh lined his eyes, giving himself a different look. With a slight curve of the pencil he drew lines that he realized only when he'd finished, precisely copied the shape of Micah's eyes, the slightly exotic cast of those deep green Sephardic eyes. The thought of that made the leather pants unbearably tight. Josh glanced down at the swelling ridge of flesh clearly outlined in the thin leather. Someone tonight was going to love that look.

He quickly finished getting ready, shoved his wallet into a black leather jacket, and headed off to find Mr. Right Now.

THE club was everything he'd wanted and more. Lots more. And even more than that. He had no idea what time it was when he finally decided he should go home. He had a vague idea he was supposed to do something in the morning, but he couldn't remember what. Not work. Something else. Well, someone would tell him. At his house someone always told you what to do and when to do it. They told you how as well, and then changed their mind and you had to do it again.

There were no cabs to be found, so he walked home. The streets were dark, but some lights were on in shops and houses. Almost morning. He smelled bread baking and realized he had no idea when he'd last eaten. He'd grab something at home. He unlocked the front door and immediately heard music and sounds of a struggle. It was just the television. Ethan was in the living room watching Saturday morning cartoons.

"What the—" Micah appeared in the hallway, his face set in a deep frown.

"Morning." Josh smiled and tossed a wave at Micah. He was feeling far too good for frowns.

"Get upstairs, Josh. Go now." Micah's tone was cold and his expression was now one of barely controlled disgust.

"Yes, Dad." Josh was a little unsteady on his feet. He headed for the stairs and felt Micah right on his tail. He went into the guest room, but before he could shut the door Micah was in there, slamming it behind both of them. Glaring at him with cold fury.

"I don't want Ethan to see you like that. What the hell were you thinking?"

"I don't know." Josh looked at his watch. Oh, right. He wasn't wearing one. "I need to sleep." He yawned and looked longingly at the bed.

"You need a shower and you need to get dressed. We're supposed to go to shul this morning. For your mom. Remember?" Micah's words were authoritative and harsh. He'd picked up that parenting stuff really well.

"Shower. Yes." Josh rubbed a hand across his eyes and realized he'd smeared his eyeliner. A lot. He glanced up at Micah and saw dark anger in his eyes. Micah wrinkled his nose. "What?" Josh looked in the mirror. He probably looked and smelled like a coke whore after an all-night gang bang. Suddenly, his legs wouldn't hold him up, and he collapsed on the bed.

"Are you okay?" Micah was next to him in an instant.

"Yeah." *And even if I wasn't, I wouldn't tell you about it.*

Micah leaned close and lifted an eyebrow. Normally, having him this close, touching Josh, would be wonderful, but it hurt. He pushed Micah's hands away.

"What did you take?"

"Nothing." Why did everyone want to treat him like a kid?

"Josh."

"Okay. A popper. One." Hadn't it just been one? Josh couldn't remember much detail after that point. He just remembered having the time of his life. And now all he wanted was to sleep for three years.

"Josh, what the fuck were you thinking?"

"That I wanted to have some fun." There's nothing wrong with that, he reminded himself.

"Did you have fun?"

"Oh, yeah."

Micah shook his head. He started to take Josh's jacket off and Josh let him. "Josh.... Look at you."

Josh looked down. He looked great. Until he realized tight leather pants and a silver mesh shirt didn't look as good in the light of morning as they did under strobe lights in a dance club. In the right context, he was hotter than hell, he reminded himself. With the slight buzz that still inhabited his sated brain, he could still convince himself it was true. "Nice, huh?" Josh felt Micah's gaze take in every inch of him. He stroked a hand along his cock to show Micah what he'd been missing.

"Take off your shirt." Micah's tone was glacial.

Josh smiled—he hadn't realized his cock would have this effect on Micah. He happily followed orders. The morning was shaping up to be at least as interesting as the night before. Or at least, as much as he remembered of the night before.

"Josh...." Micah sounded horrified.

Josh looked down. There were some bite marks and hickeys and dry white streaks along his front and back. They both knew most of the dried come couldn't be Josh's. *Shit.*

"Just one popper?"

"Yeah. I told you. Why, you want one?" Josh just bet Micah did too.

"No. I'm done with drugs. I don't want or need them. And you should stay away too."

"I'm not addicted like you." Josh hadn't expected the pain he saw flash across Micah's face.

"I've worked hard on this and I've come to terms with that... and I'm dealing with my issues. You aren't."

"I don't take drugs a lot." Well, Josh reasoned, it was true. Once in a while at a club never hurt anyone. He didn't *need* to do it. It was a choice, like another drink, or blond vs. brunet.

"You're addicted to something else. Some other form of self-destruction. You're trying to kill yourself in other ways."

"I was having fun."

"Fun. You call it fun. How many guys were you with? Did you use protection?"

Josh shook his head. "There wasn't any fucking." He didn't think there had been, although things were still a bit fuzzy. He shifted on the bed a little. He didn't feel like he'd been fucked, but he'd never bottom at a club. "No fucking." This time he said it with more confidence.

"You're not even sure what you did."

Josh just blinked. God, he wanted a shower. He also really wanted Micah. He reached out and grabbed his hips, pulling him close, but Micah pushed his hands away.

"There's nothing wrong with what I did." The words didn't come out quite as confident as he'd intended.

"If you're so proud of yourself, why do you seem to be ashamed of it? Would you tell your mom what you got up to?"

"Of course not."

"Josh, grow up. Take some responsibility for yourself and your actions."

Josh's jaw tensed with the admonition. "I'm plenty responsible. I run the restaurant. I've held onto a job all these years, and I haven't been in prison." As soon as he said it he wished he hadn't. The effect on Micah was clear but fleeting, as if he'd grown inured to the judgments, but Josh could still get to him. A week ago, it had felt good to stick it to Micah. After all, he'd hurt Josh about as badly as anyone could. Worse. And yet this time, Josh felt like a shit for having said it.

"When you're in a kitchen, you're fine. Outside of a kitchen, it's like you're still a seventeen-year-old guy. Thinking with your dick and not caring what effect it has on anyone else."

That cut Josh straight to the heart. If he acted as if he were still seventeen, it was because a part of him wanted to go back to those days before Micah had ever been anything more than a best friend. Before Micah had hurt and disappointed him. But Micah was right: Josh couldn't keep taking that pain out on everyone else.

"Get yourself cleaned up. Quietly. Don't wake your dad up. He can't handle seeing you like this."

"My dad knows I'm gay."

"Your dad's idea of gay is not this." Micah waved a hand along Josh's body.

Josh looked down at himself. At his half-erection and the streaks of multiple strangers' come and the remaining dots of glitter.

"No? What does my dad think gay is?" He was curious but still irritated that Micah was judging him again.

"You've been out of the States for a while. Around here, gay is guys getting married, having families, taking their kids to the park to fly kites. It's wedding announcements in the *Times*, not glory holes and glitter and poppers." Micah took a breath. "Your parents cater at least one gay wedding a month. That's what gay is here. It's what your parents want for you."

"You seem to know a lot about what my parents want." How long had Micah been staying here, Josh wondered. It felt as if Micah were the son and Josh was now the stranger in the house. But Micah was looking at him with an expression of concern and something else—disgust?—and he figured he'd better just listen to the guy. Not that he cared if he pissed Micah off, either. Josh was perfectly capable of deciding what lifestyle was fine for him, regardless of what the old neighborhood thought "gay" should be.

"Take a shower." Micah turned on his heel and walked out of the room.

Josh did as he was told.

The hot water was glorious, washing away the fog of the night before. The bites and abrasions stung, but he felt better. He definitely *smelled* better. When he got back in the guest room, he found a thermal mug of steaming black coffee and some clothes laid out on the bed: a pair of gray wool pants he'd brought and a respectable button-down shirt he didn't recognize. Micah's? At least he didn't have to figure out what to wear. He slurped down the hot, life-giving liquid and got dressed. He double checked in the mirror to make sure he'd gotten all the eyeliner washed off and used a tissue to wipe away the spots he missed.

When he got downstairs, he found his dad sitting with Micah and Ethan at the kitchen table and a plate of scrambled eggs and toast waiting for him. Ethan wore a white shirt and a tie, and his hair was carefully smoothed and combed. Micah wore a button-down shirt with a jacket over it, but no tie. He looked good. Too good, really. Seymour was just getting up from the table, a mostly untouched plate of food still in front of him.

Micah didn't look at him, and for that, Josh was glad. As the fog of the drugs lifted, he felt a twinge of shame he wasn't very comfortable with. More than ever, he felt like he'd wandered into a fucking after-school special, and he sure as hell wasn't comfortable with Micah playing the role of parent to him. It was hard enough when his parents did that. He didn't need an extra helping of Jewish guilt in his life.

"Gonna head over to the hospital. I don't know how long all that discharge paperwork's gonna take," Seymour said.

"You want help?" Josh asked.

"No. You're going to shul for the *Mi Sheberach*. That's all I ask. It will mean a lot to your mom."

"Sure, Dad. We're going this morning."

His dad leaned down and kissed the top of his head. "Thank you." He fluttered Josh's damp hair and shuffled out of the room. It had been twenty years since his dad had done that and Josh smiled. For the first time since he'd come back, he didn't feel like a kid, even though his dad had just treated him like one. It felt nice.

Except he couldn't quite dismiss the gray look of his dad's skin and the way he seemed to drag his feet now. His dad looked older every day. *This thing with Mom has been really hard on him.*

"We need to leave in twenty minutes," Ethan said as he happily ate pieces of fruit salad with his fingers, pausing from time to time to look over at Josh and grin. Was the kid actually looking forward to synagogue?

"Okay. Thanks for breakfast."

"Dad made it."

"Thanks, Micah."

Micah's glare was his only reply. Josh reached out and picked a grape out of Ethan's bowl. He popped it into his mouth and gave the kid a crazy grin. Ethan stuck his tongue out. At least he acted like a kid now and then. Josh kind of liked doing that too. It was a lot better than seeing the disappointment in Micah's eyes.

Micah poured more coffee into his own mug.

"Hey, can I get a refill?" Josh asked, holding out his mug and lifting off the lid.

"Sure. It's right here." Micah put the pot back on the warmer and sat at the table. "Ethan, finish your eggs."

Josh got up and refilled his coffee. "My dad didn't look so good this morning. And what are all these pills?" He picked up one of the six or seven prescription bottles sitting near the sink.

"For his heart," Ethan said as he piled eggs on top of his toast.

"His heart? What's wrong with his heart?"

"It attacked him." Ethan opened his mouth and tried to shove the egg sandwich in all at once. A little dribble of yolk ran down the corner of his mouth. Micah reached over and wiped it away, shaking his head.

"What?" Josh nearly dropped his coffee mug. "He had a heart attack? Why didn't I hear about that?"

"What would you have done if you knew? Come home?" Micah took a delicate bite of toast.

"Well...." He probably wouldn't have come home. Micah was right, and the knowledge of that made Josh's heart ache. He was a shitty son. But he still wanted to know. He *deserved* to know. "I would have called to check on him." Why hadn't his sister Jenna called? Maybe she had. He usually didn't listen to her messages, and she hated using e-mail for personal discussions.

"It was three months ago. He's not supposed to be working at all, but he won't listen to the doctors." Micah pushed his plate away and nodded to Ethan, who was just eating the last of his egg sandwich. "Brush your teeth, then we'll leave." Ethan nodded and, still chewing, stood and walked out of the kitchen. A moment later Josh heard him clumping up the stairs.

"Three months?" Josh picked up the plates from the table and scraped the leftovers into the trash before loading the dishwasher. "You've been here that long?"

Micah sipped coffee and watched Josh at the sink. "Yes. A little longer actually. I was in a halfway house when I first got out of...." Micah turned his gaze away.

"Oh." Josh noticed the flicker of pain in Micah's eyes. "Thanks, Micah. I really mean that. I can see how much your being here has helped my parents. And I'm sorry about this morning. I really was an ass when you were just trying to help."

"That's a bad word!" Ethan came into the kitchen, already wearing his coat and mittens, and clutching a dark blue velvet pouch.

*Micah has his own tallit?* Josh couldn't even remember where his own prayer shawl was.

"We can continue that discussion later," Micah said and put his mug in the sink. He switched off the coffeemaker and they grabbed their coats.

"I DON'T remember what I'm supposed to do for this prayer," Josh admitted as they walked to the synagogue.

"It's the Mi Sheberach, the healing prayer." Ethan ran ahead of them and then stopped and waited for them to catch up.

"I know that much. But what do I do?"

"When the rabbi asks if anyone is ill, you go up and stand with him and say your mom's name—in Hebrew. Usually a lot of people go up. But some just stand up at their seats, especially the really old ones. But it's easy. You say the prayer along with everyone else." Ethan sped up again and his voice trailed behind him in a cloud of pale breath.

"I can do that." How long had it been, he wondered, since he'd last gone to shul? Since college? It's not as though he'd gone in France, although there certainly were synagogues in Paris. He slept in Saturday mornings—rarely rising before afternoon—following a long night at the restaurant. And staying out late after his shift ended.

Ethan raced back toward Josh and asked, "Want me to go up and stand with you?"

"Yeah, that would be nice." Funny, Josh thought, that Ethan's offer made him feel a little less nervous.

Ethan put a mittened hand into Josh's and gave it a squeeze. "I like your mom. She makes me cake or cookies. And she taught me how to make French toast. Only with challah. It's really yummy. I wanted to see her in the hospital, but they said kids couldn't go." He sounded sad.

"It's no fun to visit a hospital. You'll get to see her later on. I'm sure she missed you too. And that French toast sounds delicious." Josh let Ethan swing his arm in a wide arc though it made keeping his balance a trick. He glanced over at Micah, who appeared lost in thought as he walked in silence.

The shul was half full when they arrived. The service had already started, so they hung up their coats quietly in the entry hall and grabbed yarmulkes for their heads. Services usually lasted more than two hours, so it wasn't unusual for people to come late. Ethan unzipped the pouch and handed Micah his prayer shawl, traditional white with cobalt stripes and silver and white fringe. He softly recited the blessing as he kissed the edge of the tallit and wrapped it around his shoulders.

For a moment, Josh just stood and watched, impressed with Micah's memory for the details of the ceremony. Josh couldn't remember the last time he'd worn a tallit. He knew he'd need to wear one if they were going to say the Mi Sheberach on the dais. Tentatively, he reached out and took a shawl from the rack provided for men who didn't have their own. The fabric was smooth and silky in his hands. He gingerly touched the fringes at each corner, the *tzitzit*, then opened the shawl wide to reveal the words of the Hebrew blessing embroidered across the top in blue and silver threads. He began to read it, then closed his eyes and recited the remainder from memory. He'd learned the prayer years ago, studying for his bar mitzvah, the Jewish coming of age ceremony. It seemed a lifetime ago. He tried to remember himself at thirteen, but failed miserably. Too much had happened since then.

He felt a hand on his shoulder and opened his eyes to see Micah looking at him, his expression once again unreadable. Josh decided unreadable was a whole lot better than disappointed or angry. Ethan took his and Micah's hands again, and they made their way into the sanctuary. A soft chorus of whispers followed their movement as they headed for the empty pews near the front. Micah led, with Ethan between them, still holding their hands. Josh caught a word here or there, his name or Micah's. Some people nodded and caught his eye. He recognized many of his parents' friends and customers.

The service was partly in English, partly in Hebrew, and Ethan helped him figure out where they were in the prayer book. Despite being years since he'd gone to shul, the familiar words and tunes soon came back, and he even sang or hummed along during part of the service.

As he followed along in the prayer book, Josh glanced around the large room. As a kid, he'd never really paid that much attention to the sanctuary—he'd been much more interested in whispering jokes to Micah and trying not to get shushed by the other congregants. Now, though, he took a moment to take in the beauty of the place. The synagogue was relatively old, built in the late nineteenth century, the interior mostly wood, but painted in surprisingly vibrant colors. He glanced up to the painted ceiling, with its depictions of the zodiac signs in shades of blue and red, one for each month of the year. The walls, too, sported murals of the ancient temple in Jerusalem, the Wailing Wall, and the Mount of Olives. Living in France, he'd done some sightseeing, and what he saw here, in his old neighborhood, was at least as beautiful as some of the ancient French cathedrals he'd visited.

When it was time for the Mi Sheberach, Ethan tugged at Josh's hand. "Let's go up." They stood and scooted past the other people in the ancient wooden pew and made their way up the aisle. The rabbi asked for everyone to say the name of the loved one who was ill or needed some extra prayer for healing. Together Josh and Ethan spoke Miriam's Hebrew name.

"Since we have you up here, Joshua Golden," the rabbi started and Josh's pulse rate hit the ceiling, "why don't you lead the prayer this morning? I know everyone here hopes your mother is doing well. She's such an active, vital member of our congregation and has been missed. Come on." The rabbi beckoned him but Josh's feet were glued in place. He couldn't do this. He didn't even know what to say when he was hiding behind the other ten people up here, much less lead anything.

Ethan squeezed his hand again. Josh looked down at the boy, who nodded. Together they walked up to the rabbi's podium. The whole congregation was watching him. He hadn't been on display here since his bar mitzvah. He could teach a room full of chefs how to slice truffles or tourné potatoes, but he couldn't say a prayer for his sick mom—and dad?

He saw Micah standing up, watching him. The stern look on his face shocked Josh. Micah was the one who took drugs and got girls pregnant. Micah was the one caught with a bag full of cocaine and who spent time in prison. And now Micah was the one judging him?

The rabbi sensed his discomfort a moment too late, but he started off the first line of the prayer: *"Mi sheberakh avoteinu: Avraham, Yitzhak, v'Yaakov...."* Josh whispered along with the rabbi and Ethan stood next to him, speaking loudly and clearly. The first familiar words triggered the place in his brain that stored old, unused memories and suddenly he didn't feel lost anymore. He stumbled a little over the next couple, but then he recited the prayer, the voice of the rest of the congregations echoing around him. *"v'imoteinu: Sarah, Rivka, Rachel v'Leah, Hu yivarekh virapei...."*

He looked out and saw Micah still watching, but this time he was smiling as he recited the same words, nodding his approval. He wondered if the approval was for him or Ethan. Maybe both of them?

Then the congregation began to sing the prayer, a mixture of Hebrew and English. It was a familiar, comforting tune and the words came back to him with a warmth and an ache that made him feel like everyone here was singing for his family. He looked down to see Ethan's joyful grin as he sang and Ethan looked up and gave Josh's hand an even harder squeeze.

> May the Source of strength
> Who blessed the ones before us
> Help us find the courage
> To make our lives a blessing,
> And let us say: Amen.

From where he stood, Josh could hear Micah's sweet tenor rise with the congregation. Micah always had a good singing voice, and he hadn't hesitated to join in, even when Josh had been more self-conscious about his own voice. "Sometimes when I sing," Micah told him, years before, "I can feel God's presence." He'd blushed with the admission, but Josh had understood, even if he hadn't felt the same.

Micah's voice was richer now. Older, but warmer too. But Josh could still imagine the teenage boy in that voice. He heard the intention behind the timbre. The emotion. Micah's strong tones resonated through Josh's chest, as if the words and music linked them by its invisible bond.

He'd always loved that feeling in shul, even when he hadn't felt the religious significance of the songs, he'd loved that connection as the congregation's voices mingled in song. Now, with Micah so close, it took on an additional comforting intimacy Josh couldn't explain. At his side, Ethan sang with the same clarity and focus. Josh could picture Micah when he was Ethan's age. Josh had looked up to Micah then, tried to emulate his quiet focus.

*Please. Take care of my parents. Watch over my mother. Keep my father safe.* The sudden emotion caught Josh by surprise. He'd never really prayed before—he'd always recited the prayers the way he'd been expected to, but he'd never really asked for anything. His eyes burned.

When it was over, Josh and Ethan went back to their seats and listened to the rest of the Torah reading. He didn't really hear the words, but for the first time in a long time, he felt a sense of peace and belonging.

AFTER the service, Josh wanted to get home and see his mom, but so many people came up to ask after her they decided to stay for a while, getting a bite to eat at the *Kiddush*, the traditional small buffet laid out after services. Josh could barely even get in one bite, so many friends of the family wanted to talk to him. Most wanted to know about Miriam, but others asked about his job and life in France, and whether he was home for good. They all greeted Micah and Ethan as if they were part of the family, and if Josh didn't know better, he would have thought some of the almost elliptical comments sounded as though he and Micah were a couple now. Wasn't that a hoot? Micah deflected the comments graciously.

How odd, Josh thought later as they made their way home. He'd expected Micah to run screaming for the hills at any intimation he was gay. Had the world changed so much while Josh had been gone? It was like he'd returned to some post-apocalyptic version of his life, like that first scene in the *Planet of the Apes*. Only this time it was some sort of gay-pocalypse, but in a good way.

When they arrived home, the house was noisy and crowded. Add some music and it might be mistaken for the club he'd been to the night before. Well, not quite. Today's visitors were a gaggle of elderly Jewish ladies—friends of his mother—who bustled around the downstairs, rearranging platters of food and catching up on the most recent neighborhood gossip.

"Joshua! Look how you've grown." A woman he didn't recognize came up and squeezed his cheek. "Oh, how handsome you turned out." She still hadn't let go of the cheek when she kissed him on the other.

Josh glanced down and saw a gleeful smirk on Ethan's face as Josh got the same treatment Ethan had endured at shul. The first pincher was replaced by a series of other half-recognizable ladies smelling of baby powder and kugel. Josh made his way through the women and found his dad sitting in his arm chair in the living room. They called it his Archie Bunker chair, after the character in the old TV sitcom. Now the chair made his dad look like a kid.

"Your mom's upstairs. I made a rule of two people at a time and the crew"—he waved a hand at two ladies guarding the foot of the stairs—"is enforcing it for me. I just want some coffee and a knish."

"Let me see what's in the kitchen." Micah came in behind Josh and then left on the food-hunting errand. Ethan waved at Seymour and then scuttled after Micah.

"How was shul?" Seymour motioned for Josh to sit on the couch.

"Fine. Good. Actually really good." Josh noticed his dad's eyes light up. "Lots of people asked about mom. The rabbi made me lead the prayer...."

Seymour let out a strangled sound Josh realized was a laugh. "Made you?"

"Yeah. I really felt like a fish out of water." He noticed his father was looking at him strangely. He couldn't think why, but his own attention was on what he hadn't noticed before. His dad just looked burned out, exhausted. Why hadn't he seen it? *Because you haven't been looking.* He'd been preoccupied with his own concerns of coming home and finding Micah here, and of course his mom's surgery. But he hadn't taken two minutes to really look at his father. He'd spent more time putting on eyeliner the night before. His stomach churned at the idea. At how he'd spent his night—thinking only of his own enjoyment—and not what and who mattered most.

"But you did it. That's the main thing."

"I almost didn't. But Ethan helped me."

"He's a smart kid, that one. He'll go far. You'll see."

"Dad, Micah said—" Before Josh could continue, Micah arrived with a plate of food for Seymour. Ethan brought him a glass of water—seltzer, his favorite. Josh could wait till they were alone again.

"Joshy," a voice called from halfway up the stairs. For once, Josh didn't cringe at the nickname. In fact, he realized he kind of liked it. "Come up here and see your mother!"

Seymour waved him away and Josh left, but he looked back at his dad with Ethan sitting on the floor near the Archie Bunker chair, still in his jacket and tie. His dad looked down and said something and Ethan cracked up. It was good they got along so well, Josh thought, since Jenna and her kids didn't live nearby. His father looked as though he genuinely enjoyed Ethan's company.

Upstairs, Miriam lay on the bed propped up with about two dozen pillows. She looked like a tiny china doll. Her two best friends, Mrs. Zimmerman and Mrs. Samuels, sat at the foot of the bed. They used to babysit Josh and his sister when they were little.

"Joshy, look at you." He knew another pinch was coming. Mrs. Zimmerman could have played a crab on TV if she didn't keep kosher. Mrs. Samuels went for the other cheek. "Oh, my you're so handsome. Why are you still single?"

"I remember you in the bathtub and—"

"Okay, Mrs. Samuels, thanks for that memory." Josh cringed at the idea of what she might say. Knowing these two ladies had seen him naked and might now be telling eligible singles about his penis scared the daylights out of him.

"Can you two get me some water?" Miriam said.

"Here you go." Mrs. Zimmerman went to pick up a glass from the nightstand.

"From the kitchen."

"Oh, sure." Mrs. Samuels nodded and gave Josh a slightly embarrassed smile. "We'll give you two some time." She took Mrs. Zimmerman by the elbow and led her out of the bedroom, closing the door behind them.

"Subtle, Mom."

"Yeah, like a stake through the heart." She laughed. It sounded good. Josh loved to hear her laughter. He used to tell her jokes when he was a kid, and she'd laugh her head off. He discovered later they weren't very funny, but he loved her even more for letting him think he'd entertained her so much.

"How're you feeling?"

"Like a stake through the heart." She rubbed her chest and laughed again at her own joke. "Better. Lots better. Apparently I'm gonna live."

"So why'd you scare me like that when you asked me to come home and help out?"

His mother shrugged and then grimaced. "Ow. Stitches." She took a shallow breath and then opened her mouth but didn't say anything.

*Oh, fuck.* This couldn't be good. If she couldn't tell him, then it must be really bad. "Mom, is it something else? Something wrong you didn't tell me on the phone?"

She didn't reply for a moment. "How's the restaurant doing?"

"Mom, don't avoid the subject. You brought it up. Just get it over with." He was really worried now.

"I know. You're right." She paused again and her gaze traveled toward the door.

Josh wondered if she'd heard about his issues with the restaurant staff. He thought he'd patched things up already. Or was it more personal?

"It's your dad, Joshy. You've probably noticed already."

"Dad?" His heart rate accelerated. "What's wrong with Dad?"

"It's his heart."

"Micah told me he had an attack recently." His voice came out a whisper even he didn't recognize.

She nodded and a grave look crossed her features. "He needs an operation. A pretty serious one. Valve replacement. He should have had it a while ago, but he didn't want to close the restaurant while he recovered. I wasn't feeling so well before and there was no way I could take care of everything while he was out. So, we decided I'd have this surgery now, and once I got healthy again, I could cover."

"Mom, that's crazy. You can't run the place by yourself."

"No. Micah helps a lot, but he doesn't really have enough experience to keep the kitchen running. I was hoping while you were here you could teach him how to manage the kitchen, but we know that would only be temporary. He's supposed to have a hearing coming up soon for his license. Once he gets it back, he won't be around to help."

Josh didn't want to talk about Micah; he wanted to know more about his dad. "When does he need the operation?"

"Sooner the better. But I'm out of commission another week, so maybe January."

"That's a month away still. Isn't it dangerous to wait?" He felt sick now. How could his father take the chance and wait? If he'd already had a heart attack, what would waiting do to him? And the restaurant… his dad had been running the restaurant.

"Sure, but that's part of why we needed you to come back. There are things we need to discuss with you. About the future."

Josh didn't like the sound of that at all. Ominous and frightening. Like the time when he was ten years old he'd lost his television privileges for a month because Old Mr. Greenblatt had told his parents he'd seen Josh at the ice cream store when he was supposed to have been at Hebrew school. No. This was far worse than that. "The future?"

"We'll talk about it later, when your sister comes for Chanukah dinner. We'll have a family discussion. About—"

"Mom, please don't talk like you and Dad are dying. You're both gonna be okay." As if saying it made it true. He couldn't lose either of his parents, not now. Not yet. They were too young. *He* was too young. He still wanted them around. Needed them around.

"No, honey"—she patted his knee—"no one's dying. But we're getting old, and we know we need to make some changes. Maybe sell up and move to Ft. Lauderdale or Arizona. Maybe Israel? Who knows? We need to talk about if there's really a future for us here, and since that affects our financial affairs, you and Jenna should help us decide."

"Sell up and retire?" Josh wasn't sure how he felt about that. They'd had the restaurant for as long as he could remember. He used to hate the place—didn't much care for it now, really—but sell it?

"The sooner we decide, the sooner we can get started. Your dad can't wait too long for that surgery." She looked wistful, even sad. She loved the restaurant—both his parents did. They'd spent their lives building the place.

"Just close the place down for a couple of months while you both get well. Why do you have to decide now?" He didn't want the responsibility of making a decision like this. He'd be back in Paris in a few days, and he wouldn't have to be part of whatever they decided.

"Won't be much business when we open again. We have to face that too. The clients just aren't coming. We're not the kind of place young people like to go, and our best customers are dead." Her words were matter of fact, but he heard her sadness too. Was it for the business or worry about his dad's health? His mother never worried much about herself.

"Mom, this is too much for you to be thinking about right now. You just got back from the hospital an hour ago." *It's too much for me to be worrying about right now too.*

"Josh, we've been talking about this for months." She smiled sadly at him and shook her head. "You're only here for a little while longer. We need your advice. But we don't have lots of time to take before we decide. I won't say any more till Jenna's here, but think about it."

"I will, Mom." He reached out and patted her arm.

"Can you turn the heat up a little? I'm cold."

"Sure, Mom." She wore a thick sweater and he could tell there was another one under that, and she had the blankets around her. If she was still cold that couldn't be a good sign. "You take a nap, get better. I'll check in later and see if you want something to eat."

"No food!" Her voice was weaker, but she got the point across. "Now you go downstairs and keep the girls out of the room. And think about what's really left here worth keeping."

Josh shut the door and walked quietly downstairs. *What's really worth keeping?*

# Chapter Nine

JOSH took the steps down two at a time, dodging one of his mother's friends at the foot of the stairs. He headed for the kitchen where he ran into several more ladies sipping coffee and eating cake and sweet noodle kugel at the kitchen table, gabbing away in Yiddish.

They all looked the same to him now: soft, gray-haired women in flowered dresses and fluffy sweaters. All with the crablike pincers. He had to get out of this noise, this craziness, this *meshugas*, and think. Too many things were happening at once. Information overload. He'd been away so long he barely knew what was happening with his own parents.

"Nothing serious," his mother had said when she asked him to come home, and now he finds out his dad needs heart surgery and they're thinking about shutting the restaurant. If that was nothing serious, he'd hate to see serious. He could barely breathe as he went out the back door and stood, chest heaving as he sucked in freezing cold air. It hurt. He could see his breath with each exhalation, but he drew in more, each breath more painful than the last. His throat burned as the cold settled into his body, wove its way under his clothes and spread goose bumps across his flesh.

"Joshy! Come in here or put a coat on!" One of the women was shouting at him. He didn't care. He needed the cold. Needed to feel. Needed to let out the emotions boiling inside. The cold was good for that. He slipped into the back alley and wandered toward the street, shoving his hands in his pockets. He was cold. Now he wished he'd gone back to get his coat. Odd how the yenta was right.

Odd how many things people told him to do turned out to be right.

The kitchen and the house were stifling. Too hot and crowded with his mother's friends checking in on her. His dad was smart, sitting in the living room away from the chaos.

Dad.

Josh thought about how his dad looked, small and gray in the big armchair. His dad was really sick, but he'd never said a word. Micah knew more about his family than Josh did. How had that happened? Jenna should have told him! He needed to talk to her. What else were they hiding from him?

Josh turned the corner. He'd lived in this neighborhood as long as he could remember. He knew every crack in the sidewalk and every shop on the street. He knew which neighbors had big TVs and what kind of music they listened to. In the summer, everyone had their windows open and no one kept secrets. He knew which husbands yelled at their wives, and which wives had male friends visiting when the husband was at work.

But now, as he shuffled down the block, he didn't recognize anything. Even the pavement was new. Old, run-down shops had been replaced with sleek boutiques and restaurants he'd actually eat at. No wonder his parents' restaurant was failing. They couldn't compete with these places. He'd seen their figures, and while they weren't losing money, they weren't making much either.

He nearly ran into a couple walking a dog, and the little terrier yapped at him and managed to tangle its leash around his leg.

"Sorry about that." The man reached down and pulled the leash back, admonishing the dog for being a naughty little terror.

Josh looked up and realized the couple was two men. They smiled apologetically at him, got the dog under control, and continued on their way. He turned and stood on the sidewalk watching them walking arm in arm, huddling close for warmth as the sun disappeared behind the buildings on the other side of the island.

Micah's words came back at him. "Around here, gay is guys getting married, having families, taking their kids to the park to fly kites." And walking dogs. Boy had this place changed. It wasn't a gay neighborhood, but no one else on the street paid a second thought to the men. He'd never hidden who he was, but he'd never thought he would stroll with his boyfriend that casually around here.

What boyfriend?

There was always Dr. Nathan Silver. His mother had probably decided where she'd register them. She was always trying to fix him up. Last time he'd visited, she found some gay Jewish singles group and signed him up for some mixer event. God, that had been a nightmare. He'd skipped out on it, but she'd asked so many questions. He hated lying when she just wanted him to be happy.

But except for the doctor, she'd been pretty low-key about his relationship status. Probably she was preoccupied with her own issues. Of course, she still wanted him to be happy, like she and his dad, and like his sister Jenna. Jenna had a nice husband, a nice job, two nice kids—a perfect life as defined by Miriam Golden.

Which reminded him, he had a bone to pick with that sister of his for not letting him know about his father's heart attack. He reached for his cell phone and realized he'd let Ethan borrow it. He'd been fascinated by the fact everything was in French, even if the games and apps were exactly the same.

Josh decided to go home and brave the yenta gauntlet. He'd call Jenna on the kitchen phone with the long cord if he had to sneak out to the backyard to get away from the eyes and ears of his mother's friends.

But back at the house, it was quiet except for his dad snoring in the living room, mouth open, slumped to one side of the Archie Bunker chair, with the TV on mute. Josh found Jenna's phone number on the ancient corkboard next to the even more ancient wall phone in the kitchen. One of those old black plastic things with a rotary dial. Who had those anymore? They would probably outlast a nuclear war.

He dialed, painfully, because he had to put in the area code for Connecticut. And she had to have three nines in her number. No ones, but plenty of nines. Like she'd planned it just to inconvenience him.

Her husband, Steven, answered.

"Hey, Steven, it's, uh, Josh. Golden."

"I know who you are, Josh." Steven chuckled on the other end of the line. "Though it's been a while since we've talked. How're you doing? Jenna talked to your mom a couple of times already today.

Everything okay?" Of course Steven had his finger on the pulse of the Golden household. Everyone knew more than Josh did.

"Mom's fine. Is Jenna around?"

"Yeah, Joshy, I'm here, on the extension."

"Oh, hey, Jenna." He paused. He didn't really want to have this discussion with Steven on the line. "Family business, Jen."

Steven must have gotten the message because Josh heard a click.

"What, Josh? Is Mom okay? I talked to her less than an hour ago. Or is Dad—?"

"Yeah, it's Dad."

"Oh, no, what happened?" Her voice rose with clear concern.

"Nothing. Not yet." He took a deep breath and his heart was pounding. He didn't know why. "Jen, why didn't you *tell* me about Dad?"

"What's to tell?"

"What's to tell? Heart attack? That's not something serious enough to let me know?" Was he the only one who thought someone should have told him about this?

"He survived. You were too far away to help or to get here, just in case...."

"Jen, that's not what I mean. How come Micah Solomon knows more about my father's health issues than I do? You should have called me."

Jenna exhaled slowly, but loud enough for the sound to rattle through Josh's head. "You're right. But I knew how the conversation would go. Like they always go. You're busy and you can't help. Same old Josh, same old conversation."

"When was it, exactly?" He dreaded the answer but he had to know.

"Mid-September. Why?"

"No reason." The lie burned in his throat. He'd been in California then, cooking at a big event for his friend Austin Kelvin's winery up in Napa. How had he found time off for Austin but hadn't made it home in more than five years? It was a career move, he rationalized. That had always come before family.

"Well, I'm surprised you came home now." Jenna's strident tone broke through the rapidly building layers of Josh's guilt.

"That's not fair. I had to. Mom needed me. You couldn't—"

"Right. I couldn't. If I could, I'm sure you wouldn't have come. Are you going to accuse me of having a difficult pregnancy just to sabotage your life?" Her tone cut right through him. His chest ached.

"No, Jen. I didn't mean that. Oh, shit. I'm sorry. I really am sorry you're having trouble. I hope it's gonna be okay." Josh gulped. He didn't even know what the problem was with Jenna's pregnancy, only that she was supposed to be off her feet most of the time.

"It's manageable. But I don't think you called to talk about my pregnancy. Let's finish one thing at a time." She was treating him like a child, the way everyone else had treated him. For the first time, he wondered if he deserved it. If Micah was right and he *was* a seventeen-year-old when he wasn't working.

"I'm sorry. Tell me what's going on with Dad. Mom said he needs a valve replacement. How long can he last without one?" As soon as the words were out he regretted his word choice. "I mean when does he need it?"

"Pretty soon. A month at the outside. Even if Mom is back to a hundred percent, it's gonna be tough on them. On her. If I could help out I would, but it's too big a risk."

"What do they need?"

"They need to retire. That's what they need. It's good you're here. They want to have a family conference after Chanukah dinner. You and I have to convince them to slow down. Dad won't unless Mom does, and you know her, she's like a Jewish Energizer Bunny."

Josh laughed at the image. The first laughter he could remember for a while. It felt good. "Oh, yeah. You should have seen her with the doctor."

"Dr. Nathan Silver? I hear he was interested in you."

"Shut up. Liar!" Somehow they'd reverted back to being eight and five years old again. It felt good not to be arguing with Jenna. "He was nice. And good looking."

"Seriously? What are you waiting for? Maybe he'd do Dad's surgery for the family rate!"

"One thing at a time. Let's get through Mom's recovery before you start marrying me off to the doctor."

"Well, Mom wanted one of us to marry a doctor or lawyer. I got a college professor. Your turn."

"Yeah. That'll be the day. And speaking of lawyers...."

"Were we?"

"Micah."

"What about him?"

"Why's he living here?"

"Did you ask him?"

"Sort of."

"He was at a halfway house, and then he moved in with Rina and Ethan. She's got one of those tony co-ops near Delancey. Damn, that neighborhood has changed a lot! Anyway, they gave her a hard time about Micah."

"Can they do that?"

"Apparently they were ready to get a restraining order or something pretty serious. He didn't want to get the courts involved, which I guess you can understand. He was staying with Mom and Dad for a couple of weeks while he looked for his own place, and then Dad had his heart attack. It made sense for Micah to stay with Mom and Dad. He helps out around the house and the restaurant, and he's not too far from Ethan. He probably couldn't afford a decent place nearby. He'd have to live in Brooklyn or Staten Island, and I guess there are a lot of restrictions for his probation."

"So who's helping who?" Josh was beginning to wonder. He had a feeling he knew the answer too.

"I think he's helping them out. He even offered to pay rent, but of course they wouldn't take anything. And they've always loved him, since you two were kids. Mom was heartbroken when you two fell out. Micah was like—"

He cut her off. "Like a son to them?"

"Well, yeah. They miss you, Joshy. For a little while, Dad had a son, and a grandson. And you'll be leaving again soon."

"You make it sound like with Micah around they don't need me." Josh's chest hurt again.

"Oh, God, no. Dad won't say anything, but he was so excited you were coming home. But with Mom in the hospital and him so sick, he probably hasn't been able to show it. If you had come home sooner, he would have dragged you to a Yankees game."

"I'm not ten years old anymore." He really wanted to believe her, but at the moment, he wasn't feeling as confident as she. He'd certainly not been a very good son. Micah had been kinder, more helpful, and he wasn't even their flesh and blood.

"No, but Dad still would love to go to the ball game with his son."

Josh loved going to the games with his dad too. They used to bring Rina and Micah along until Rina's parents wouldn't let her go to ball games and forced her to take ballet lessons. He felt a little pang at the thought of his dad at the new Yankee Stadium with Micah and Ethan. He wouldn't ask.

"Joshy, I gotta go and help tuck the boys in. I'll see you in a few days, or call me if you want to talk some more."

"Yeah, Jen. Take care of yourself." He paused. "I guess I have a lot to think about before the family meeting."

*Understatement of the century.*

# *Chapter Ten*

BY MONDAY morning, Josh felt as though he'd run a double marathon between taking care of things at the restaurant, worrying about his mother, and worrying about his father. She, at least, seemed to be doing better every day. His father, on the other hand, Josh wasn't so sure about. Maybe it was knowing there was something seriously wrong with his father's heart that made Josh see him differently. Now every time his dad climbed the stairs to bring his mother something, Josh thought he moved a bit more slowly, but he refused any offers of assistance. He seemed paler, too, as if her surgery had weighed just as heavily on him. Josh was worried, more now than he'd been before he'd spoken to Jenna.

At breakfast Josh and his father sat in the kitchen talking. It was the first time since his mother had come home from the hospital that they'd actually said more than a few words to each other. Since her return Seymour had been at Miriam's side almost constantly. Seymour had been so worried about her it had been all Josh could do to make sure his father got something to eat. After his dad had taken up her tray Josh volunteered to make something special for his father—nothing fancy, his father had insisted. At least they weren't eating Mrs. Kreutzer's potato kugel for a third day in a row, Josh thought, happy to be doing something that felt as though he was helping at home.

He scoured the cupboards for a leftover box of matzoh so he could make his father's favorite dish: matzoh brei. His mother had only made it around Passover—the traditional time of year for eating matzoh instead of leavened bread—but Josh considered it comfort food any time of year. Sort of a Jewish version of French toast, with unleavened matzoh dipped in eggs and fried. As usual, Josh improvised with other ingredients, making it something beyond the typical. He first sautéed garlic and thinly sliced onions, then added some cumin and a bit of paprika and mild chili powder before adding in the matzoh and egg. That had been another source of argument in the Golden household: how many eggs to pieces of matzoh. His mother made it one-to-one and his dad two eggs to one matzoh. Josh split the difference with two eggs per three sheets of matzoh. Not too eggy and not too dry.

He fried it up in a few minutes and brought the plate out to his father. He expected an argument about the onion and spices. Instead, Seymour just smiled at Josh and ate the entire plateful without complaint. Not an out-and-out compliment, but from his father, Josh figured it was a victory of sorts. That, or his father was just too tired to complain.

"How are things at the restaurant?" his father asked, making an obvious effort to talk to him as he ate.

"Good. I think the staff are getting used to me." He wouldn't tell his father about his run-in with the staff.

"Micah helping you?"

Josh bit back the urge to tell his father where Micah could take his help. "Sure."

"Good." Seymour took another sip of his water, set it back down again with a clunk, then stood up and walked over to the calendar on the fridge. "Damn."

"What's the matter, Dad?"

"I forgot we're supposed to watch Ethan after school." Seymour rubbed the bridge of his nose and shook his head. "But I have to take your mother to the doctor's again."

"Why are you watching Ethan? Why isn't Micah doing it? He's not on the work schedule."

"Micah does his community service on Mondays."

And this was his father's problem why? Because Micah had fucked up and had to be rehabilitated? Josh repressed a snort. *As if.* "Can't that neighbor Mrs., uh, Feinstein do it?"

"Mrs. *Finkelstein* plays mahjongg on Monday afternoons. That's why it's our day to watch Ethan." He paused and took a few labored breaths. "Please, Joshy. Do you think you could watch Ethan until we get back from the doctor's? Help him with his homework? It's a slow day at the restaurant, so you can take a break before dinner service."

"I... ah...." Josh reminded himself it was his father asking, not Micah. Besides, Ethan was a good kid. Micah had screwed him over just like he'd screwed over the rest of them. "Okay," he said at last, not wanting to add any stress to either of his parents.

"Great. Thank you."

"Do you need me to get him from school?"

"No. Micah arranged for a classmate's mother to bring him home. He knew your mother wouldn't be up to walking over to the school after the surgery."

Josh wondered how often his parents had been babysitting Ethan. Then again, Jen said Micah had been a godsend to their parents, and maybe they didn't mind looking after the kid now and then in return.

"All you need is to get him a snack when he gets home and get him started on his homework. He won't give you a hard time. He's a good boy."

He'd do this for Ethan and his parents, he told himself.


JOSH met Ethan at the front door a little after three that afternoon. Josh thanked the classmate's mother, a rather large-boned woman who looked vaguely familiar and told Josh she remembered him and Micah from grade school. He gave her a pleasant smile and shepherded Ethan inside.

"Hi, Uncle Josh." Ethan took off his backpack and set it on the kitchen table.

Josh was still getting used to being anyone's "uncle." "Hi, Ethan. How was school?"

"It was okay, I guess. I got an A on my social studies test."

"Great job. You like social studies?" Josh rummaged through the cabinets to find something for a snack.

"It's my favorite class."

"It was mine too." *Except for geography.*

"Really?" Ethan looked up at him, green eyes bright to hear this.

"Yep. I had Mrs. Morrison and she was a really good teacher. She told stories about people all over the world, so it wasn't just memorizing maps."

"My teacher's like that too. It's really interesting, not a bunch of boring dates and facts. I don't like memorizing stuff."

"Neither did your dad." Josh pulled out a box of crackers and set it on the counter.

"Was my dad in your class?"

The question took Josh by surprise. "Your dad? Yes. He was."

"He told me you guys met when you were in elementary school." Ethan's interest perked up. "Said you were best friends, like me and Jason."

"We were." Josh nodded, ignoring the usual pain that accompanied any thought of what he and Micah used to be like. "He helped me with my English homework—I was really bad at that—and I helped him with math."

"You're good at math? That's my worst subject." Ethan scrunched up his face. "It's boring."

"I'm pretty good at it." Josh smiled and pulled a couple of plates down from the cabinet. He'd been good enough to get an accounting degree, even if he hadn't really enjoyed his classes.

"Can you help me with my homework?" Ethan's voice was tentative. "Dad usually does, but he's got community service today."

"Sure." He wasn't sure he knew the first thing about fifth-grade math, but he'd certainly give it a try. Josh cut up some carrots and celery, put a dab of peanut butter and a dab of cream cheese on the plate, and set it in front of Ethan. "This okay for a snack?"

Josh half expected Ethan to complain about the healthy snack, but he just smiled and said, "Sure. Thanks."

"So what does your father do for his community service?" Josh asked as he poured Ethan a glass of milk and set it down in front of him.

"He works at a boys club not too far from here." Ethan grabbed a carrot stick off the plate and began to crunch it.

"Oh." Josh wasn't sure what he'd expected, but it hadn't been working with kids. The guy was a drug addict. How was that good for kids?

"Sometimes I go with him," Ethan continued, mouth half-full. "When I don't have school. Mr. Simmons said it was okay. He's my dad's probation officer."

"Do you like going to the boys club?" Josh wondered why he was even asking—he didn't really care what Micah did, did he? He told himself he was just making small talk with the kid. Besides, what could it hurt? It wasn't any great secret what Micah did on Monday afternoons.

"Yeah. It's fun sometimes. We play basketball and stuff. My dad's good at basketball."

Josh remembered. The two of them had dreamed of being NBA players when they'd been in middle school. Josh hadn't been as good as Micah—he'd always been the more athletic one. He remembered watching Micah dunk the ball and how the muscles in his shoulders would tense as he reached for the hoop.

"… and sometimes my dad talks to the kids about drugs. You know, about how he got messed up," Ethan was saying as Josh came back to himself.

"He talks about that?" This took Josh by surprise. "What does he say?"

Ethan swirled a piece of celery in the glob of cream cheese. "He says he did really stupid things. Stuff that hurt other people. Not like *hitting*, you know, but he hurt their feelings. He says it makes him feel sad that he hurt anyone with his mistakes. My mom and me too, I guess."

"Oh." Josh wasn't sure how he felt about that. A few days ago, he would have just passed it off as more of Micah's bullshit. Hell, it was easy to talk about things. *Doing* things was a lot harder.

"My dad's pretty cool. I mean, now he is. I was really mad at him before. You know, when he was in jail and all." Josh noticed Ethan had smeared the cream cheese in big circles on the plate.

"I guess that must have been hard for you."

"Yeah." More cream cheese circles. "Mom says it was hard for Dad too. She said he was really sad he had to leave me. We went and visited him sometimes at the prison. When we left, I could tell he was really sad. One time, I saw him cry when he thought I couldn't see."

In spite of himself, Josh's chest tightened to imagine Micah saying goodbye to Ethan. The two were obviously really close.

*Stop it!* Why was he feeling sorry for Micah? He should be feeling sorry for Ethan—*he* was the one whose father was gone all that time while he was in prison. And whose fault was that, anyhow? It hadn't been Ethan's. Or Rina's. *Or mine.* For once, though, those thoughts didn't make Josh feel any better.

"So what do you have for homework?" he asked, deliberately changing the subject.

Ethan reached into his bag. "Social studies, math, and spelling."

IT WAS nearly five when Micah got home.

"Hey, Dad!" Ethan's face lit up as bright as a pair of Shabbat candles when Micah came into the kitchen.

He planted a kiss on Ethan's head, then mussed his hair. "How was school today?"

"Great. Jason and I played basketball before school."

Micah laughed. "I meant class."

Ethan grinned. "I aced my social studies test."

"Way to go, Eth!" Micah shouted before giving Ethan a high five. "I knew you could do it."

"Uncle Josh says you took social studies together when you were my age."

Micah glanced at Josh, one corner of his mouth edging upward in a half-cocked smile. "Yes. We did."

"I should really get going." Josh stood quickly, nearly knocking his chair over. He grabbed for it awkwardly. "It's just about time for the dinner prep."

"Thanks for watching Eth," Micah said. "Seymour told me about Miriam's appointment."

"Sure."

"What do you say to Josh?" Micah prompted Ethan.

"Oh. Thank you, Uncle Josh. I had fun."

"I had fun, too, Ethan." Josh grinned at the boy, making a point to avoid Micah's gaze. "And don't forget, if you need any help with math, just ask, okay?"

"You bet!" Ethan's smiled reminded Josh of Micah's.

"I'll be at the restaurant as soon as your parents get back," Micah said as Josh walked out of the kitchen. "Thanks again."


WEDNESDAY night was another holiday charity tasting event at the restaurant. The main course was Miriam's famous brisket—a recipe she'd based on her own grandmother's. It called for the meat to marinate for two days, then simmer half a day to achieve the cut-with-a-spoon tenderness that made the dish so sought after by their customers. The Monday crew had prepped an extra dozen briskets and a dozen chickens just for this dinner, all of which would be prepared on the morning of the event, along with half-a-dozen side dishes and a variety of cakes for dessert.

When Josh arrived Wednesday morning, he went into the walk-in to retrieve the briskets. The brining liquid should have been a pale golden color, but this time it was dark red. He sniffed. A spicy tang filled his nostrils.

*Oh, no. This is not happening.*

He pulled a spoon from his apron pocket and took a taste of the brining liquid. *Paprika.* Someone had made a mistake with the measurements, and the whole batch of briskets tasted more of strong, spicy paprika than the half-dozen other herbs and spices that usually balanced out the piquancy.

"Need help with the briskets?" Micah's voice carried from outside the walk-in.

"Oh yeah. These need more help than I can manage. Maybe a miracle." He'd made a Chanukah joke. Who would have guessed?

"What's wrong?" Micah walked into the room and glanced down at the container of beef. "Smells funny."

"Who prepped the brine?"

"Raphael? Maybe Sharon? I can't remember. It was Monday. I was off that afternoon."

The day Josh had been home helping Ethan with spelling. He slammed a fist against the metal rack and it rattled and echoed in the closed space. "Too much paprika. The meat's been marinating in it for two days. You can't just sprinkle something on that and fix it."

"How bad is it?"

Josh handed Micah another spoon and he tasted it. Micah's expression was almost comical, his nose scrunched up and his eyes wide. "Blech. What do we do?"

Josh thought for a minute. He liked the way Micah didn't complain or try to blame someone for a problem. Micah wanted a solution and was ready to try it. "Let me cook one, just to see how bad the situation is."

"What can I do?"

"Can you get started on the chickens? Oh crap, I didn't even check those yet."

Micah opened the next tub. "They look okay. Smell okay too."

"Grab one. Let's cook one of each and make sure."

Back in the kitchen, Josh carved the raw brisket into thick slices. He could cook it more quickly that way, and find out how badly the seasoning was tainted. Micah followed suit, cutting the chicken into pieces and tossing them into a roasting pan. Josh placed a few slices of beef in, as well, and shoved the pan into the oven.

"While that's cooking, let's sauté these." He heated a pan on the range and drizzled in some oil, then put in some more of the beef, letting it form a brown crust and cook through on one side before turning it. A few minutes later he plated the slices and handed Micah a fork.

Micah took a bite and Josh watched his nose wrinkle and mouth turn down. "It's awful. All I can taste is paprika."

Josh popped a slice into his mouth, chewed twice then spit the whole thing into the nearest trash can. "They're all ruined."

"So what do we serve them tonight for the dinner?"

"Excellent question." *Time to think. You can do this.* He'd managed disasters in the kitchen in Paris before, but none on quite the scale as this one. He couldn't possibly get a dozen briskets brined and cooked in less than a day unless he did something drastically different.

"Is there some quick marinating method?" Micah suggested.

"No. Marinating still works the old-fashioned way. But...." Josh went over to the spice rack and looked at the rows of bottles and jars of various sizes, from the tiny vials of saffron to the huge jugs of salt and whole peppercorns. He ignored the section with three different kinds of paprika.

"What are you thinking, Chef?"

"I might be able to come up with some kind of a sauce that will counteract the paprika." He grabbed various bottles. He pulled a notepad out of his apron and set it on the counter.

"Can I help?" Micah's voice surprised Josh. He'd been deep in thought.

"Not yet. You can taste test once I come up with some options."

The lunch crew started arriving, greeting Micah and Josh before settling into their tasks. Josh made sure his experiments weren't in their way as they prepped and cooked. Micah watched with obvious interest as Josh sprinkled various proportions of different ingredients into a small dish, noting measurements on the pad and ripping the paper off, then placing it under each small Pyrex bowl. He added oil to one dish, broth to another and vinegar to a third dish.

"Can you get the meat from the oven, please?"

Micah did as Josh requested, and Josh prepared his sauces. He had four different spice blends. He made pastes of each blend with the three liquids, so he had a total of twelve sauces in small glass bowls.

"Wow, it's amazing watching you work. I never realized how carefully you keep track of everything."

Josh grinned. "I learned the hard way it's best to write it down. Then you can play around with details later. But you have no idea how many great things I can't remember and never could make again." It was nice to share something he was good at, to explain what he did. Comfortable, even.

"I thought there would be more spontaneity to it." Even without seeing Micah's face, Josh could sense he was genuinely interested.

"There is sometimes. That's the fun, creative part, but the truth is, in the restaurant biz, you need to be able to make it again. And for some idiot who never went to culinary school to be able to make it."

"You mean like me?" Micah didn't have a trace of irony or hurt in his voice.

"I didn't mean it like that." Josh shrugged one shoulder. He hadn't meant it as an insult to Micah or anyone. He made a mental note to be more careful about what he said in the kitchen—the last thing he needed was to alienate the staff again. Or alienate Micah, especially when he needed his help.

"I know I'm not much of a cook. I don't pretend to be."

"You're not bad. You pick up things really fast, but I know your interest really isn't in the kitchen."

Micah laughed. "It is, actually, but not in the way you think."

Josh glanced up to see Micah grinning, but he couldn't figure out what Micah meant. He decided to let it go; he had more pressing things to think about. He also needed Micah's help, and he didn't want to push his luck. "Ready to taste?"

"Sure."

Josh cut the roasted beef into chunks he set out on a platter, then he and Micah went down the line of sauces, dipping and tasting. Micah had drawn up a grid on a paper and he wrote his notes about which sauces tasted best.

"None of these really work, if you ask me." Josh pushed the platter with the meat away and felt like he'd be sick. He knew he never wanted to eat paprika again.

"I kind of liked seven and eleven. Definitely better than the others."

"Those were the vinegar-based sauces."

"Yeah, I liked the bite. It balanced out the spice."

"Good observation." Josh tossed out the rest of the samples and tried some new combinations, this time choosing three different types of vinegar to create the pastes. Then they did the tasting all over again.

"Why are you doing this? Spending all this time trying to save the briskets? Can't we just make a run to the suppliers and get something else to serve tonight?"

"Because this group asked for brisket. Because Goldens has a reputation for giving people what they want. Because if I screw up something in here and a customer leaves unhappy, it chips away at everything my parents have worked to build their whole lives. I'm not going to let that happen."

"I thought you hated this place."

Josh straightened up and looked Micah full on. It irked him that Micah had so easily read his emotions. The last thing he wanted was to be so transparent to the staff. Especially with Micah. "That has nothing to do with it. I made a promise to my parents. I'm not going to let them down." He went back to mixing. It was far easier to focus on his work than on Micah.

An hour later they had two mouthwatering sauces that would allow them to serve the mis-spiced beef briskets.

"Now what? We don't serve the brisket with sauce. What if they don't use it? It's still going to be a disaster."

"That's the tricky part. It's impossible to get people to put the right amount of sauce on something. Usually."

"Usually? You have a solution?" Micah peered up at Josh in obvious awe.

"I know just how to do it." For the first time that day, Josh smiled.


FOUR hours later they had cooked all the briskets and roasted all the chickens. They'd mixed up huge batches of two sauces. "Now you need to shred the beef."

"What?" Micah put down the knife. "Normally it gets sliced."

"Right. We're way past normal tonight. The dinner starts in two hours and we've got to get this prepped. Take a fork like this." He grabbed a fork and a brisket and showed Micah how to shred the beef. "They do it like this in Texas, and this method is also used for barbecued brisket and pork."

"Barbecue?"

"Yeah. We're making a Jewish version of hand-pulled brisket. We'll mix in the right amount of sauce so no one will ever know the meat was ruined, then we'll serve it in different kinds of wraps. Flatbread, lavash, I don't know, whatever's around here."

"That's not what's on the menu they agreed on. Won't they get mad?"

"Not if it's delicious. It's still brisket." Josh grabbed a variety of breads from the bin and made a few samples. "What do you think?"

Micah took a flatbread filled with the beef mixture and took a tentative bite. "Oh, wow. That's really good. Nice and tangy and a little spicy and... just wow." His eyes closed and he let out a tiny little moan.

Josh couldn't help but grin at Micah's response. "Still think they'll be mad?"

"They can come back another day for Goldens' regular brisket. This is a one-time thing."

"Now you're talking." Josh smiled at Micah. "You ever take any marketing classes?"

"No."

"Well, you're a natural. You dress up what you've got and make the customers think you did it just for them. Works almost every time."

"But the rest of the stuff on the menu, that's all just the regular recipes. Won't they wonder why you did something different with the briskets?"

"Just watch."

The other two dinner staff came in and Josh explained about the change in menu. They all tasted the finished samples before getting started on the food for the dinner. The look of pleasant surprise on their faces was obvious.

"Somehow, even with the sauce, it still tastes like your grandma's brisket. Just a little zingier. But basically, it's the same. How did you do that?" Micah asked.

"Trial and error. You saw how many mixtures I tested until we found one that balanced out the spices."

"It's more than that. You're really good. I think I'd like to eat at your restaurant in Paris. Someday."

Josh glanced up to see the wistful look in Micah's eyes. "Really? I guess I could make something for you while I'm here."

"I'd love to taste your French cooking too." Raphael came over. The rest of the staff murmured similar sentiments.

"I didn't think anyone would like it."

"We loved what you came up with tonight. Sure, it's not what we've been cooking all these years, but it was incredible and it still had the flavors people want. But something more." Raphael shook his head. "I can't explain it. I liked it. I'd like to taste something you created from scratch, though."

Josh glanced around at the staff. They all watched him and he saw a new look of respect in their gazes. It felt good. Really good. "Sure. How about I do a staff lunch on Friday before we close?"

His suggestion was greeted with unanimous applause.

WHILE everyone else worked, Josh showed Micah how to take the standard recipes and give them a twist with some new techniques, using French methods of cooking or swapping in a Sephardic flavoring for a traditional Eastern European spice. By the time the first guests arrived, they'd recreated three of the most popular side dishes with minimal additional work or change of ingredients.

"Josh, you better go and explain what you've done here," the front room manager told him when they were ready to begin service for the fundraiser guests.

"Sure." Josh wiped his hands on a towel and tidied up his apron. Micah followed him to the kitchen door and stood there watching as Josh introduced himself to the guests. "Since it's a special cause and to thank you all for your generosity, Goldens Restaurant wants to offer you a very special meal. I've designed a tasting menu with new twists on some of your old favorites." A murmur of surprise and disapproval traveled around the room but Josh wasn't deterred. "When I cook in France, they pay five times what you paid." Laughter greeted his comment and he relaxed a little. "But if you don't enjoy this, I'll bring you some plain old brisket. Just ask." He gave a little bow and the diners responded with a smattering of applause, and a few louder grumbles.

"Oh, shit," Micah said once they were back in the kitchen. "How are you gonna give them plain old brisket?"

"Time to pray." Josh grinned and helped finish plating the meals.

TWO hours later, he pushed open the kitchen door to see only Micah still there. The dishwashers were clattering away in the next room, but he'd sent the dinner crew home once the meals had been served and the desserts prepped. Josh was exhausted but flying high. He hadn't had this much fun since he'd cooked that first dinner for Raymond Vessy years before. Sure, he'd loved working in the Paris restaurant, but he didn't often have the opportunity to strut his stuff in the kitchen—he was still only second in command in Raymond's kitchen. It had been good to be completely in charge tonight. Really good.

"They loved it, Josh. I never expected that." Micah reached out as if to shake Josh's hand, then stopped and looked down at it. A moment later, he shook his head and pulled Josh into a hug.

*Oh, damn.* It felt so good to have Micah's arms around him again, but almost as soon as the hug started, it was over. Josh couldn't ignore the disappointment he felt when Micah pulled away. He gave Micah a half smile before grabbing a bottle of wine from the cabinet and pouring himself a glass. He needed something to steady his frayed nerves, and part of him also wanted to celebrate the victory. How was it he could handle a disaster in the kitchen so easily, but all it took was one touch from Micah and he was a nervous wreck?

"I was a little worried myself for a while," Josh said, trying to sound nonchalant. "You saw their faces when I said it was something different." He took two long swallows, nearly draining the glass. He refilled it and leaned against the counter. He couldn't help but notice as Micah appeared to appraise the level of the liquid in the glass.

"They practically gave you a standing ovation. Very impressive." Despite the compliment, Micah's smile seemed a bit forced. Josh could tell something was bothering him.

"I couldn't have done it without you, Micah." He meant it too. It had been good having Micah there tonight.

"I didn't help much."

"You did, actually, just by being there and supporting me with what I needed. That's what a good sous chef does." Josh grinned.

"That's how you see me? Your assistant?" The tone of Micah's voice made Josh take notice. Was that sadness he saw in Micah's eyes?

"No. No, I see a lot more. More than I ever expected to see after all these years." God, why did this man set him so on edge? Why did he care so much what Micah thought?

Micah looked at Josh, his eyes dark under the thick lashes. God, it felt like that night at the pool again with them alone late at night, so close but for a million miles of uncharted territory between them. They'd been as close as two people could be, long ago. But now?

Would Micah's lips taste the same as they had that weekend more than ten years ago? Would his skin feel the same?

Josh had to know. He couldn't stand it anymore. He closed the distance between them, brushing his lips against Micah's. Josh's physical response to that delicate contact was so intense, he thought he might lose his balance. Micah's hand snaked around his waist and they merged lips, tongues, moans. Micah's dusky stubble scraped Josh's cheek, so unlike the last time they'd been this close. Rougher. A grown man and not the college boy Josh remembered. Josh liked it.

He ran his fingers through Micah's hair, soft and smooth, like silk. He let out a small groan as he pressed his hips forward. He felt Micah's cock swell against his thigh, igniting every fiber and nerve ending in his body. He wanted Micah so much it hurt.

"Micah," he groaned into Micah's sweet mouth.

"Josh, wait." Micah pulled away with obvious difficulty, breaking contact except where their arms rested on the other's hips. "Not like this."

"There's a couch in the office." Josh reluctantly let go of Micah, keeping the fingers of one hand interlaced. "My parents are at home...." He tugged Micah in the direction of the office, stopping to bring the half-full bottle of wine.

Silently, Micah followed. In the office they settled onto the couch, a bit awkwardly at first. Josh finished his glass of wine, then pulled Micah close and leaned in to take his lips again.

"Josh, not yet." Micah pushed Josh away—gently, but the message was clear.

"What? Why not?" Josh settled back on the couch and poured another glass of wine. He took a sip to steady himself and offered it to Micah, who waved it away.

"No. Josh, I don't want to do this, not here."

"Afraid someone'll catch you and they'll all know you're gay—or bi, or whatever you call yourself?" Josh felt a hint of the old anger and insecurity return. It had felt so right. So good. And now Micah was pushing him away. Again.

"No. I'm not afraid. Everyone knows now." Micah spoke softly, but the confidence in his voice was obvious.

That threw Josh for a loop. "You're out? Here? When?"

"It's actually been a few years. It was part of my recovery even before I was in jail. Twelve-step programs… acknowledging who I am. I'm not running or hiding from that anymore."

"My parents too? They know?" Josh could barely process the news. Everyone knew? But what did that mean? Micah was still pushing him away, wasn't he?

Micah nodded. "I told them before I told my own parents." He laughed, a short, slightly pained laugh. "My parents… my dad about hit the ceiling. After everything else I've done, you'd think my being gay would be a relief. I think they'd rather have a drug-dealing son than a queer one." This time, the pain in Micah's eyes was obvious.

"I'm sorry about that. God, really sorry." He fought the urge to touch Micah. To comfort him.

Micah shrugged. "I didn't expect more, so it wasn't a surprise. Still, I was disappointed."

"What about us?"

"What do you mean?" Micah paused. "Oh, did I tell anyone about us? No. That was between us."

"All in the past?" Josh said the words softly, wishing he hadn't asked. Why the fuck had he brought this up now? He had Micah in his arms a moment ago, and now he'd killed the atmosphere. When would he learn to keep his mouth shut?

"Is it all in the past? It doesn't have to be. I don't want it to be."

"You don't?" It was the last thing Josh had expected to hear, and it nearly floored him. They'd grown closer during the past couple of days, since they'd gone to shul, but he hadn't been sure if it had been Micah opening up or that he was starting to see Micah differently. Whatever the reason, he was all for a reconciliation. He'd been thinking about it—and dreaming about it, literally—since he'd slipped into those sheets that still had Micah's scent on them, and the feeling had just grown since then. He wanted Micah back. He wanted his body, too, but more than anything, he just wanted to kiss Micah. He leaned forward for another kiss, this one rougher and more insistent.

Micah didn't kiss back this time.

"What's wrong?"

Micah shook his head. "It doesn't feel right. Not yet."

"Come closer and it will feel just fine." He reached out to stroke Micah's thigh, but he could sense Micah was uncomfortable.

"Josh, I'm worried this is just something you need right now."

"Of course I need this." Josh needed Micah so badly right now, he was about to scream in frustration.

"That's not what I mean. It's like the club. The drugs."

"I told you I only did the poppers a few times. It's not a regular thing."

"I'm glad to hear it. But what about the drinking?" Micah motioned toward the glass.

"A little wine with dinner or to relax." Well, that's all it was. Everyone had a drink once in a while to relax, didn't they?

"And the sex?"

"Yes." Josh grinned. Now they were getting somewhere.

"It wasn't a yes or no question."

"Oh." He glanced at Micah and didn't like the deepening frown he saw there. Micah looked genuinely concerned. "What about it?"

"I learned a lot from the mistakes I made over the years, Josh. I hurt too many people who loved me. I don't want to make the same mistakes again."

"What are we talking about now?"

"This is step nine for us. This is where I make amends for the harm I've done to you."

Josh did not want to be having this discussion right now. He wanted to feel Micah's naked body in his arms. He wanted to show Micah how much he'd missed him over the long years. How glad he was they had made up and smoothed over the past. The last thing he wanted was to dig up the past again. To go over that painful ground would be like digging his own grave. "Okay." Josh sat up and took a deep breath instead of the gulp of wine he needed.

"I'm sorry for how I treated you and I need to explain to you what happened and why." Micah waited until Josh nodded his understanding, then continued, "After college, when I got back that summer, it was all so confusing for me. I made all the wrong decisions, or I let other people make the decisions for me. And the biggest mistake I made was not trying hard enough to explain it all to the most important person in my life: you."

"Micah, don't. Please. It's over and done with and I don't want to—"

"If there's any chance for something between us, I need to tell you."

Josh could see determination burning bright in Micah's eyes.

A chance for something with Micah? Could that be a real possibility? For years he'd convinced himself that he hated Micah and eased his own pain by telling himself Micah wasn't someone he ever wanted in his life. But now, this new Micah, this responsible, caring man, the good parent, this was a man Josh had never met but was powerfully attracted to. He'd loved the old Micah, the Micah who had broken his heart. He could barely breathe as Micah started talking, the weight descending on his chest was so heavy. He was terrified, although he wasn't sure of what: losing Micah for good—or getting back together with him?

"You already know how much I struggled during college, with drugs and with accepting who I am. When I came back that summer after school, I really wanted to tell you how I felt. I called, I even came over, but you wouldn't talk to me. I don't blame you—I didn't blame you then, either. I fucked up our friendship. Pushed you away because I couldn't understand it, or myself.

"Anyhow, by August I'd just about given up on talking to you. You had been my best friend for so long—and I wanted more than that too—but I still needed a friend. Rina was there for me. We hadn't been really close during college, but she helped me that summer, talked with me. Then one night we got some wine and we were at her parents' house, kind of drunk, and she said, just as a joke, 'Maybe you aren't gay after all. You haven't even had sex lately, so how do you know what you even want? You should try it with a girl again. Like a test.'"

"And by that point, I'd given up hope you'd talk to me." Micah stopped speaking for a moment and took a deep breath, eyes focused somewhere beyond Josh. "I was so naïve. I figured it would be great if I wasn't gay, then if you rejected me it wouldn't matter. So we had sex, just like that time in high school when she wanted to lose her virginity with me. It was awful." Micah let out a bitter laugh and shook his head. "Worst. Sex. Ever. Even worse because her mom barged into her room before we got our clothes on. It would've been funny if it hadn't been such a disaster."

"Micah, don't go on. I get it." He tried to smile at Micah, wanting to reassure him, but he didn't really want to hear any more about Rina and the sex. It just hurt too much.

"But after that, I knew for sure I wanted you. It took me a couple of weeks to get up the courage to come by and force you to see me. And it was so perfect with you. Like I'd been expecting it to be. Until right after I got up to Cambridge and Rina called. She got pregnant. Her parents knew we'd had sex and that I had to be the father. Then our parents took over and wanted us to get married. Rina didn't want it any more than I did. She said she wanted to get a termination, or put the baby up for adoption, that it'd be easier for both of us. She wanted to go to grad school, not have a kid. But I knew she wasn't really sure, and I couldn't let her make a decision she might regret just so I could be happy—even for you."

Micah looked away from Josh. His voice had gone low and raspy, as if each word were as painful to speak as it was for Josh to hear. Cold guilt flooded Josh's gut and veins. He'd been so selfish when Micah had been trying to make the best of an impossible situation where someone—everyone in this case—would suffer.

Micah took a slow deep breath. "I knew I had an obligation to her and to our child, and I would go along with whatever she decided. In the end, our parents pressured both of us. But I'm not sorry for having Ethan. I love him, and I'd do anything for him." The hint of a smile returned to his face at the mention of his son.

"Too bad you didn't get *me* pregnant. We'd still be together." Josh tried to laugh, but it hurt too much. "I'm sorry, that was really low. Ethan's a great kid. You're lucky."

Micah's warm smile reassured him. "Rina and I were always just friends. She helped me after you left for Europe. I didn't handle it very well. I probably would have completely self-destructed if I hadn't had her and Ethan. But I never stopped caring for you, even though I knew there was no way to make up for how I treated you."

"Thanks for explaining it."

"Do you mean that? Because it's fine if you can't decide right away. Because if you never want to see me again, I can accept that." But the look on Micah's face told him he would crumble to dust if Josh rejected him.

"I forgive you," Josh said again, meeting Micah's gaze and holding it. "I mean it." He pulled Micah close so his head was on his chest, and he combed his fingers through the soft silky hair he'd wanted to touch every day of the past ten years—even longer. Despite the hurt that had grown into anger and even animosity over the years, he really did forgive Micah. He'd been in a terrible situation.

And that's when it came to Josh with a force that nearly knocked the breath out of him. Had Micah chosen not to commit to Rina and the baby, or had he let Rina terminate the pregnancy, Micah never would have belonged to him completely. Micah was, at heart, too good a man to make a selfish choice like that and not let it affect everything in his life. Josh only now understood what a sacrifice Micah had made, knowing he would have killed their love no matter which decision he made. But the path Micah chose meant he hadn't destroyed Rina and Ethan as well.

"Oh, Micah." Josh leaned down and kissed away the tears sliding down Micah's cheeks.

THE following day, Josh was having a late breakfast upstairs with his mother when his dad came into the room, breathing hard.

"Seymour, take it easy. Don't run up and down the stairs." Miriam scolded, but her expression reminded Josh of how sick his father was.

"Josh, you may want to get to the restaurant a little early today." If his mother's expression was clear as day, his father's expression was unreadable.

"Why, Dad? Is something wrong?" Things had been going so well, he sure hoped someone hadn't quit or screwed up the marinade again. He wanted so much to help his parents—really *help* them—for a change.

"Didn't you hear the phone ringing off the hook?"

"I turned the ringer off up here," Josh replied.

"What's wrong?" his mother asked as she sat up a bit straighter in bed.

"Nothing's wrong, but dinner is booked solid for the next week and people are asking for crazy things we don't even have on the menu. Some brisket taco or something. What kind of meshugas is that?"

"Oh." How had anyone found out about that?

From downstairs they heard the front door slam with extra force. "Josh! Josh? You here?"

"Up here, Micah." Holy crap. What now?

Micah thundered up the stairs and came into the room waving a newspaper. He was nearly as breathless as his father. "Did you read the review?"

"What review?" Josh was still too tired to process Micah's words. He needed more coffee.

"One of the *Times* food writers was at the dinner last night. Apparently he loved what you served and he did a whole write-up on the restaurant, and your career."

"Really?" *The New York Times*?

"Look." Micah offered Josh the paper, but Seymour snatched it out of his hand before he could take it.

"Listen to this." Seymour sat down on the edge of the bed and read. "'Last night I was prepared for another of those indistinguishable meals one attends to support a good cause, which is rarely one's own stomach.' How do you like that? He never even thought he'd like our food?" Outrage was painted all over his face.

"Keep reading." Miriam smacked him on the back. "Or give that to me."

"I'm reading. I'm reading. 'Well, imagine my surprise to learn that internationally known but locally grown Chef Joshua Golden had prepared a special meal rather than serve off-the-menu mundanities at Goldens. I was in the minority as my fellow diners greeted that news with resounding disappointment. But I was thrilled beyond belief to see how a classically trained chef with global sensibilities could transform dishes my grandmother used to cook into a sublime treat.'" Seymour stopped reading aloud as he gazed at the rest of the column. "Joshy, what did you do?" There was an undercurrent of horror in his tone.

"We had a little mix-up with the brisket and there wasn't time to marinate any more. I had to improvise."

"You changed your grandmother's recipe?" Seymour sounded as if Josh had just admitted to devil worship.

Miriam patted Josh's hand. "Who cares? People loved it, and you said the tables are booked a week out. What's wrong with that?" She smiled. In fact she looked better than she had since Josh arrived.

"Micah, let's go. We're going to need a bigger kitchen."

Micah chuckled and started toward the door. Josh gave him an affectionate pat on the arm as he passed by.

"What bigger kitchen?" Miriam sounded confused.

"It's a line from a movie, Mom. Never mind." Josh shook his head and followed Micah down the steps. It was going to be a very busy night.

THEY were closed Friday night and Saturday night, no matter how loudly people complained, but from opening on Sunday, the tables were booked up through the following weekend, when Josh would be leaving. The hostess had left a few open tables during each seating for regulars, but even then she was bombarded with bribes and diatribes from diners demanding a table. Sunday night, Josh, Micah, and the rest of the staff were rushed off their feet with no end in sight for the duration of Josh's visit—except for Wednesday night, which he'd vowed to take off to spend the first night of Chanukah with the family, especially since Jenna was coming down from Connecticut with her husband and kids.

Come Monday morning, it was all Josh could do to drag his aching body out of bed when the alarm went off. Why had he set it so early? He didn't need to be in to the restaurant until lunch time.

"Morning." Micah looked up from the frying pan and smiled at Josh as he saluted him with a spatula. "I'm doing breakfast."

"Morning." It was wonderful having Micah cook after the night they'd had in the kitchen. Nonstop. Even without his morning coffee, Josh felt good. Even better now that Micah was nearby. Not that they'd really had any time alone, but ever since they'd talked, Josh had felt like this. More so after the review in the *Times*, not to mention the phone calls he'd gotten congratulating him. For once, the night before, he hadn't even thought about the Paris restaurant and what he might be missing out on there.

"Over easy?" Micah asked.

"That'd be great, thanks."

"There's some turkey bacon in the oven too."

"Sure." Josh thought he could get used to having Micah around for breakfasts—and he appreciated the break from cooking. "Ethan already ate?"

"Yeah, he's getting his stuff together for school." Micah turned back to the stove. "Listen, Josh," he said a few minutes later as he set the plate full of eggs and bacon in front of Josh, "I hate to ask, but I'm kind of in a bind with community service today, and your mom's got another doctor's appointment. I know it's asking a lot, especially with things at the restaurant so crazy, but—"

"No problem." Josh waved a piece of bacon. "I wouldn't mind a break today before the dinner rush. Yesterday was insane. I prefer not to do that again."

"Are you sure? Because Mrs. Finkelstein might be persuaded to give up an afternoon of mahjongg."

"I'm sure." Josh smiled reassuringly at Micah. "I'll stop by the restaurant first, then walk over to the school."

Micah looked incredibly relieved. "Great. You could just take him over there if you'd like, rather than coming all the way back home. He can work on his homework, and I'll take him home when I finish up around four and then get right back to help you."

"Sure." Josh popped another piece of bacon in his mouth. Hell, even the turkey bacon tasted better than he remembered. Could it be because Micah had cooked it? "Ethan said you work at the boys club." Micah nodded. "What do you do over there?"

"Not much, really." Micah began to wash the breakfast dishes. "Just hang out with the kids, play games, listen if they want to talk. Sometimes I think they just see me as the old guy who did some time in prison."

"Ethan also told me you're honest with them—about the drugs. I was surprised. Not that you wouldn't be honest, but that you'd talk about it with them at all."

Micah chuckled. "I was a little surprised, too, when the counselors suggested it. But they encourage all the volunteers to share their experiences with the kids. If they ask, I tell the kids the truth. That I was an addict."

"I don't know." Josh picked up his plate and brought it over to the sink. "If I ever have kids, I'm not sure I'd want them to know about some of the stupid shit I did when I was younger." *Younger? What about the stuff you still get up to sometimes?*

"It's better to talk about it. I learned that the hard way." Micah set the dish he was drying down on the counter and turned to look at Josh. "If I'd been honest with you years ago—with myself, mostly—things might not have turned out the way they did."

Josh reached out and brushed Micah's jaw with a few fingers. "He's really lucky to have you as a father, you know."

"Nah," Micah answered. "I'm lucky to have him."

The sound of feet coming down the staircase startled Josh, and he pulled his hand away as Ethan ran into the room carrying his book bag. "I'm ready to go," Ethan announced.

"You're early, Eth." Micah straightened Ethan's collar and looked him over.

"Jason said he'd shoot some hoops with me before class, so I said I'd get there early."

Micah's smile was for Josh—Josh knew he, too, was remembering when the two of them would meet early to play basketball before class.

"I'll finish the dishes." Josh waved a soapy sponge. "You two get going."

"Thanks," Micah said. "Oh, and, Eth, Josh is going to pick you up from school today. I'll come get you at the restaurant and bring you home afterward, okay?"

"Cool." Ethan looked up at Josh and grinned. "Do you like basketball, Uncle Josh?"

"I love basketball." At least Josh used to. He couldn't remember the last time he'd even held a ball.

"Really? Maybe you and dad and I can shoot baskets some night after school, then?"

"Ethan, I really don't think Josh—"

"I'd like that, Ethan," Josh interrupted.

Micah ruffled Ethan's hair, but his gaze was fixed on Josh. He looked both surprised and happy. "We'd better go. See you later, Josh. And thanks again."

Josh watched them leave, then leaned back against the counter. He was sure he was grinning like an idiot, but he didn't care.


JOSH waited for Ethan outside the elementary school courtyard. The sun had finally come out from behind the clouds, chasing the biting chill away. Josh unzipped his jacket and played with his scarf. He was nervous, he realized with some surprise. *He's just a kid*, he reminded himself. He'd never been that comfortable with kids anyhow, but knowing it was Micah's kid seemed to have somehow ratcheted up his nerves. Doing homework in the kitchen was one thing, but spending time with the kid without something to keep him busy was another.

"So what's Paris like?" Ethan bounced along beside Josh.

"It's... different, I guess." It was hard to sum that up for a kid. And right now, Josh just couldn't find the enthusiasm he'd usually felt about France—the reminder that he'd be going back soon was unwelcome. More so to think he'd be leaving Micah behind, after they'd just started to get to know each other again.

"When are you going back?"

"Soon," Josh said.

"Oh." Ethan looked disappointed, as if he'd been about to ask Josh something.

They stopped at the corner for a red light. As Josh glanced up at the street sign, an idea came to him—something he'd been thinking about doing since he'd gotten home, but had never found the time for. "Hey, Ethan?"

"Yeah?"

"How'd you like to get some pickles before we head over to the restaurant?"

"Pickles?" Ethan's face brightened. "You mean the ones in the big plastic thingies?"

"Plastic barrels?" Ethan nodded. "Yeah. I haven't had one of those in a long time, and it's not too far out of the way." The barrels had been made of wood when Josh was a kid.

"Cool!" Ethan nearly jumped up and down. "Did you and Dad buy pickles when you were kids?"

"Sometimes." Josh didn't mention they'd both gotten into trouble more than a few times for being late to Hebrew school because they'd stopped for pickles. The memory made him smile.

Three blocks later, they stopped in front of a small storefront. The enormous red plastic pickle barrels—waist high for Josh—were set out in front of the store. Other than the barrels now being plastic instead of wood, Josh was surprised at how much it looked the same as he remembered. One of the store's employees was scooping pickles into a plastic container for a customer. The smell of garlic and saltwater brine danced in the air, and Josh's mouth watered.

"So, what kind do you like? Half-sour? Sour?"

"Sour." Ethan looked proud of his choice. "My friend Jason says I could eat a whole lemon. I ate a whole bag of these mega-sour gummies once. He said I looked like a fish." Ethan made a puckered face and they both cracked up.

"A dozen half-sour, a dozen sour, and two sours to go," Josh told the man behind the pickle barrels before glancing back at Ethan. "I like them really sour too. My mom and dad like the half-sour ones."

"My dad likes the half-sours."

*I remember.*

Five minutes later, they were headed toward the restaurant and happily crunching their pickles. Josh had forgotten how good they tasted, even enjoying the juice running down his chin. He wiped it off on his sleeve, just like when he was a kid. Ethan grinned and followed suit. It would be impossible to find traditional kosher pickles in Paris. Not that he'd thought to look for them. The French version of pickles—*cornichon*—weren't even remotely similar.

Ethan chattered happily away as they walked, talking about his favorite TV shows, movies, and music. Josh listened to him, nodding from time to time or asking him about something he'd never heard of before. He hadn't really been paying attention to where they were—he'd walked this way so many times as a kid, it was like being on autopilot. It wasn't until they got halfway down the next block that he realized where they were: the community pool. The one he and Micah had broken into years before, that last summer before college.

It looked exactly the same as he remembered it, down to the peeling paint on the metal gate to the cracks in the concrete next to the entryway. There was no one inside, of course—the pool wouldn't open till May. Still, Josh could almost hear Micah's voice telling him, "Just jump. I don't care if you dive. Whatever you do is fine."

Josh shivered. A few days ago, the memory would have at least made him angry. But now….

"Dad promised to take me swimming when it warms up," Ethan said. "Mom says I'm as good a swimmer as he is."

"You must be really good, Ethan. Your dad's a great swimmer." Josh smiled as he recalled the way Micah used to beat him every time they'd raced in the pool.

Ethan grinned and trotted off down the street. For a moment, Josh just stayed there, lost in the past. Then he rubbed the back of his neck and took a long, slow breath before heading after Ethan.

# Chapter Eleven

THE next two days passed in a whirlwind of cooking, two requests for interviews, and three job offers from Manhattan restaurants. Goldens's business was booming, and they were way ahead of budget. Everyone was happy. The kitchen staff had all returned, now eager to learn something new from Josh. Josh had barely seen Micah except in the kitchen, but they had settled into a comfortable working relationship. They'd even talked a little about personal things. Josh had told Micah about his work at the restaurant in France, and Micah had talked a bit about Ethan and Rina.

Miriam made her first visit to the restaurant since her surgery, greeting guests and staff and waving like the Queen of England. "Josh, you let Micah come home early to help Jenna cook dinner, okay?"

"I thought you wanted me to cook for Chanukah?" Josh had actually been looking forward to it.

"You're too busy here. The restaurant needs you. Just make sure you're home in time for our dinner, okay? Let Raphael or Brenda run things the rest of the evening. They can handle everything for one night."

"Then I should just leave with Micah."

"No. People want to meet you, and there might be more interviews. I'll supervise the Chanukah dinner prep, from a chair in our kitchen." She grinned and headed off his complaint before he even had a chance to make it. "See you later."

"Be careful, Mom. Take a taxi home!"

She gave him a hug and a kiss. "I will."

Back in the kitchen, Micah was shredding more brisket. He looked up and flashed Josh a smile, the kind of smile that made Josh feel as though it was meant just for him. It gave him a little jolt of excitement. They hadn't even slept together, but for once, Josh felt as though there really was hope for some kind of a future with Micah. After their talk, they'd moved to a new phase of their relationship. Micah's honesty had gone a long way to cleansing away much of Josh's long pent-up animosity. It was as though they could start with a fresh, clean slate. Or nearly clean. Josh couldn't quite forget the pain of losing Micah years before, but he felt as though he was ready to move past it.

Which only reminded Josh he had some important decisions to make. He'd worked hard to land his dream job with Raymond Vessy in Paris, but there was no way to keep Micah—and Ethan—in his life if he was living in France. They would stay here—it was home to them and Ethan needed his mother in his life. The thought of leaving Micah again just when they'd reconnected was just as devastating to contemplate. What was most important to him now? And was he really considering giving up his prestigious Parisian restaurant position for a man he'd pined after for more than ten years?

*Yes.*

JOSH was tired when he finally left the restaurant to head home for Chanukah dinner with his sister's family. Just what he needed, more family drama. For the first time in the past few days, Micah had left before him. Josh realized he'd gotten used to heading home with Micah at his side. It had only been a few days since they'd reunited, but he already missed having Micah there.

Josh's very pregnant sister Jenna met him at the door with a hug and a kiss on his cheek. He was careful not to get too close to her protruding belly. She and her husband, Steven, lived in Connecticut with their two children, and although she'd checked in regularly while their mother was in the hospital, her pregnancy kept her from coming down to visit or help with the restaurant while their mother recuperated from her surgery.

Josh had barely stepped inside the house when there was a low rumble and three children sped down the stairs with Ethan in the lead. "Can't catch me!" Ethan shouted, diving onto the carpet and allowing himself to be attacked by the two smaller children.

"Boys!" Jenna shouted over the din. "Come here and say hi to your Uncle Josh."

A few grumbles and a scowl from Jenna later, and Jenna's boys Cory and Jacob marched into the hallway. His nephews had barely been able to speak the last time Josh had seen them. Now, it was all Jenna could do to keep them from babbling. Josh, who had intended to go help out in the kitchen, ended up surrounded and inundated with questions about France. When Micah came out to tell everyone it was time to wash up for dinner, Cory was happily counting to thirty in French for Josh.

"Go wash up," Jenna ordered.

Josh leaned down and whispered in Cory's ear, "You can count your *gelt* later for me. That is, if you don't eat it all first."

Cory laughed and trotted off down the hallway.

"What did you tell him?" Jenna asked, appearing surprised.

"Only that there'll be plenty of chocolate coins for him to count in French for me later." Josh smiled. "When did they get so big?"

"When you were in France, little brother." There was no anger in her voice, although her tone was wistful.

"Dinner, *Mommy*!" Jacob shouted from the dining room. "Now we're waiting for *you*!"

"Okay, okay. Be right there." Jenna turned back to Josh and squeezed his hand. "It's good to have you back, you know. Even if it's just for a little while. I've missed you."

Josh swallowed hard but said nothing, instead following her into the dining room.

THE dining room was festooned in blue and white decorations and construction-paper streamers, most of them handmade by the kids, guessing by the lopsided Stars of David and the jagged edges on what looked to be a paper menorah, the special Chanukah candelabra. A real menorah of shiny brass was set on the sidebar. Each menorah held two candles: the *shamesh* to light the other candles, and the first candle for the first night of Chanukah. Over the eight days of the holiday, the menorah would slowly fill with candles until the last night, when all eight would burn at once.

Josh smiled at the memory of long-ago Chanukahs when he'd watched all the candles lit with that dreamy, childlike wonder. His parents hadn't given him or Jenna large gifts like some families, choosing instead to give them eight small presents, more tokens to celebrate the holiday than anything else—markers, baseball cards, stickers, a doll or action figure. Josh hadn't minded, though; he'd loved it. Micah had come over after his family's dinner, and they had all played most of the evening at dreidl, the traditional Chanukah game of chance.

"Would you like to light the menorah for us, Ethan?" Miriam asked as they all settled into their seats.

Ethan's eyes widened in obvious surprise. Josh figured he'd been about Ethan's age when his parents first let him light the menorah. "Is it okay if my dad helps?" he asked, glancing at Micah.

"Of course, dear," she said with a bright smile.

"Can Uncle Josh help too?" Ethan added.

"If he wants to. Sure."

Micah looked at Josh, who for once did not look away. "I'd love to, Ethan," Josh said, willing his heart to stop pounding. But then Micah also smiled, and Josh relaxed a bit.

"Remember," Micah told Ethan a moment later as Ethan held an unlit match in his hand, ready to strike, "there's a second prayer on the first night. And the *shehecheyanu*."

Ethan grinned. "I know. I learned them all at Sunday school."

Josh wasn't sure he remembered the extra blessing after all these years, but as Ethan lit the candles and began to speak the words, *"Baruch atah adonai, eloheinu melech ha-olam, asher kidshano b'mitzvotav, vitzivanu...."* Josh found himself murmuring the prayer from memory.

After Ethan had finished, Micah leaned and kissed him on the top of his head. "You were great, Eth," he said, his face lit with happiness. "Really great."

Josh marveled at how good Micah was with Ethan and how much Ethan obviously adored his father. Looking at them like this, Josh couldn't help but wonder how Micah had ended up in jail for drugs. Micah obviously doted on his son—would do anything for him. It made no sense that Micah would have risked it all so easily: his son, his career, his life. Then again, Micah was an addict, wasn't he? Addiction drove people to make bad decisions and hurt the ones who meant most to them.

"Time for latkes!" Squeals of delight from the children and the adults greeted Jenna's announcement and pulled Josh out of his morose thoughts.

He helped Micah pull the platters out of the oven, piled high with golden brown potato pancakes that smelled heavenly. "You made these?" he asked Micah as they walked back into the dining room.

"Your mother watched over me and Jenna the whole time," he answered with a chuckle. "She said if we wouldn't let her make them herself, she'd make sure we made them right."

"Looks like you did her proud." Josh nodded in Miriam's direction. She was beaming, seated with one grandchild on either side of her.

"Applesauce!" Cory shouted over the din of conversation.

"Sour cream!" Jacob added, clearly not wanting to be outdone.

"Both!" Ethan added happily, after which both of the other boys looked at him in surprise, then shouted, "We want both, too!"

"At least he's not drowning them in ketchup," Micah said with a wink at Josh, who screwed his face up in mock disgust.

Jenna, who had just finished up plopping large piles of sour cream and applesauce on the boys' plates, took one of the platters from Micah and said, "You've worked hard enough tonight, Micah. Time for you to eat something."

Micah opened his mouth to protest, but she just pointed at his seat and shook her head. "Don't make me put you in time out."

Josh laughed.

"You too, Joshy," she added with another shake of her head for him. "Eat. I can get Steven's plate and mine."

DINNER was a lively affair. Jacob, Cory, and Ethan told jokes, most of which were met with laughter all around. Josh, who hadn't eaten anything since lunch except a few tastes of items at the restaurant, ate more than half a dozen latkes drowned in applesauce. Then came the main dishes: Jenna's brisket, a vegetable kugel made with sweet potatoes, apples and carrots and a simple but tasty noodle kugel which the kids hardly touched after filling up on latkes.

"This brisket is fantastic, Jenna," Josh complimented his sister, not caring that he spoke with his mouth full.

"Really?" Her tone was skeptical and she raised an eyebrow.

"Yeah, really. Different from Mom's special recipe." He'd had enough of that this past week and the tomato-y tang was a tasty change. "What's in it?"

"The big shot French chef is asking me for a recipe?" Jenna's comment was greeted with chuckles from the adults. "No. You won't want this recipe. Just enjoy it."

"Tell me."

Jenna looked him in the eye and cocked her head, visibly contemplating her options. "It's made with ketchup and wine and some garlic and—"

"Ketchup!"

"I told you that you wouldn't like it."

"How the hell can you—" Josh stopped himself as he saw a pained look flash across Micah's face. Steven's eyes held a glimmer of annoyance as well. "You know what, it's good. You'd never guess how it was made." Josh took another bite. It *was* good. "I mean, you'd think it had a lot of fancy ingredients." He hoped that sounded less insulting. He looked at his plate again and then at his mother. She wasn't smiling.

"I'm glad you like it, Joshy." Jenna smiled but Josh knew he'd hurt her feelings.

"Jen, Sorry." Josh felt Micah's hand give his knee a little squeeze. A small gesture of support and encouragement. "Thanks for making dinner. Everything's wonderful." Micah's grip tightened and he could see Jenna relax a little.

"That means a lot coming from a famous chef." Jenna's smile broadened and he knew she really meant it. Josh felt like a real dick. Jenna's brisket tasted great, even if it wasn't prepared to his exacting standards.

"Isn't food supposed to be about how it tastes and not about what's in it or how complicated a recipe is?" Micah asked.

Micah was exactly right. Josh was the one who had lost touch with that concept. Yes, he could prepare incredible dishes his family couldn't even imagine, but at the end of the meal what mattered was that it tasted good. Why did it take him this long to learn such a simple lesson? He'd been focusing on the wrong thing since he'd gotten off that plane at JFK.

"Thanks, Micah." Josh turned and nodded. Micah gave Josh's knee another squeeze, and Josh wondered whether he'd imagined a flicker of anticipation in Jenna's and his mother's faces.

"So who can tell me why we celebrate Chanukah?" Steven piped up to fill the awkward silence.

"I can!" Ethan raised his hand as though he were in school. Cory and Jacob looked on in admiration as Ethan began, "A long time ago, Jews couldn't study their religion. It got so bad, they had to pretend they were playing a game to teach their children about their religion."

"That's where dreidls come from," Cory interjected.

"Cory," Jenna warned. "Let Ethan tell the story, okay?"

"Yes, Mom," Cory said with a slight blush on his cheeks.

"So this man named Judah Maccabee got a whole bunch of Jews together to fight the Romans. They took back the temple which had been decreated…." He stumbled over the word.

"Desecrated," Micah prompted with a broad smile for his son.

"Right," Ethan said. "Desecrated. But there wasn't much oil left to burn the eternal flame in the temple, only enough for one day, and it would take eight days to get more. But the oil lasted long enough for them to get more."

"It was a miracle!" Jacob chimed in.

"Right," Cory agreed.

"And we get to eat latkes," Ethan added with a grin.

"That's the best part," Jacob said as he shoveled another pancake into his mouth and a mixture of applesauce and sour cream dripped onto his chin.

Cory laughed, followed by Ethan, and finally all of the adults laughed too. Under the table, Josh reached for Micah's hand without really thinking and squeezed it. Micah turned and smiled at him, causing Josh's heart to race yet again.

AFTER they'd finished with the main meal, Josh helped Steven and Micah clear the dishes over Miriam's vocal protests. "Good to have you back in town, Josh," Steven said after he'd set down some of the dishes by the sink, clearly having forgiven Josh's earlier faux pas. "I know your parents really appreciate what you've done the past few weeks. I only wish Jen and I could have helped more."

"It's been good coming home," Josh said as he caught Micah's eye. "I'm glad I came." He was more than glad, really.

Micah and Steven did the dishes while Josh plated two dozen donuts—the traditional Israeli variety filled with jam. They, like the latkes, were fried—another reminder of the miracle of the oil in the temple.

AFTER dinner, the kids retreated to the living room to play dreidl after first stopping in the bathroom to wash their powdered-sugar-covered faces. The sound of the wooden top spinning on the floor, punctuated by shouts and laughter, reminded Josh again of how much he'd enjoyed holidays like this.

"The letters stand for *Ness Gadol Hayah Sham*, 'a great miracle happened there'." Ethan explained. "You spin and then see if you win anything. You spin the dreidl and it lands on *nun*, you get nothing. *Gimmel*, you get the whole pot. *Hay*, you get half, and *shin* means you put one coin in." He glanced up at Micah, who nodded his approval. "Who wants to play?" He made a big pile of chocolate coins on the floor, and moved them around.

"He reminds me of the dealers in Monte Carlo, but he knows his stuff." Josh chuckled as he and Micah watched the boys play.

"He's a good student," Micah said proudly. "And he likes Sunday school."

"Like father, like son. I remember you always liked it too."

"I liked it because you were in my class, not because of Mrs. Rothstein," Micah said with a chuckle.

"I forgot about her! She made us memorize the entire *Amidah* one day because we wouldn't stop talking."

"Came in handy later, when we had our bar mitzvahs. One less thing to learn."

"We made her nuts, didn't we?" Josh smiled at the memory.

"Yeah, I guess we did. Just don't give Eth any ideas." Micah's eyes sparkled with mischief.

"Promise I won't."

Josh saw his mother nod to his father from the couch, and Seymour nodded back.

Cory shouted, "Gimmel! I get it all!" This was followed in short order by groans from Ethan and Jacob.

"Maybe we should handle the business in the kitchen while the kids are occupied," Seymour said as he watched the children play.

"I'll keep an eye on everything in here. Go, talk." Steven settled on the floor by the boys. "My turn next!" He grabbed a few of Cory's coins and held out his hand for the dreidl.

Josh's stomach did a few flips. He didn't know how the family discussion would go. Honestly, he didn't know how he wanted it to go. He wasn't sure he was ready for the kind of big changes he guessed were in store. One way or another, their lives would never be the same, no matter what was decided tonight.

Micah stayed in the living room with Steven until Miriam called, "Micah, you should be part of this, too."

"No. I don't think I should." Micah shifted on his feet and looked very uncomfortable.

Josh wondered why his mother wanted to include Micah in the discussions. They hadn't told anyone they'd patched up their differences, and he didn't think his mother was that good at reading people.

"You have a share, so you have a say."

*What?* Josh stopped halfway down the hallway. "Mom?"

"The Solomons were minority partners in the restaurant. Micah's parents invested when we were short of funds and couldn't get a bank loan. A long time ago."

"I didn't know that." Josh glanced at Micah.

"I bought their share out when I was working, before…."

Josh didn't need for him to finish that sentence. "And now?"

"It's just ten percent." Micah seemed almost embarrassed by this statement.

Josh wasn't sure how it made him feel to know Micah owned part of the restaurant. A few days ago, he was sure he'd have been angry to hear this.

"Enough to stay for the discussion," Seymour said. Micah didn't argue.

The five of them settled around the kitchen table, supplied with fresh coffee and a pile of gold-wrapped chocolate coins.

Jenna unwrapped a coin and popped it into her mouth. "No other chocolate in the world tastes like these. I wonder why? Joshy, what's in them?"

He shrugged. "I don't know. Why are you asking me?"

"You're the expert." She grinned and unwrapped another.

He pulled it out of her hands and ate it, laughing at the look of surprise on her face. He probably looked just as shocked because she hadn't paid him a compliment in a long time. Maybe never. As the older sister, she had always lorded her position and knowledge over him like a weapon.

"Enough with the chocolate," Miriam said. "You should watch what you eat."

Josh groaned at the possibility for disaster if his mother started lecturing Jenna on her weight.

"Business." Seymour clunked his mug on the table, and everyone turned their attention to him. "We need to decide whether or not to keep the restaurant."

Everyone glanced around the room, no one daring to look at anyone else. Josh had never heard his father speak so directly before, especially about a topic this important. It made him even more nervous.

His mother, always the practical one, took the lead. "Let's face facts. For the past few years, business has been falling off. Too many upscale restaurants have moved in lately, and our main clientele has either moved because the neighborhood got too expensive, or died. Our business is dying off. And with your dad's surgery, we'll need to close for a while. I can't take care of him and run the restaurant. And we can't afford to hire an outside manager."

"What about promoting someone? Raphael or Brenda? Or the front of house manager?" Jenna suggested.

"I don't think they can do it." Seymour shook his head. "Josh, you've seen the place the last week or so. Can they handle it?"

"Brenda is pretty focused on desserts. I don't think she has the skills to take on the rest of the kitchen, either in terms of cooking or managerial ability."

"Then it's settled. Now we just have to decide if we're going to try and find a buyer—or close." Miriam nodded but her eyes were bright. Josh could see she was trying hard not to get emotional. He knew how much the restaurant meant to his parents.

"It's for the best." Seymour reached out to pat her hand. "We've worked a long time, and we have a lot to show for it. Best to close up now before we get in financial trouble. We'll be in good shape even if all we do is sell the fixtures and equipment. The building alone is worth a fortune in today's market."

"That's it?" Josh nearly stood up. "That's the decision?" It all seemed too final. So depressing. His parents had run the restaurant for nearly forty years, and it would be gone. Just like that. All the memories, the hard work, the sense of family he'd never realized he'd wanted when he'd worked there as a kid. Gone.

"Well, we were hoping you might help us approach some buyers while you're still in town. Some big shot restaurant friends you have at the swanky places. You must know some investors?" Miriam blinked a few times, her eyes welling with tears.

"Sure. I have some contacts but…." He stopped. He didn't know what he wanted to say. He just knew he didn't want it to end like this. It *couldn't* end like this.

"Joshy, you've never liked the restaurant. I don't see why you're putting up such a fuss now."

"That place has been your whole life, ever since I can remember. My whole life. I can't believe you're not gonna try to keep it open. Micah?"

"Josh, I don't see any options. Your parents can't run it, and with profits falling, there's no money to hire an executive chef."

"But the place is packed. People are booking tables weeks out. How can you say there aren't enough customers?"

Miriam shook her head. "Josh, that's just the past week. Since you showed up. Once you leave, everything goes back to normal. Our staff can't really cook the kind of things you can, keep making up interesting specials. They can follow directions, but they don't have your imagination in the kitchen. Our regular customers don't really want imagination anyway." She shrugged and met Josh's gaze directly. "That's what these new customers want, something new all the time. They come once and they're happy. They come back the next time, and they see the same menu. They don't come a third time."

"Well…. Why can't I run the place?" Josh hadn't planned on saying that, but his heart overtook his brain and the words just tumbled out. And once they were out there, it felt like the right thing. Like the solution to everything.

"What?" Josh's parents looked at each other before turning toward him. There was something more than just surprise on their faces. Hope, perhaps?

"I thought you couldn't wait to get back to your big job back in Paris, France." Jenna never minced words.

"I… I…." Josh needed a minute to think. What the hell had he just suggested? He wanted to get back to Paris, didn't he? Back to civilization, not this dinosaur life he'd been running from since— Unconsciously, Josh glanced over at Micah, who was smiling with a look of relief on his face.

And then it hit him. Years before, he'd run away from the thought of a life without Micah. But Micah was here now, and he wasn't going anywhere this time. He'd made that clear enough. Micah was out and ready to make a life. Josh was the one who had doubts. "I do have a good job there, but…." *But you're not in charge. You work for someone else—probably never get to run your own restaurant in*

*France,* he reminded himself. "But everything I really want is right here. In New York." He sat back down and put his hand over Micah's.

Miriam burst into tears. "Thank you," she whispered and looked toward the ceiling.

If she were Catholic, Josh thought, she probably would have crossed herself.

# Chapter Twelve

JENNA, Steven, and their kids had left, Josh's parents had gone to bed, and Ethan had been tucked in. Josh and Micah were finally alone again after another exhausting and emotionally eventful night. It was getting to be normal here at the Goldens'.

They went into the guest room, and Josh closed the door behind them. Micah sat on the bed and Josh settled next to him.

"You're really going to stay?" Micah's voice was slightly breathy, as if he didn't really believe it.

"Why not? I have everything I want here."

Micah cocked his head, a question in his gaze.

"I mean jobwise. I wanted to run my own place. I wanted to be world famous and have investors clamoring to hire me. I got three job offers already this past week from some high-powered people in the business." Josh had seen Micah's disappointment but he wasn't ready to respond to it. He needed to think things through, one at a time.

"But you're not taking any of those jobs, are you?"

"No. But that's not the point." He could see Micah still didn't understand. "I don't think I want to work for anyone else. But they wanted to hire me. I guess I just want to be wanted."

"I want you, Josh." Micah's tone forced the issue at hand, making it clear he wasn't talking about restaurants anymore.

Josh let out a slow breath, trying to steady himself. He hadn't expected Micah would press the issue, but he realized he was ready now. "I want you too." He moved closer and leaned in so their shoulders were touching. As always, the feel of Micah's body, solid against his own, made his body thrum with need.

Micah wrapped his arms around Josh and pressed his lips against his. Oh, the softest kiss. Josh knew just one or a hundred wouldn't be enough. Not now. Not tonight. He opened his mouth to Micah's and their tongues touched. He pushed just the tip into Micah's mouth, tasting him. Micah's fingers brushed against Josh's throat. He knew just where to caress him. He still remembered, even after so many years. It was like coming home. Familiar. *Wonderful.*

Josh's body definitely remembered. He wanted nothing more than for them to get out of their clothes and have a proper reunion. He shifted on the bed, his swelling cock making his pants too uncomfortable to wear for much longer.

"Dad?" Ethan's voice filtered through the door. "You coming to bed?" The door started to open and Micah sprang off the bed, untucking his shirt to cover his own bulging trousers.

"Not yet. Let's get you back to bed, okay?" He threw Josh an apologetic look and led Ethan back to Josh's bedroom.

Josh lay on the bed looking up at the ceiling, his heart pounding, thinking of the way Micah had tasted. How his hair smelled and how softly his fingertips had brushed against Josh's skin, awakening every nerve ending in one simple stroke.

A moment later, Micah was back. "Sorry. I told him I'm going for a walk and I'll be back late. He got used to sharing the bed with me, and he needs to know I'm just across the hall. He worries sometimes."

"Worries?"

Micah shook his head and looked away. Josh could see pain flash across Micah's face even in the low light. The shadows stood out starkly against his pale skin.

"Once in a while, he'll have a nightmare that I'm not coming home. Rina said it started after I got arrested."

"Oh. You should go back. I can wait."

"As long as he knows I'm coming back, it's okay. And I don't want to wait. I have an idea. Let's take a walk." Micah offered his hand to Josh, who took it without hesitation.

Once downstairs, they put on coats and scarves. It was bitterly cold outside, but Josh barely noticed. He felt alive and refreshed as he watched Micah's breath make a silver cloud. Micah hooked his arm through Josh's and they strolled toward Clinton Street, past shops and bars and boutiques. "Where are we going?"

"Almost there." Micah smiled back at Josh reassuringly.

Two more blocks and Micah turned into a small side street and unlocked an elaborate wrought-iron outer door that led to a small entry hall paneled in walnut. He fitted the key into the elevator and they rode in silence to the top floor. Thick carpet muffled their steps and Micah put his finger to his lips.

"Where are we?" Josh whispered.

"Rina's." He stopped at the second apartment and slid the key into the lock, then closed the door behind them.

Josh reached for the hall light and Micah pulled his hand back. "No lights. Just in case the neighbors are snooping. I'm not exactly welcome around here."

Josh banged into a table in the hallway. "Ouch!"

"Wait there for a minute."

Josh heard him walk away and then the sound of a drawer opening and what he guessed was Micah going through the contents. This was followed by a series of clinking and clicking sounds Josh couldn't identify. Micah returned a moment later with a lit candle.

"Come with me." He took Josh's hand and led him into the living room, a wide sparsely furnished room lit by a row of tea-lights along one wall. The flickering light illuminated Micah's pale skin, and his eyes looked like blazing emeralds.

"Beautiful. And so appropriate." Josh decided Chanukah wasn't such a useless holiday after all.

"Let me get something to lie on."

Josh sat on the couch and waited for Micah to return with a thick comforter and some pillows. No cartoon characters, thank goodness. Not Ethan's. "From the guest room," Micah said as if he'd read Josh's mind. "But I think it's nicer out here, with the candles. Or if you're cold, I can light the fireplace."

"Why don't you keep me warm?"

"I thought you'd never ask." Micah spread the comforter on the floor, well away from the candles, and tossed his jacket over the couch before helping Josh out of his own jacket.

They settled onto the makeshift bed and just studied each other in the candlelight for a few awkward moments, as if both of them were trying to get their bearings, or perhaps coming to terms with the years they'd been apart. Micah was beautiful like this—ethereal, not quite real—like the Micah from Josh's dreams over the years. Wanting to reassure himself this was not a dream, Josh put one hand behind Micah's neck and drew him close, taking his mouth in a kiss he hadn't realized how much he'd hungered for. Micah returned the intensity, bumping it up even further. For as calm as Micah had seemed these past few weeks, it took Josh a bit by surprise to sense Micah's strong physical need. Josh moaned against Micah's mouth.

They then undressed each other, stopping along the way to kiss and explore with hands and mouths. For Josh was coming home yet again, to a body he'd known in so many different ways across the years. From the pale, scrawny kid in elementary school, to the almost-man he had known that night they played in the swimming pool and were a breath away from their first kiss, to the time after college when they'd become lovers—Micah's body firm and slim. Now, however, it was a man's beautiful body that welcomed Josh in the candlelight. A body Josh couldn't wait to explore, and one he knew could give him immense pleasure.

"Josh." Micah's whisper sent chills along Josh's spine. The pent-up need and raw emotion in Micah's voice told him Micah wanted this every bit as much as Josh did, and for all the same reasons.

Micah slid his boxers down, giving Josh a good long look at his naked body for the first time in ten years. Micah's cock curved up out of a jumble of silky curls, darker than the pale skin of his torso and thighs. Josh watched, wanting to take it in his hands, to caress Micah's balls, to explore every inch of that amazing body. Micah leaned down, fingers slipping beneath the waistband of Josh's shorts and tugging them down. Micah looked up and their gazes met. He licked his lips and bent to nuzzle Josh's cock.

"Oh, God. Micah." Josh bit his lip, the sight of Micah's tongue darting into the slit of his cock every bit as arousing as the electricity that jolted along every sensory fiber in his entire body. But Micah stopped there. He lay down next to Josh and pulled him onto his side so they were face to face. "You are a tease, aren't you?"

"No need to rush, is there?"

Now, now, now! Josh's body said. "No," he replied, hoping he kept the disappointment out of his voice.

Micah pressed his hips against Josh's, their cocks sliding and rubbing together against the groove of his hipbone, the friction thrilling. Josh ground back against Micah, and they battled like that for a moment, hips and cocks together. Then Micah leaned down and took one of Josh's nipples between his lips.

*Sweet lord*, Josh thought. *Holy hell*. Micah tugged and sucked, occasionally nipping while his cock rubbed against Josh's. Josh tangled his fingers in Micah's hair and let the sensations wash over him. He was so keyed up from the decision he'd made earlier, from the wonder of being in bed—or on the floor—again with Micah and the things Micah made him feel. He couldn't catch his breath at the sensation. He could barely think straight. All he could think about was Micah. How much he'd missed him. Missed *this*.

He pulled Micah up for a kiss and then licked his way down Micah's pale throat, the stubble coarse, but the friction against his lips made everything come alive. He fastened his lips on a nipple and felt it harden to a tight bud against his tongue. He toyed with that tight flesh, sucking, nipping, teasing until he found what Micah liked best. He rolled him onto his back and with his mouth alone explored Micah's body, lingering when Micah's gasps or sighs told him he'd hit on the right spot. He felt Micah's hard response in the groove along his left hip, inside his thigh, and turned his full attention on Micah's cock.

After playing around the head and slit, and thoroughly tasting Micah's balls, Josh wrapped his mouth around the head and slid down the full length. He felt Micah's entire body shiver, and Micah grabbed at his hair. "Slow down."

"I haven't even started yet," Josh mumbled around Micah's cock, which more than filled his mouth. "Mmm." It was heavenly but he went slowly.

"No, I mean stop. It's too much."

Josh stopped and looked up at Micah, not relinquishing his cock that easily. "What?" Micah was no virgin. They hadn't been lovers long, but they'd certainly gone all the way. And he must have been with other men after Josh, hadn't he? Unpleasant images of prison flashed through Josh's brain and he let go.

"Are you okay? Is this too fast? We can stop." *Please, don't say stop.* But he would if Micah wanted it.

"No. Yes. I mean it feels too good. I don't want to finish like that, but I'm so close. You get me too worked up." Micah pulled Josh in for a kiss. "I'm sorry."

"Shh. Don't be sorry. What do you want to do tonight? Just hands? Just mouths? Tell me."

"What do you want, Josh?"

"Whatever you want."

"No, tell me what you want." When Micah turned his dark green gaze on Josh, he knew immediately what he wanted. What he'd been craving for so long.

He fumbled for his coat and dug into the pocket. He pushed a condom into Micah's hands. "I want to feel you inside me, filling me up. Will you?"

Micah took the packet and kissed Josh hard. A shiver shot through Josh's spine and lodged at his core, behind his balls, where it turned into a warm ache. There was only one thing that would make it go away. He lay on his back and let his knees fall apart, opening himself up, offering himself, wanting Micah to want him as much as Josh needed him.

Micah looked at the condom and back at Josh. "This all you got?"

"Huh?"

"Lube?"

"I don't have any."

"I thought you would have."

"Jesus, Micah, is that what you think of me? That I carry lube around all the time just in case I run into someone I might want to fuck at the grocery store?" Hurt welled up in Josh's gut as he remembered the look in Micah's eyes when he'd seen him after the club.

"God, no," Micah said, running soft fingers over Josh's jaw. "Nothing like that. I thought you'd have some tonight though."

"It's in my suitcase. I didn't know that 'walk' is a code word for let's go fuck at my wife's apartment." Josh blinked away the frustration. This wasn't how he pictured tonight going.

"Ex-wife." Micah's voice was serious, and he looked genuinely offended, until he quirked one corner of his mouth.

Josh couldn't help laughing. "Ex-wife." He lifted Micah's hand from his face and kissed it tenderly.

"Okay, I have an idea. Wait here." Micah got up and Josh hoped like hell he wasn't going to find something in Rina's bathroom. Yuck. However, he liked knowing Micah didn't have supplies on-hand either. Micah walked into the kitchen and banged around in the cupboards. "How do you feel about olive oil? Extra virgin?" He held the bottle up.

Josh laughed again. "Too late to put that genie back in the bottle. But that'll do."

Micah laughed and slid back onto the comforter with Josh. "It's organic." He said it like he was sharing a secret.

"Good. I'm very picky about what goes in my cooking *and* my ass."

"Is that so?" Micah rolled Josh over and planted a few kisses on one cheek, before trailing his fingers down the crack. It sent sublime shockwaves of pure pleasure to his balls, and the warm glow he'd lost began to heat him once again. Micah poured some oil into his hand. "Letting it warm up a little."

*Sweet touch*, Josh thought. Then Micah gently spread his ass cheeks and he felt a slippery finger tracing a line along his perineum and circling his hole. A fingertip circled again, and a third time—softly relaxing—then slipped a little ways inside. *Whoa!* It hadn't come as a surprise; he'd known Micah would do that, but still. He couldn't help but tense up, and Micah removed the finger.

"You're really tight."

"You say that like it's a surprise. I told you I'm picky. I don't bottom."

"Then why now?"

"Not 'now.' *You.* It's you. You're not just any guy and this isn't a one-time thing. Is it?" Josh turned his head to look at Micah. "Is it?" It hadn't occurred to him until that moment how much he needed to know this was about more than just one night. The ache of their last time together like this was still there, beneath the surface. Josh was afraid, he realized, of being heartbroken again. He wasn't sure he could take that kind of pain again.

"No." Micah's voice was soft and reassuring. "No. It's not a one-time thing. Not this time. I don't want to be just any guy for you."

The tension in Josh's shoulders abated with Micah's words and the pain faded, replaced by something else other than just his thrumming sexual need: hope. Hope that they had a future together. Hope this was the first of many nights spent together. "You're not. You'd never be." The words came out in a hoarse whisper.

"Roll over again."

"Arf!" Josh gave a playful bark and received a little smack on the ass. He was glad to leave the intense emotion of a moment before behind. It was still too overwhelming. He needed time to come to terms with his feelings for Micah and move past his fear. He needed encouragement.

Then Micah's slippery finger circled once, twice and bingo, it pushed inside. Micah worked his finger in, loosening the tight ring of muscle and treating Josh to a satisfying burn as he slid in, out, and brushed across his sweet spot with just enough pressure to get him hard as a rock again without making him come. Carefully, Micah added more oil and a second finger, and continued to massage until Josh's body opened up, a pool of heat and liquid warmth that had him breathless and pressing back against each little thrust.

"I am so ready for you right now." The words seemed distant to Josh's own ears, as if someone else were speaking them. He was so far gone, wanting Micah, wanting to feel him inside.

"Not yet."

"Stop teasing, Micah," Josh groaned.

"I'm not. Not boasting or anything, but I'm not going to fit in there just yet."

"Yes, you will. It expands. It fit before…." Josh's cock twitched a little at the memory and his ass tightened around Micah's fingers.

"Okay." Micah rolled Josh onto his back and opened his legs wide. Josh bent his knees and let Micah work a pillow under his ass. He watched Micah open the condom wrapper. Micah's cock was hard and jutting out from his body, and Micah didn't even need to stroke himself before he began rolling the condom down. He poured more oil on and moved between Josh's knees. "Chanukah. It's all about the oil." Micah grinned.

"You smell like a salad."

"Fuck you."

"I've only been waiting ten years. Get to it already." Josh opened his knees a little wider to emphasize the point.

Micah positioned himself, and Josh felt the tip of his cock slide past his balls and right to his hole. He pulled his knees up, giving Micah easy access. Then just the tip slid in. Oh, sweet fuck that was good. "Oh, yes," he panted. "More."

But Micah didn't slide in yet. He was holding back, easing himself in. From the look on his face, it required all his concentration.

Another inch. Despite the oil, there was more friction than Josh could handle just yet. He really hadn't bottomed for a very long time. Years. Ten, or was it eleven? But he wanted Micah to fill him up and make him feel the connection. Then Micah did.

*Owfuckinghellit'slikeafuckingmissile.*

"You okay?"

"Yeah." Josh forced the word out between gritted teeth and tried to breathe. *Ouch. Bad idea. Bad fucking idea. Inhale, exhale. Inhale, exhale.* Micah's arms slid around him and held him tight. He felt Micah's hot breath on his cheek, heard his stuttered breaths. Josh finally relaxed and the pain subsided. "Yeah, I'm good. I'm great." Josh tentatively shifted his hips and felt the stretch, now a good stretch, the heat subsiding to a heavenly warmth radiating through his center. "I'm fantastic."

"Good. You had me worried." Micah planted a kiss along Josh's throat and slid in all the way.

Josh thought Micah had been in all the way. But holy mother of God, this was going to be better than he remembered. Once Micah filled him completely, it awakened an even greater need than Josh had realized. An emotional one. Josh closed his eyes and forced himself to breathe through the feelings: love, loss, pain, happiness. He'd never felt such a confounding mixture of emotions in his life.

Micah moved slowly, in and out, trying different angles until they found a rhythm. Clearly it had been a while since Micah had done this, and in some ways, it felt like their very first time together, again. They relearned each other's bodies' secrets and surprises. Micah had amazing control. A light sheen of sweat shone on Micah's skin in the candlelight, his hair damp at the temples as he moved as much for Josh's pleasure as his own.

"You ready?" Micah asked.

Josh nodded and reached down for his cock, but Micah took control. With a few skillful thrusts and one hand wrapped loosely around Josh's cock, Micah coaxed the impending orgasm into a full-blown eruption. The warmth that had begun to build deep in his belly was now fire, rocketing to his fingers and toes and setting his body ablaze. The dull ache in his balls turned sharp and tight as creamy plumes splashed along his chest, and Josh fought to keep his eyes open. He watched the flicker of satisfaction in Micah's eyes at the sight of Josh's pleasure. Only once Josh had ridden the wave completely did Micah let himself go. Josh felt a jolt of additional delight as Micah's body shook with his own orgasm, and his groans of pleasure filled Josh's ears.

Micah fell on top of Josh, and they rolled to their sides, bodies still connected, hot and sticky, sated. Josh listened to Micah's breathing, playing through his damp hair. When Micah's arms tightened around him, Josh felt like only now had he really come home. Had it been his fault they'd spent these years apart? When he'd run, had he pushed Micah back to the drugs that eventually got him in such trouble he'd ended up in prison? Now, as he listened to Micah's slow, even breaths, hovering on the edge between exhaustion and exhilaration, he marveled at how they'd come together tonight, their hunger for each other as deep and fierce as Josh's hatred for Micah had been only a week earlier. Then again, Josh finally understood that he'd never really hated Micah. He'd only told himself he hated him. The truth was that he'd never stopped loving Micah. He'd hated the pain that love had caused him over the years.

When Josh woke up, Micah was staring at him. They lay face to face, and Josh realized Micah had cleaned him up while he slept. The man was a saint.

"Are you ready to rest now?" Micah asked, his expression unreadable.

"I just woke up. But don't we need to get home? In case Ethan wakes up? And there's Rina's neighbors."

"That's not what I mean."

"Okay, what do you mean?"

"You know that '*chanu*' of Chanukah means a rest. The Maccabees rested after they won the battle for the temple." Micah pushed a strand of hair out of Josh's eyes. "Are you done fighting and ready to rest?"

Josh hadn't seen it like that until just this moment. He had been running and fighting his way through the world, trying to build a life as far away from his roots as he could get. And he was tired. In Paris he worked late, partied until early in the morning, and then dragged himself to work again, keeping in constant motion so he'd never have a quiet moment to think about what he really wanted. Or about the pain that had haunted him for years. He was burning out, just like the candles sputtering and flickering around them.

"Yes. I'm ready for a rest. Ready to come home. To make a home here. A new life in an old place I thought I never wanted to see again. Everything's the same, but somehow this time it's so much better than I remember it."

"You're different." Micah leaned down and kissed Josh's lips, but before he could return the kiss, Micah had moved lower. He hovered over Josh, soft silky hair tickling its way down Josh's chest, flicking across his nipples as Micah kissed and licked and sucked a trail of fire.

"So are you," Josh gasped out as Micah swept his tongue across the tip of his cock. "Oh, God, are you different." A little over a week ago, Josh had hated the sight of Micah, though his body had craved Micah's touch. And now, they'd stepped back in time.

*No. Not back in time. Back to a feeling.*

"I've never changed, Josh. I made mistakes, but I'm still the same man. Maybe someday you'll understand."

Josh didn't know how to respond, so he kept quiet and let Micah do better things with his mouth than talk. Micah took his time, licking and teasing with tongue and fingers, applying light suction to Josh's balls until the pleasant heat at his core grew in intensity to an insistent thrum.

"You're killing me, Mish. Please finish me off or let me do it."

Josh felt Micah's shiver at the old nickname only Josh had used.

Micah shook his head, soft stubble of his chin scraping pleasantly across Josh's inner thigh. "Not yet."

Josh groaned. "When?"

"Your turn. I want to bottom now."

They reversed the roles they'd taken earlier. More olive oil, more playing, and this time they were both more relaxed, had more fun.

When Micah spread himself open to welcome Josh inside, Josh thought he'd never felt a deeper contentment in his life. He pushed into Micah's dark heat and felt as though he was falling into another world where there was nothing but warmth and pressure and the fire burning deep inside, ever hotter as he pumped and thrust, with Micah's fingers caressing him, pinching a nipple or holding tight and focusing the power of his hips, channeling the intensity.

They came almost at the same time, Josh unable to wait another second once he felt Micah's body tense and squeeze down on him. He'd never felt a more incredible release in his life, unless it was when Micah had made love to him hours earlier.

Later, they cleaned up the living room and showered together, trading soapy hand jobs and sloppy wet kisses. They dressed and left. As Micah was locking the door a gray-haired woman with a lemon-puckered face called from down the hall. "Mrs. Solomon isn't home. How did you get in here?"

"I know. I'm Mr. Solomon." Micah looked like he was about to start laughing.

"Well, you're not supposed to be here when Mrs. Solomon isn't home." She walked up to them and gave them a withering stare, taking in their wet hair and guilty smiles. "And who are you?"

Josh cocked his head. "I'm Mr. Solomon's lover." He'd said it with a straight face but Micah lost his composure. They laughed their way to the elevator, leaving the neighbor standing in the hall with her jaw nearly on the floor. Still chuckling as they rode the elevator down, Josh realized he hadn't had so much fun since the night they did high dives at midnight.

"No cops this time," Micah said, reading Josh's mind.

Josh leaned over and kissed him. He wouldn't miss that chance ever again. "Not yet."

# *Chapter Thirteen*

MICAH looked in on Ethan when they got back home, but he was sound asleep.

"Come stay with me?" Josh squeezed Micah's hand and tugged him in the direction of the guest room.

"Better not tonight. He's expecting me and if he does wake up...."

"Sure." Josh schooled his expression, hoping he hid his disappointment. He wanted to go to sleep curled around Micah and wake up the same way. Wanted to feel Micah's heat and hear his breath across the pillow.

"Tomorrow night. We'll figure it out. Promise."

"Okay." Josh stepped close and planted a kiss on Micah's lips before dragging himself to his own bed. He turned back to see Micah standing in the doorway watching him.

"Goodnight, Josh." He blew a kiss across the hall.

Josh grinned and shut the door behind him. The butterflies were back, joined by an army of crickets and a flock of seagulls. He leaned against the door and realized he was acting like a twelve-year-old girl. Nothing wrong with that. Not this time. He moved toward the bed, body exhausted but mind still reeling with the changes that had happened in just a few days.

Not looking where he was going he slammed his knee against the dressing table and something rolled off. He picked it up: the eyeliner pencil he'd used when he went to that club the previous Friday. Was that only a week ago? His life had been turned upside down and inside out in the space of one short week?

A week. A little over a week ago he'd arrived, ready to head back to Paris before he'd even gotten off the plane. Nothing had gone as expected. And now, far from being shocked and angry to find Micah here at his parents' house, Josh had not only forgiven Micah for everything that had happened between them the past ten years, but they'd gone far beyond mere forgiveness. As Josh settled into bed under the ancient afghan, he felt the soreness, the wonderful, beautiful reminder of what he and Micah had shared only a few hours earlier.

And this time, it wouldn't be one night or one week, or even one month. Josh was moving home, and maybe he and Micah could make things work out for... well, he wouldn't say forever just yet. But he thought about walking arm in arm with Micah, taking Ethan to the park to fly kites. The new gay.

He liked it.

WHEN he got up the next morning, he dressed quickly and glanced out of his room to see if Micah and Ethan's door was open. It was. They must already be downstairs. The aroma of fresh coffee wafted toward him, and he realized he was famished.

Seymour and Micah were at the stove while Ethan and Miriam sat at the kitchen table.

"Good morning, sleepyhead," his mother said and poured him a mug of coffee.

"Morning." Josh said, his attention on Micah's back.

Then Micah turned and smiled. Not just any smile. Everyone else in the room would have to be blind not to see the affection radiating from that incredible smile. Josh returned the smile because it echoed everything he felt at that moment. He thought his chest would burst from the sheer joy welling up inside. Josh glanced at his mother, but she was reading the paper and thankfully hadn't noticed.

"Dad's making his secret pancakes again." Ethan slurped orange juice then went back to perusing the funny pages.

The secret pancakes. Josh didn't think his spirits could rise farther, but they did. Micah glanced back over his shoulder, and Josh just knew the pancakes were a message. A reminder of the night years ago when they'd first made love. A message meant only for him.

"Maybe it shouldn't be a secret recipe anymore." Micah placed a plate full of pancakes on the table as he raised an eyebrow at Josh.

"Not really much of a secret," Seymour muttered as he brought the frying pan, full of perfect over-medium eggs.

Josh's cheeks burned. Micah sat down next to him. Close, but not so close that their arms touched. Josh wanted to reach out and take his hand, but he tried to play it cool. That meant not looking at Micah.

"So what do you have planned for the day, boys?" Miriam asked.

"Dad promised me we'd go ice-skating at Rockefeller Center."

"Oh, I did, didn't I?"

"It's so cold. You shouldn't be skating in such cold. You'll get sick." She clucked like a mother hen as she conveyed her disapproval of the plan.

"I've got a ton of work ahead of me at the restaurant. More orders and I need to work on the schedules if we're going to be so busy." Josh wished he could go skating with Micah and Ethan, but with the restaurant booked out, he didn't have time. He had to standardize the recipes he'd come up with so they could scale them up. It would take some trial and error. And he needed to bump up the orders with the suppliers.

"I should help you." Micah glanced at Josh and his entire body tensed. Images of the night before flashed through his brain. The feeling of Micah's lips on his. Micah's—

"Nobody's going to shul?" Miriam made another sound. "I was hoping someone would go with me."

"I'll go with you, Mrs. Golden. Then we can all go skating." Ethan was determined to go skating. His exuberance made Josh smile.

"I'm a little too old for skating, honey." Miriam ruffled Ethan's hair. "And my doctor wouldn't like it probably."

"We'll head off to Rockefeller Center. Afterward, I'll drop Ethan off and head over to the restaurant to help you, Josh."

"Sounds like a plan."

"Ethan, teeth." Micah finished his coffee as Ethan rushed from the room and thundered up the stairs.

Micah got up and Josh followed him into the hallway, watching as he pulled on his coat and wrapped a scarf around his neck. Josh helped with the scarf even though Micah was capable of dressing himself. He needed to touch Micah, to reassure himself he wasn't dreaming. Even more, he wanted to show Micah how he felt.

"See you later." Josh leaned in and gave Micah a soft kiss, wishing it could be so much more.

Micah's arm snaked around his waist, pulling him closer, promising more. "Later." The word was a rumbly breath from deep in Micah's throat, and the sound went straight to Josh's core. He let out a little groan and stole another kiss.

"Dad?"

"Yup, we're leaving." Micah winked at Josh. Ethan didn't comment on the kiss as Micah helped him into his coat and made sure he was bundled up with mittens and scarf.

"Have fun." Josh waved from the door as they walked toward the sidewalk. Micah glanced back and blew another kiss.

*I am so in love with that man*, Josh thought and went back toward the kitchen. He could hear his parents talking, voices raised in that familiar tone that would sound like an argument to anyone else. For his family, it was normal conversation.

"Well, that worked out just like I told you," his father said. "But you with the doctor! You almost blew it."

That stopped Josh in his tracks. Doctor? He hovered in the hallway, listening.

"Blew it? What blew it? It was perfect." His mother shook her head.

"You overacted. You're no Meryl Streep."

She raised her hands and turned her head away with a shrug. "It worked. That's what matters." She let out a sigh. "But I was worried for a while there. You should have told him Micah was here. That nearly blew it. I thought he was gonna get right back on a plane and we'd never see him again."

"If I'd told him, he would have stayed at a hotel. But he's moving back. That's what matters now."

"I know. Our little boy is coming home again. It worked!"

Josh felt his blood boil. His parents had been manipulating him, like a pawn on a chess board? Scheming to make him stay? Everything clicked into place. Her surgery, planting the seeds about the restaurant and how his father couldn't handle the work anymore. Josh couldn't keep quiet.

"Do either of you care to explain?" He strode into the kitchen and both his parents turned around, wearing identical expressions: mouths open and guilt written all over their faces.

"Oh, Joshy. I didn't hear you." His mother shrugged.

"Obviously." He crossed his arms over his chest and glared down at them. "You planned all this? You wanted me home so badly you cooked up some scheme to get me to move back and take over the restaurant?"

"Sit down."

"No!" He bellowed the word and wished he hadn't. His parents looked like they wanted to crawl under the table. His dad looked grayer than usual. "I'm sorry I yelled. But I don't like being lied to or manipulated."

"Please, son, sit down." Seymour motioned to the chair. Josh sat, but only because he really was concerned for his father's health.

"We've been talking about closing the restaurant for quite a while now. We just hadn't decided when," Miriam said. "We did want you to be part of the family conference, but we would have decided without you if you didn't come home. We didn't expect you'd have such a success in just a week. But staying and keeping it open was your idea. We never expected you to suggest something like that." She shook her head and his father nodded in agreement.

"Then what was this big plan you were congratulating yourselves over?"

Miriam glanced over at Seymour. "You and Micah," she said with a shrug. "We wanted to get you two talking to each other again, and of course we hoped—" She wrapped one hand over the other and shook her hands, looking up. "—hoped but never imagined you two would sort everything out so quickly. We just wanted to give you a little push."

"A little push." His father shrugged and raised his eyebrows.

"But I can see you're getting along just fine." The smile on her face was deeply unsettling. It seemed his parents had a pretty good idea what he and Micah had gotten up to.

"Look, you need some privacy, right? Why don't you two stay at Rina's? One night won't kill any of her neighbors. Oy! Some neighbors! Who needs neighbors like that? No one!"

Josh chuckled at his mother's habit of asking questions and answering them herself. He realized he wasn't angry anymore. He couldn't stay angry with them.

"But you should stay there and we'll keep Ethan here."

His father nodded again.

Josh's cheeks heated. His parents were arranging a night for him with his boyfriend? The world really had changed. It was more than upside down and inside out.

Boyfriend? Josh had a boyfriend. He smiled and nodded, and his parents smiled back like he'd just agreed to marry the doctor. Well, Micah was a lawyer, even if he couldn't practice. No wonder his mother was so happy.

"What made you think Micah and I could ever be a couple?"

"Oh, Joshy, you can't hide how people feel about each other." She beamed.

"You knew? About me, about Micah? I was that obvious?"

"No, honey. Micah was. He would call or come by and you wouldn't talk to him. But I could see how he felt. How he looked when you ignored him. A mother always knows these things!"

Josh dreaded finding out what else she knew. Apparently, he didn't have as many secrets as he thought.

"Then when he married Rina, he never looked happy. He'd come by to visit, and he'd always look at the photos of the two of you around the house and ask about you. He'd mention Rina as an afterthought. Until Ethan was born. He doted on that baby. He started smiling again, but he still wasn't really happy. One day he came for a visit and told me how he'd made a big mistake, and he wished he could go back and do things differently. Then, you know, a lot of bad things happened, and he made some more mistakes. When he got out of prison, he came for a visit and he asked about you again. It hurt seeing him so sad, and I decided I was going to figure out how to get you two talking again."

"*Beshert*." It was Josh's father who spoke the word.

Josh just stared. His father—the no-nonsense man who thought romance was a silly thing for teenagers—apparently subscribed to the ancient Jewish belief that certain matches really were made in heaven. That even before birth, there were souls whom God had created for each other.

"Seymour." Miriam's eyes brimmed with tears, and she hugged Josh's dad with enthusiasm, kissing him soundly on the cheek. Seymour looked entirely uncomfortable with the emotional response.

"So Micah didn't know about your big plan?" Josh asked a moment later, seeking to dispel his own discomfort at his father's romantic sentiment.

"No. He wanted to stay in a hotel while you visited, and I had my work cut out to make him stay."

"I'm glad you did, Mom. I'm glad you did." Josh leaned over and pulled his mother into a hug, until she begged him to stop squeezing her to death.

"Well, you know, getting a couple together, it's a mitzvah!"

"I CAN'T believe my parents sent us off for a romantic evening together. It's kind of embarrassing." Josh and Micah were wrapped up, collars pulled up around their ears against the night wind. Josh put his arm through Micah's as they strolled toward Rina's apartment.

"I think it's sweet." Micah tightened his grip, pulling Josh closer. He turned and their gazes met, simmering.

"That's because it's not *your* parents." Josh shook his head. It was sweet, but he didn't enjoy the thought his parents knew what he and Micah would be doing later. Well, that was how his family was. Everyone knew everyone else's business. Maybe he should have stayed in a hotel instead of at their house.

"Thank God for that."

"What're you gonna tell your parents, Mish?"

"Nothing. At least not yet. They're not around, and there's no point in making things with them any worse."

"Hey, let's stop here for something for dinner." Josh stopped in front of a small grocery store. "Let's see what they've got and I'll fix something nice for you. Not more brisket." He grinned

Micah laughed. "In that case, it sounds perfect."

They opened the door, greeted by the sound of a tiny bell attached to the inner handle. Thankfully, there was no Christmassy Muzak pouring out of the speakers in this shop. It wasn't crowded, being near dinnertime and so close to the holidays. People were at parties or eating at restaurants and not cooking at home. A few couples drove carts along the aisles as random single shoppers mostly carried baskets slung over one arm.

Josh had given Rina's kitchen only a cursory glance the night before. All he recalled was a row of gleaming pots hanging above a granite-topped island. And the olive oil. She had a good brand, which meant she probably had a decent collection of spices. She'd been away for two months so he'd need to pick up anything fresh. It took only a few minutes of thought as to what he'd make. Something simple but delicious. He wanted to impress Micah, but didn't want to spend all night in the kitchen.

Micah insisted on pushing the cart as Josh collected the few ingredients he needed. At the end of every row, Micah stopped for a kiss. Shopping took longer than Josh expected, but it was far more fun. How had he never realized this? He paused in the wine aisle before choosing a mid-priced Burgundy.

"Wine with dinner okay?" He held up the bottle. "You drink wine, right?"

"I'll have a sip of yours."

"Sorry. Are you not allowed to drink? We don't need it." Josh put the bottle back. He remembered Micah's criticism of his drinking habits. And he didn't want it to be a temptation if Micah was not supposed to drink as part of his substance abuse recovery.

"I'm done with my twelve steps, and I know what my limits are." Micah retrieved it and placed it in the cart. "Let's have a glass with dinner."

"You sure?"

"Yes."

Josh couldn't read Micah's expression, but he bought the bottle anyway. He would show Micah he didn't need to drink, but that he could enjoy a moderate amount with dinner.

Micah carried the groceries the two blocks to Rina's. "I can't believe all you bought was some chicken, a bottle of herbs, carrots, olives, garlic, an onion, and lentils. How can you make a whole dinner with that?"

"That's my magic. You'll see."

They entered the lobby of the building, and Micah used the key to call the elevator. Josh hoped they wouldn't run into the busybody neighbor from that morning. They'd acted like kids, and at the time it had been fun, but they didn't need her calling the cops on them. He could just see them busting down the door and shouting "Put the spatula down and step away from the sauté pan!" He let out a chuckle.

"What?" Micah cocked his head and grinned.

"Nothing."

"What?" Micah's tone was more insistent.

"Shh. Just in case."

Micah nodded and grinned. They made it upstairs and into Rina's place without incident.

Josh washed up and uncorked the wine to let it breathe. He rolled up his sleeves and set about cooking while Micah watched from a stool at the island. He started water boiling for the lentils—the tiny green French lentils du Puy. Then he peeled and sliced the carrots on the diagonal, so each slice looked like an oval rather than a circle and set them sautéing in a pan with some olive oil. Then he butterflied each chicken breast and lightly pounded them to an even thickness before sprinkling with sea salt, freshly ground black pepper, and a thick layer of herbes de Provence.

"Don't you need any help?"

"Sure. Come on over and help."

"How?"

"Stand behind me." Josh pointed to the floor a few inches from where he stood.

"Okay." Micah came up behind him.

"Now put your arms around me."

Micah did. "Now what?"

"Just hold on." Josh grinned back at Micah, pleased when he felt Micah's arms tighten around his waist.

"I'm not really helping much."

"Yes, you are. But you're not close enough."

Micah chuckled and pressed himself against Josh's back. "How's this?"

"Perfect." Josh pressed back, pleased as he felt Micah's cock stiffening against his ass. "Mmm."

Micah leaned down and kissed Josh's ear and neck, letting out a little moan that thrummed through Josh's body too. With Micah holding him, Josh carefully chopped the onion and a few cloves of garlic and set them aside. He put the lentils in the water and flipped the carrots with a few skillful shakes of the pan, the orange ovals flying in midair.

"Ooh, they're getting a little brown. But they smell fantastic."

"I'm caramelizing them, concentrating the sugars. You won't even know you're eating carrots. Just wait."

"I can't wait. For dinner or for you." Micah pulled Josh around to face him and planted a hot, eager kiss on his lips. Josh opened his mouth to let Micah in and melted against the firm planes of muscle, easing into Micah's arms. Their bodies fit together perfectly, as if they belonged together. Back-to-front or face-to-face. Josh felt so comfortable. He could lose himself in Micah's embrace and kisses.

*Beshert.* The word had taken root in Josh's thoughts. Maybe his father was right. He breathed deeply and smiled.

A hiss from the stove got his attention. The water boiled over and he pulled the pot off the heat. "You're a little bit of a distraction."

"I thought you were used to working in a busy kitchen."

"Not when I'm the one getting busy." Josh drained the lentils and added them back to the pan with onion and garlic, salt and pepper, and turned his attention to the chicken, which he cooked in olive oil just a few minutes on each side before letting it sit.

"Why do you do that?"

"So I can finish the carrots."

"That's what they taught you at chef school?"

"It's not called chef school any more than you went to lawyer school."

"Culinary school?"

"Right. And you let the chicken sit for a few minutes so the juices redistribute. It makes it moister."

"It smells divine. I can't wait to eat."

Josh tossed whole cloves of garlic in with the carrots and sliced oil-cured olives and put the lid on. When he turned around, he discovered Micah had set the table and lit candles. More candles. This was a Chanukah like none he'd ever celebrated.

"Just supposed to be two candles tonight," Josh said as he put their plates down.

"Who's counting? I like how you look by candlelight." Micah's eyes almost twinkled in the low light.

"You too. I like how the candlelight makes your skin glow."

Micah pulled his shirt over his head and the candlelight played across the contours of his shoulders and chest, leaving the hollows in shadow. Josh was ready to completely skip dinner. He pulled his own shirt off and started on his belt but Micah stopped him with his hand.

"Just shirts or we'll never eat."

"I'm not hungry."

"I am. For you and for this dinner. If it tastes as good as it smells I'll... well, I don't know."

"How about you'll make love to me all night."

"That was already on the agenda." Micah kissed Josh's neck. Josh shivered.

"Eat already, then, or I'm going to lose my mind!"

They sat, not facing each other, but on adjacent sides so their knees touched. Micah poured a glass of wine and handed it to Josh. He took a sip and waited for Micah to take a bite of chicken.

"This is incredible. And it's just herbs and salt and pepper? That's it?"

"That's it."

"So much flavor." Micah spoke with his mouth full.

Josh took a bite. It was good. He'd made it dozens of times but watching Micah's enjoyment made it more flavorful this time.

"And the carrots. You were right. They're so sweet. Like essence of carrot. With a hint of garlic and the salty olives. So simple and just perfect." He made little moans of delight as he ate.

Nothing Josh made was difficult, but each dish showcased the basic flavor of the food, the herbs and the carrots, the firm bite of the almost-spicy lentils. He loved playing with flavors and creating something impressive, but tonight he'd made simple farmhouse-style dishes, and for the first time in a long while, he was reminded of the power of food. He ate slowly, sipping at the wine, holding the glass for Micah to take a sip. Their hands touched, elbows and knees brushing more often than just by coincidence. Every touch heightened the tension, the excitement of what would follow the meal. But Josh was in no particular hurry tonight. They had the whole night. No need to rush home for Ethan.

When Micah finished eating, he sat back and studied Josh. Josh watched as the flickering candles made Micah's dark hair shimmer with gold highlights, and gave his green eyes an extra warmth. Josh put his knife and fork down and gazed deep into Micah's eyes. "I'm finished."

He stood up and Micah also stood. Josh pulled him into an embrace and kiss. They swayed, bodies moving to some inner music as hungry mouths and inquisitive hands explored and stroked and caressed. They finished undressing each other and Micah led Josh to a bedroom. They tumbled onto the bed, the moonlight all the illumination they needed.

"Do you have—?"

Micah put a finger to Josh's lips. "Yes." He opened the night table. There was a pack of condoms, some lube, and the bottle of olive oil.

Josh stifled a laugh. "Did you want to make a salad?"

"Yes. Let's make a salad. Only two ingredients. You and me. And olive oil. Three."

"You sure?

"Mmm." Micah kissed Josh hard and deep. "Top or bottom?"

"Bottom." Josh lay across Micah's lap and let Micah slick him up with oil. Micah's fingers were steady tonight, strong and careful, not particularly practiced or skillful, but Micah soon learned what Josh liked. Josh pushed back against Micah's hand, alternately thrusting down into his lap. When he couldn't wait any longer, he sat up and grabbed a condom. Leaning forward he kissed Micah while stroking his cock. Little moans bubbled out of Micah between kisses, their power vibrating down through Josh. He rolled the condom down on Micah, feeling Micah's cock harden under his touch.

"Sit back, against the headboard."

Micah complied and Josh straddled his lap. He positioned himself so he could slide down on Micah's cock, taking him inside, slipping in inch by inch. The sheer pleasure of the invasion made Josh want to close his eyes, to focus on the heat invading him, but he forced himself to watch Micah, see the growing pleasure in his eyes as he slid inside.

Finally, Josh had Micah deep inside. He pressed against Micah's chest, feeling strong arms circling him, and they kissed for a very long time. Then Josh moved up very slowly, and down again, with Micah's hands at his hips, helping him, taking some of the weight off him and intensifying the movements. But he kept each stroke slow and steady.

"Ahh. Josh. This is incredible." Micah panted against Josh's ear.

Josh was out of breath too, his chest heaving against Micah's from the exertion of the movements and the willpower it took not to speed up and explode into a million shiny sparks of pleasure.

Micah's chest was slick with sweat and oil, giving just enough friction as Josh's cock slid up and down against the flat, hard planes. Micah's hands stroked his back or spread his ass so he'd push in deeper on the down strokes. They kept this up for longer than Josh expected, his thighs screaming in protest, his balls aching, and his cock and ass a mass of raw nerves. Every touch started tremors moving through to his core. Then Micah held him tight, and the extra pressure sent Josh over the edge, splashing hot pearly strands all over their chests.

Laughter bubbled up from Micah's throat and sent shockwaves that started his orgasm, thrusting quick and hard up into Josh. When the last shudders of pleasure subsided, they held each other close.

"You make quite a good dessert, Mish."

"Oh, I forgot. There's dessert. In the fridge."

"We didn't buy any."

"I got something this afternoon."

"What?"

"After skating. I got a few things and dropped them off. Like the lube and the dessert."

"What kind of dessert?"

"Tiramisu.

"I died and went to heaven. I can't believe you remembered. Not from Ferrara's, is it?" It had been Josh's favorite. Whenever they'd gone to Little Italy, he'd ordered it. Sometimes he'd gone just for the tiramisu.

"Where else?"

"You didn't. You did?" Josh snuggled closer to Micah. Sweet, amazing, full of surprises Micah.

"Want some now?"

"In a bit. First I want to kiss you a few thousand more times."

"Just don't wear out your mouth—or mine—or we won't be able to enjoy the tiramisu."

They cuddled and kissed for a while before Micah got up and returned with two forks and a slab of tiramisu the size of a brick. Josh took a bite, letting the perfectly beaten whipped cream melt in his mouth. "Mmmm. Fabulous." Just the right amount of rum soaked into the ladyfingers and a hint of espresso to balance everything out. Heaven on a fork. "Mmmm. I can't believe it tastes the same. Maybe even better."

"Everything tastes better after sex."

"Considering how many times we've been together, hearing you say that really doesn't make me feel all warm and fuzzy."

"Sorry. I didn't mean it that way." Micah looked away and Josh wished he hadn't said anything. His heart ached at the thought of Micah with other lovers. How many had there been? Between Josh before and Josh now? It had been ten years. There must be plenty, especially after he came out. Then Josh recalled the conversation a little over a week earlier when Micah had caught him coming home from the bar, after he'd been fooling around with complete strangers. How had that made Micah feel? Josh hadn't realized Micah cared for him at that point, and he'd flaunted his sexual exploits in Micah's face. That had been cruel.

"Me too, Mish. It's not my business what you did before."

"Not that it was very much, to be honest."

They stared at each other in awkward silence for a few moments then Josh took another bite of dessert, but it didn't taste good anymore. "Micah, I'm sorry. It was such a sweet gesture getting this for me. Thank you." He leaned forward to kiss Micah and got whipped cream on a nipple.

Micah leaned down to lick it off.

"Mmmm. Tickles."

"Tastes even better on your nipple than on a fork."

"Ferrara's can use that in their ads."

"Let's see how it tastes on your cock."

"Let's."

Once they'd exhausted themselves and eaten their fill of dessert, they rinsed off under a warm shower then settled back under the covers.

"This is nice here. Too bad we can't spend every night here."

"Rina's coming home in a few days. The project is supposed to wrap up before Christmas." Micah pulled Josh close. "Ethan will move back here once she returns."

Josh nodded. He wasn't sure if Micah was happy or not about Rina's return and not having Ethan full time. "You'll miss him."

"Yeah. I'll see him during the week, and then I think he'll stay with me on weekends, depending on my work schedule. The restaurant schedule works out nicely."

"You and Rina get along pretty well then, even after the divorce?"

"We always got along fine. When it comes to Ethan, we've never had any disagreements. We put him first."

"What are you going to tell Rina? About us?"

"The truth. I've always told her the truth."

"About being gay."

"Yes."

"What about us, before?"

"Yes."

"She *knew*?"

"Rina's always been my friend. She was never a lover in the real sense of the word. She's always cared about me and my happiness. And yours."

"Rina knew about us, about that week before you left for Harvard?"

Micah took Josh's face between his hands and he looked directly into Josh's eyes. "Josh, when will you understand you're the only person who didn't realize I've been in love with you for more than half my life?"

Josh gazed back, dumbstruck. "R-really?"

"Yes, you idiot. Really. I think that's why my parents sent me away for college. They would have sent me to Stanford if there had been more Jews there. I wanted to go to Columbia. I would have been happy going there for law school too. They seemed determined to keep us apart. And then when Rina…." He paused. "I know my dad, at least, jumped on the opportunity."

Josh still couldn't quite think or breathe. Micah had been in love with him that long? As long as he'd been in love with Micah? And a few bad choices had kept them apart for so many years. No, Josh realized. Micah made a couple of bad choices, but Josh had run away and kept running, avoiding everything that might possibly remind him of Micah and the happiness they had shared, as best friends and as lovers.

He was done running. He'd stay put this time and take whatever the universe sent his way. He wrapped his arms around Micah and held on for dear life. He loved the idea of going to sleep with Micah and waking up next to him. He could get used to this.

# *Chapter Fourteen*

THE next week flew by in a series of seemingly endless days of cooking, several interviews with the food press, and the excitement that accompanies big changes. Josh had broken the news to Raymond Vessy that he needed to stay in New York for a couple more weeks. He would fly back to Paris afterward because it would be better to quit in person than over the phone; then he could catch Raymond at the right time. Micah divided his time between the restaurant, his community service commitments, and Ethan. And at night when everyone else in the house was asleep, he slid into bed with Josh.

They perfected the art of nearly silent lovemaking and relished the mornings when Ethan was at school and Josh's parents took a stroll around the neighborhood. He wondered whether they might have started their exercise kick as a way to give him and Micah some time alone. He didn't care, though if he thought about it too much, the idea embarrassed him.

The week before Christmas, Rina came back from her business trip, and Ethan went back to spend most nights with her. She'd missed him, and they needed time to catch up while Josh and Micah needed to, well, be a couple. Micah had a long talk with her and explained that Josh was moving back to take over the restaurant. She'd been thrilled.

The following Saturday, Miriam and Seymour had gone to visit friends for dinner, and Josh and Micah had the house.

"So, what should we do now that we have the place to ourselves?" Josh sidled up to Micah who had settled himself on the couch.

"Oh, I figured you already had plans. I know Saturday is a big party night. I can help slide you into those tight leather pants if you want."

Heat suffused Josh's cheeks. He looked away for a moment then back. Micah was grinning. "Asshole. I'm not going to clubs anymore. Unless you want to come along. We've never gone out together. I want to dance with you. Show you off." Josh pulled Micah off the couch and started gyrating his hips, pressing up against Micah.

"You're crazy." Micah shook his head and pushed Josh away with a laugh. "Really? You want to go dancing?"

"Yeah, why not?"

"Maybe. But later. There's something I was planning first."

"I like the sound of that." Josh lowered his voice to a soft rumble and pulled Micah close, planting a kiss against his throat.

"That's not what I was talking about."

"Then what?"

"Football. The New Orleans Bowl."

"What?"

"I want to watch the game, then I'll let you talk me into dancing. But no eyeliner for me."

"You don't need any. You're already beautiful."

"You wear it because you think you need to look good?" Micah shook his head.

Josh shrugged. "I don't know. Sure, I want—wanted to look good for those guys." A knot the size of a basketball formed in his gut. He didn't want to bring up that night or any of his past behavior now. He couldn't bear Micah judging him.

"I love you, Josh, with or without eyeliner and tight leather pants."

Josh let out a breath. "I'm sure you love me more without the pants, right?" He brushed off Micah's words, not believing they were anything more than a joke.

"Josh." Micah pulled Josh's chin toward him with a finger. "I love you, and I can't believe how lucky I am to have you back." He leaned down and gave Josh a soft kiss.

*Wow.*

"Micah, I'm sorry I was such an ass to you when I got home. I just remembered too much about the man I wanted, and after everything I heard, I—"

"It's past, okay?"

"No. Let me finish, please. I shouldn't have blamed you for the fact that I hadn't grown up. You... you're a great dad and more responsible than I am and...." He paused. He didn't know what he meant, he only knew what he wanted to say. "Micah, I never stopped loving you, since we were fifteen. I just hated that you weren't the man who could spend his life with me. But I always wished you would."

"Oh, Josh." Micah pulled him close and they kissed, bodies pressed together from knee to shoulder. They came up for air and settled back on the couch, Josh's head against Micah's chest.

"My mom is going to kill me if I don't feed you."

"Halftime." Micah turned the television on with the sound on low. "Let's watch the game."

"I didn't know you were into football."

"Not gay enough for you?" Micah laughed and shook his head.

"No. Just a surprise." *You're full of surprises, Micah.*

"There's a player I like at SMU, and I like to catch his games when they're on TV."

"Oh? Who?"

"There." Micah pointed as the SMU team came out on the field. The announcer named the starters and photos and stats popped up on the screen. "Walker, the wide receiver."

"I'd go for a tight end myself."

"I told you, later." Micah kissed the laughter from Josh's lips and they watched the game.

SMU won in a surprisingly close battle, though it was Neville Walker's six receptions for nearly two hundred yards that allowed them to clinch the game.

"Your pal's a hero."

Micah sat up, attention fixed on the screen when the MVP was announced. He clapped and hooted, and Josh just stared like he realized he'd fallen for an extraterrestrial.

As the teams raced off the field, the sportscaster stopped Walker for a quick interview.

"So, Neville, did you ever think you'd be standing here today, MVP and one of only four sophomores ever to win a Heisman Trophy?"

"No, sir. I almost didn't even make it to college. I almost didn't make it to age eighteen." Walker's excitement was visible as he panted and wiped an arm across a sweaty brow.

"So, all your hard work paid off for you right here tonight."

"I wouldn't have got this far without help from one person who believed in me when I didn't believe in myself. Mr. Micah Solomon saved my life and gave me a chance." He looked directly into the camera. "Thank you, Mr. Solomon." Then he nodded to the reporter and ran after his teammates.

Josh turned to Micah, who had a huge grin on his face.

"What was that all about?"

"He was a client of mine and I helped him."

"I thought you worked for some expensive law firm, not the public defender."

"I did. Mostly defending guys accused of white collar crimes, but I took on PD cases and some clients from children's legal defense. Neville was one of those."

"So, what did he do?"

"He hadn't done anything. Yet. But he was about to make a huge mistake—for all the right reasons. He was seventeen, with a juvenile record for various low-level drug-related offenses, and anything else would push him into the adult side of the legal system. I made sure that didn't happen or he'd be dead right now. Either on the streets or in prison." Micah turned off the television and moved to get off the couch, shutting down the discussion. "Dancing anyone?"

In his head, Josh did the math. Neville must have been one of Micah's last clients before he got nailed with the drugs. Everything sank in, in one blinding flash of realization. He pulled Micah back down and looked into his eyes. "Micah, tell me what you did."

"Attorney-client privilege. Now let's go out."

Josh wouldn't give up so easily. "Why don't you want to talk about it?"

"Because I fucked up. Neville was lucky, but I miscalculated. Someone phoned in a tip about the drugs and…." He paused. "As Paul Harvey used to say, you know the rest of the story."

"You went to jail for the drugs that belonged to that kid? Why on earth would you do that?" Josh felt sick inside at the realization of what Micah had done, what he'd sacrificed.

"I can't tell you specifics. I can tell you that I had the drugs, but not how or why. But I'm not sorry. I wouldn't turn Neville in to save myself. He hadn't done anything."

"He had all those drugs, Micah! Of course he was going to sell them."

"The dealer threatened Neville's mom and sister. He was afraid to defy the dealer. It wasn't about money. Josh, you have no idea what life is like for these kids. They do what they need to survive, or to protect someone else. That dealer was a pimp. Neville's sister was thirteen. You do the math."

"You—" Josh stopped himself. His mouth went dry and he couldn't speak. He'd never in a million years suspected anything like this. That Micah had gone this far to protect a client. No wonder he'd been secretive and acting strange, the symptoms Josh had told Rina were proof of Micah's relapse into drug abuse.

"Why didn't you ever say anything? Why'd you let me go on treating you like shit over the drugs?" God, he'd been such a schmuck for how he'd behaved toward Micah.

"I deserved what you said. Not for this, but for everything else that went before it. And I'd made enough mistakes with drugs myself. I got out of that easily. It was one of the reasons I wanted to help the kids in trouble with drugs. I knew what that was like. Or I thought I did. I'd grown up sheltered and privileged. But once I saw the world Neville fought to survive in, I had to help."

"But don't they have rules for lawyers who turn in drugs or things for clients? They're not supposed to charge you for the possession."

"I didn't handle it through the system. I thought I could sort it out another way, so I wouldn't have to throw Neville under the bus. He would have ended up in prison, not juvie, and he wouldn't have survived and neither would his little sister if that had happened. I won't say more until after my reinstatement hearing. I broke a law."

"But it was to save someone else." Josh took a slow breath, recalling something his dad had said that first day about Micah doing a mitzvah, a good deed. One of the highest forms was a self-sacrifice, and even higher to do it in a way where you don't take credit for the deed because the true purpose is simply to help. "A mitzvah."

Micah waved Josh's words away, closing the discussion.

"Oh, Micah. Oh, damn it, Micah. Can you forgive me for how I treated you?" Josh's whole body ached now, and his eyes burned. How could Micah ever forgive him?

"I already did. And you already apologized to me. Even before you knew the whole story. That's your mitzvah. For me, that's all I need from you. Don't keep kicking yourself."

"Micah, you amaze me. Every single day I learn some new reason why I should love you."

"Don't love me for what I did."

"I love you for being the man who would go so far to help someone. I just don't understand why you love me."

"Because you've made sacrifices for what's important to you. Like your family."

Josh shook his head and tried to look away, but Micah reached out and turned his head back so their eyes met.

"You came home for your mom, and then when you thought your parents were going to close the restaurant, you made the decision to come back here to run it, rather than let their life's work disappear. You don't see how you help people, but you do. That's a mitzvah, too." Micah pulled Josh into his arms, enveloping him in warmth and comfortable strength before placing a kiss against his hair.

"It doesn't seem like much, in comparison." Josh looked into Micah's eyes.

"Okay, you're right. It's really because you look hot in eyeliner and skintight leather. Now are you taking me dancing, or what?"


ON THE following Monday, an official-looking letter arrived for Micah at the Goldens' house. It sat on the dining room table propped up against the Shabbat candlesticks when they got home after the dinner shift at the restaurant. Josh watched him look at the front then turn it over and peer at the back. Micah let out a sigh and closed his eyes for a couple of beats before opening them again.

Josh moved to his side. "What is it? Bad news?" He glanced at the envelope, but Micah had moved it out of his line of sight. "Mish, what's wrong?" Josh's heart skipped a beat. It was the first time he'd seen Micah not look in control.

Micah shook his head. "It's from the bar. About my appeal, probably. I don't want to look."

Josh bit his lower lip. This could be the end of his law career, and smart as he was, it would be tough to start looking for something new with the drug conviction hanging over him. No wonder Micah was worried. "What can I do?"

Micah looked up at Josh, the green eyes dark with worry suddenly brightening. "Would you open it? It's thin. That can't be good news. Like a college rejection. Nothing to fill in and send back."

"Come on into the kitchen. I'll make some tea and you relax."

"I need to check on Ethan."

"He's back at Rina's, remember?"

Micah ran his fingers through his hair and shook his head. "Yeah. I forgot. I'm so—" He glanced up at Josh again.

Josh moved an arm around Micah's waist and leaned in for a soft brush of lips. "We'll face whatever it is. First, tea."

"You sound like your mom."

"You meant that as a compliment, right?" Josh grinned, more for Micah's sake than his own. He really didn't know how to help him over bad news. He got Micah out of his coat and ushered him into the kitchen, then set the water to boil.

Once they sat down at the table with mugs of steaming mint tea, Micah handed the envelope over. Josh saw the front had several crossed-out addresses, with the Goldens' home address the latest. The letter had been bounced around before finally catching up to Micah. Josh took a deep breath and ripped it open.

"Well?"

"Let me read it first." Josh's gaze traveled down the paper. "Your hearing before the disciplinary committee is on Friday."

"This Friday? But it's already Monday! That's only four days from now? How can they do that?" Micah spat the words out in a nervous staccato.

"The letter is dated three weeks ago. They sent it somewhere on Staten Island first and then it went to Rina's...."

"The halfway house was on Staten Island."

"Figures."

"And it must have come to Rina's while she was out of the country and the post office forwarded it here?"

"Yeah, that's probably what happened. So you'll know this week, right?"

"How can I prepare in only four days? I need to call my lawyer. What time is it?" Micah looked at his watch and frowned. "In the morning."

"You have a lawyer?"

"Sure. There're guys who represent attorneys before the disciplinary committees. They know the rules and can explain your actions. I know the law, not the bar rules. I can't risk it."

"Oh. Well, let's get to bed. I'll wake you up first thing and you can call, okay?"

"Thanks."

Josh spent a wakeful night as Micah tossed and turned, but he held him close and hoped like hell he'd know what to do if Micah's world fell apart at the end of the week.


ON FRIDAY, Micah put on his best suit. It didn't fit as well as it must have when he first bought it, Josh thought. He'd lost weight around the middle, but his shoulders were bulkier. The pants hung around his waist and he had to use the tightest notch on the belt. Josh donned the one suit he'd brought with him, and Seymour and Miriam insisted on attending the hearing. Rina would be there, too, but she had been called as a witness and wasn't supposed to speak with Micah until after she had testified.

No one spoke in the taxi on the way to the courthouse. Josh held Micah's hand the whole way and gave a reassuring squeeze. He wanted to put his arms around Micah and hold him tight and tell him it would all be fine, but he knew empty reassurances wouldn't help. Thankfully, even Josh's parents stayed quiet, though his mother, sitting on Micah's other side in the back of the cab, patted his knee and nodded as they zigged and zagged in the Manhattan traffic.

The taxi let them out and they made their way up the steps.

"Mr. Solomon!"

Josh glanced in the direction of the shout. Neville Walker was at the door to the building. He gave a thumbs-up and a friendly smile before he turned and entered the building.

"Neville's here?" Josh glanced at Micah, who smiled for the first time that morning.

"My attorney said he wanted to testify."

"That's got to be good news, right?"

"It could go either way." Micah stopped halfway up the steps. "Go on ahead. I need a few minutes."

Josh's parents nodded and continued up, but Josh stayed with Micah.

"Go on."

"No. I'm staying with you till it's decided. And no matter what happens, I'm sticking with you."

"Better than I did, huh, Josh? I should have stuck with you. None of this would have happened."

The look of failure that flashed through Micah's eyes hurt Josh even more than the tone of the words. "That's not what I meant." He paused, stumbling over the words to choose the right ones. "I could have gone after you and I didn't. I ran away. I'm no less to blame for anything. But going forward, we're together. A team. A family—" Micah glanced up and met Josh's gaze head-on with a surprised smile. "—and we'll face this and go home together and work through it. Do you think you can handle that?"

Micah stared at him for a moment and nodded. "I do."

Josh felt a little thrill at the significance of the words. He grinned and Micah followed suit, eyes twinkling and one corner of his mouth quirking into a wicked smile. Josh pulled Micah into an embrace and whispered, "Hold that thought, Micah Solomon."

AND they made their way up the steps, hand in hand, to face the future together.

# Traditional Matzo Brei

3 sheets of matzo (available year-round at most grocery stores)
2 eggs
Vegetable oil
Salt and pepper to taste

Note: The correct ratio of egg to matzo is a time-honored topic of argument among every family. One egg per sheet of matzo is fairly standard, with some recipes calling for two eggs per sheet, or two sheets of matzo per egg (in communities where eggs were scarce). We like it somewhere in between, so two eggs for three sheets. Not too eggy or too dry.

1. Heat oil in a nonstick pan on medium-high heat.
2. Break matzo in 1-2 inch pieces and place in a medium bowl. Cover with water while beating eggs in a separate bowl. You just want to moisten the matzo in the water for a minute or two.
3. Drain matzo. Add the beaten eggs into the bowl. Season with salt and pepper. Stir carefully to coat matzo with egg.
4. Pour matzo mixture into hot pan and spread out evenly. Lower the heat to medium and let it cook until the egg firms up.
5. Break into several pieces so you can easily turn the matzo brei. Flip and continue to cook until the edges brown. The more pieces you break it into, the crispier it will be. Turn a few times until the egg is cooked to your liking and serve.

# Josh's Gourmet Matzo Brei Variations

Sauté sliced onions and chopped garlic in olive oil until onion is caramelized and translucent. Sprinkle in a pinch of cumin and coriander. For something really gourmet, try a pinch of saffron instead.

Add cooked and seasoned onion to the egg and matzo mixture in step 3 above. Continue as directed.

You can also add in your favorite omelet ingredients to the egg and matzo mixture. To really impress, add onion to the traditional recipe and serve with a dollop of caviar and sour cream, blini-style. L'chaim!

# Sweet Matzo Brei

3 sheets of matzo (available year-round at most grocery stores)
2 eggs
2 tablespoons sugar
1/2 teaspoon vanilla
1/4 teaspoon cinnamon
Butter or vegetable oil
Jam, syrup or sour cream, for serving

1. Heat butter or oil in a nonstick pan on medium-high heat.
2. Break matzo in 1-2 inch pieces and place in a medium bowl. Cover with water while beating eggs, vanilla, sugar and cinnamon in a separate bowl. You just want to moisten the matzo in the water for a minute or two.
3. Drain matzo. Add egg mixture to the bowl. Stir carefully to coat matzo with egg.
4. Pour matzo mixture into hot pan and spread out evenly. Lower the heat to medium and let it cook until the egg firms up.
5. Break into several pieces so you can easily turn the matzo brei. Flip and continue to cook until the edges brown. The more pieces you break it into, the crispier it will be. Turn a few times until the egg is cooked to your liking and serve.
6. Serve with jam, syrup or sour cream and enjoy.

# Jenna's Slow Cooker Chanukah Brisket

Beef brisket (not corned), approx 4 lbs.
Salt and pepper to taste
2 medium onions, sliced into 1/4" rounds
2 tbsp olive oil or pareve (nondairy margarine)
1 cup tomato ketchup (ideally the no-corn-syrup variety)
1 cup white wine (or substitute 1 cup of your choice of broth – onion soup works well here)
½ - 1 tsp garlic powder
4 carrots, peeled and cut into 2" pieces
Preparation Time: 15 minutes
Cook Time: 8-10 hours

1. Caramelize onions in oil or margarine over low heat in a frying pan (if your slow cooker insert is meant for stovetop use, you can even do this in the insert). Lay the onions on the bottom of the slow cooker insert. Pat the brisket dry, then season with salt and pepper to taste. Lay the brisket on top of the onions. Whisk together the ketchup, garlic powder, and wine/broth until combined. Pour over the brisket to coat it. Add carrots.
2. Cook in slow cooker on low for 8-10 hours, until the brisket is tender but not falling apart. Slice brisket on a 45-degree angle to the grain of the meat.

Optional: If you like more sauce to pour over the brisket, double the ketchup and wine/broth.

Variation: Substitute a good barbecue sauce for the ketchup for a bit more "kick" to the sauce.

# Traditional Latkes

2 cups peeled and shredded potatoes

1 tablespoon grated onion

3 eggs, beaten

2 tablespoons all-purpose flour

1-1/2 teaspoons salt

1/2 cup vegetable oil for frying

Applesauce and/or sour cream for serving

1. Put the potatoes in a cheesecloth or several layers of paper towels and wring, extracting as much moisture as possible.
2. Stir the potatoes, onion, eggs, flour, and salt in a medium bowl.
3. Use a large, heavy-bottomed skillet. Heat the oil on medium-high until hot. Place large spoonfuls of the potato mixture into the hot oil, pressing down to form 1/4 to 1/2 inch thick patties. Brown on one side, turn and brown on the other. Let drain on paper towels. Serve hot!
4. Slather with sour cream and/or applesauce and enjoy!

# Josh's Chicken with Herbes de Provence

1.5 pounds of chicken breasts or chicken cutlets (thin-cut breast meat)
3 tablespoons herbes de Provence (available at the grocery store, or blend your own with equal portions of thyme, fennel seeds, savory, and basil)
Kosher salt and coarsely ground black pepper
3 tablespoons of butter, or olive oil (for a kosher version)

1. Place chicken breast between sheets of plastic wrap and pound to an even thickness of a half to three-quarters of an inch. It doesn't have to be exact, but you want to flatten it so it will cook quickly and evenly. If you don't have a meat pounder, use a rolling pin or a heavy pan.
   If you buy thin-cut cutlets as a shortcut, you can skip Step 1.
2. Sprinkle both sides of the chicken liberally with salt, pepper, and herbes de Provence. You want a very liberal coating of herbs, even if it looks like too much.
3. Melt a few tablespoons of butter (oil for kosher version) in sauté pan over medium-high heat. When the foaming subsides, add the chicken breasts. Aim for a hard sear, to seal in the juices, so keep the heat up high. Cook for 3 minutes on each side. Cover the pan and set it aside off the heat.
4. Let the covered pan sit off the heat for 8 to 10 minutes. This continues the cooking. Now place the meat on the cutting board for another 8 minutes. This allows the juices to redistribute throughout the meat.
5. Slice the chicken breast and place on a plate of greens such as arugula or baby spring greens. Pour over any pan drippings and enjoy!

—Recipe inspired by Jacques Pepin

# Josh's Provencal Carrots

2 pounds of regular carrots
2 tablespoons of olive oil
6 whole cloves of garlic, peeled
Salt to taste
Handful of oil- or dry-cured black olives such as Nyon. You can find these at the olive bar and they are more wrinkly than brine-cured olives.

1. Peel the carrots. Slice on the diagonal. It looks like a lot of carrots, but they cook down, so keep slicing.
2. Heat the oil in a heavy skillet over medium-high heat. When it's hot, add the carrot slices and stir to coat evenly with oil. Lower heat to medium and cover.
3. Braise the carrots for about 20 minutes, stirring every 5 minutes.
4. Add the garlic and a sprinkling of salt. Reduce the heat to low and continue to cook another 15 minutes, stirring every 5 minutes. The carrots will have cooked down and begun to caramelize. Make sure they don't stick to the pan.
5. Chop the black olives and sprinkle on the carrots. Serve. You can discard the garlic if you choose. It has perfumed the carrots, but it's still rather strong.

A *Delectable* Novella

# Brand New *Flavor*

a *Delectable* novella

EM LYNLEY

http://www.dreamspinnerpress.com

EM LYNLEY has worked finance, the wine industry, and high-tech, though she'd rather be writing hot man-on-man romance. She spent ten years as an economist and financial analyst, including a year as a White House Staff Economist, but only because all the intern positions were filled. Tired of boring herself and others with dry business reports and articles, her creative muse is back and naughtier than ever. She has lived and worked in London, Tokyo, and Washington, DC, but the San Francisco Bay Area is home for now.

Visit her website at http://www.emlynley.com

her blog at http://emlynley.livejournal.com

her Twitter page at http://twitter.com/emlynley

and her Facebook at http://www.facebook.com/emlynley.

SHIRA ANTHONY, in her last incarnation, was a professional opera singer, performing roles in such operas as *Tosca, Pagliacci,* and *La Traviata,* among others. She's given up TV for evenings spent with her laptop, and she never goes anywhere without a pile of unread M/M romance on her Kindle.

Shira is married with two children and two insane dogs, and when she's not writing, she is usually in a courtroom trying to make the world safer for children. When she's not working, she can be found aboard a 35' catamaran off the Carolina coast with her favorite sexy captain at the wheel.

Shira's Blue Notes Series of classical music themed gay romances was named one of Scattered Thoughts and Rogue Word's "Best Series of 2012," and *The Melody Thief* was named one of the "Best Novels in a Series of 2012." *The Melody Thief* also received an honorable mention, "One Perfect Score" at the 2012 Rainbow Awards.

Shira can be found on:

Facebook: https://www.facebook.com/shira.anthony

Goodreads: http://www.goodreads.com/author/show/4641776.Shira_Anthony

Twitter: @WriterShira

Website: http://www.shiraanthony.com

E-mail: shiraanthony@hotmail.com

Also from EM LYNLEY

HOSTILE
TAKEOVER

EM LYNLEY

http://www.dreamspinnerpress.com

# Also from EM Lynley

http://www.dreamspinnerpress.com

# Romance from SHIRA ANTHONY

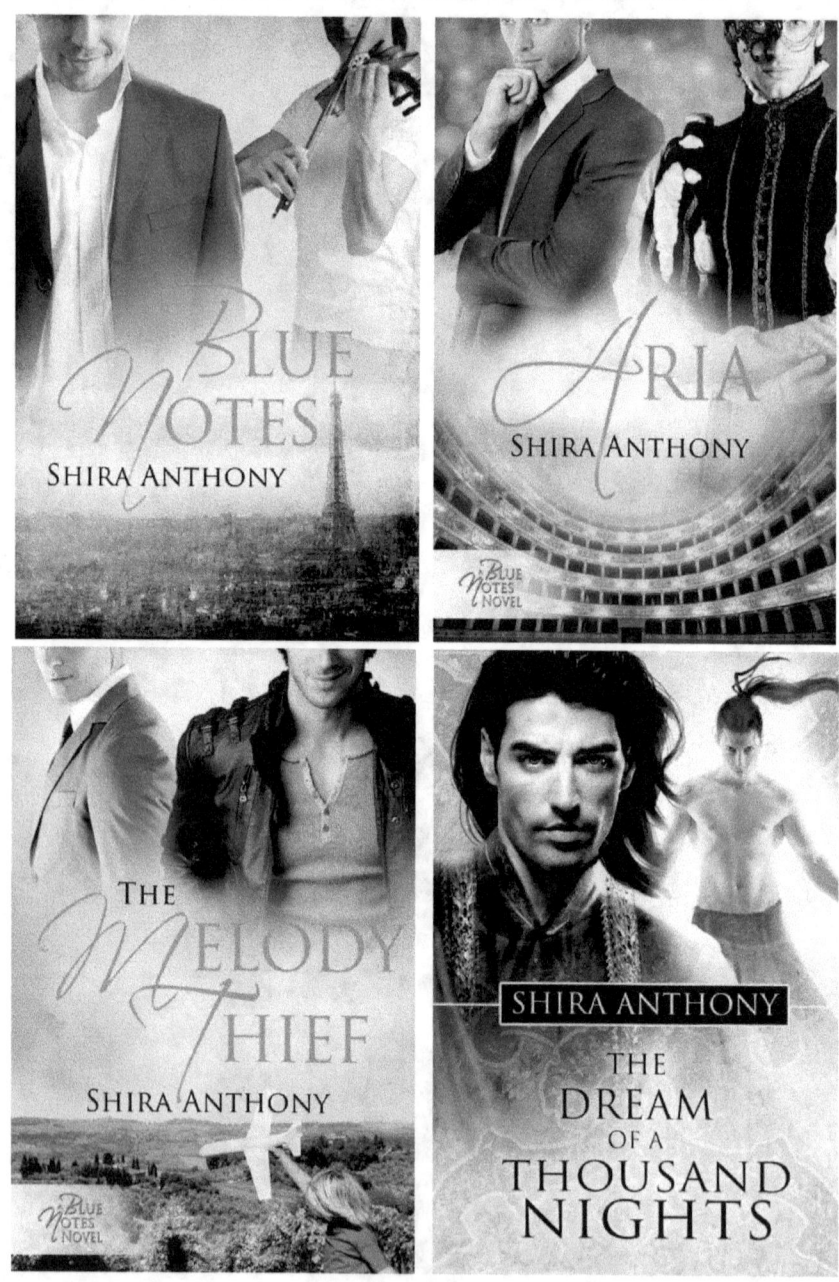

http://www.dreamspinnerpress.com

Also from SHIRA ANTHONY

# the trust

## Shira Anthony
## Venona Keyes

http://www.dreamspinnerpress.com